The Last Summer

by

Brandy Bruce

THE LAST SUMMER BY BRANDY BRUCE
Published by Bling! Romance
an imprint of Lighthouse Publishing of the Carolinas
2333 Barton Oaks Dr., Raleigh, NC 27614

ISBN: 978-1-946016-19-5

Cover design by Elaina Lee
Interior design by AtriTeX Technologies P Ltd

Available in print from your local bookstore, online, or from the publisher at: lpcbooks.com

For more information on this book and the author visit: http://www.brandybruce.blogspot.com

Brought to you by the creative team at Lighthouse Publishing of the Carolinas:
Marisa Deshaies, Managing Editor
Meghan M. Gorecki, Publishing Assistant to the Managing Editor
Brian Cross, Christy Distler, and Lucie Winborne, Proofreaders

Library of Congress Cataloging-in-Publication Data
Bruce, Brandy
The Last Summer / Brandy Bruce 1st ed.

Printed in the United States of America

Praise for *The Last Summer*

Brandy Bruce captures the heart of every woman with this charming tale of well-meaning friends caught in a love quint-angle!

~Marianne Hering
Author of the Imagination Station series

Like the beauty of a sunset, *The Last Summer* will bathe your heart with a colorful display of grace. From the opening lines to the last poignant moments, I was enraptured by this story of broken hearts, healing tears, and above all abundant hope in the power of friendships and the unending love of God. *The Last Summer* has found a place on my keeper shelf to be read again and again.

~Candee Fick
Author of *Dance Over Me* and *Catch of a Lifetime*

Brandy Bruce has imagined an ensemble cast of unforgettable characters into a wonderful story reminiscent of my own twenty-something days. I loved this story and hope to see more from this author in days to come.

~Pamela Meyers
Author of *Second Chance Love* and *Thyme for Love*

I loved this book! Filled to the brim with superbly spun ingredients that make for a tender-hearted, truly unforgettable tale, *The Last Summer* is a must read for everyone who enjoys drama, romance, and relatable characters in the thick of it all

~Sara Hanson
Author of *Chosen*

Reading *The Last Summer* immediately stirred up memories of tearing through Robin Jones Gunn's Christy Miller series with a vengeance. A compelling and fast-paced tale of friendship, faith, and the sort of guys who'd be any girl's undoing, *The Last Summer* is perfect for your book club or simply enjoyed with a cup of your favorite brew.

~Christa Banister
Author of *Around the World in 80 Dates*

For Jeff

I would choose this journey with you all over again
because you, and these three babies
we've made, are everything.

If you ever doubt it, my love,
know that grace covers us all.

Chapter One

I never meant for any of it to happen.

But sometimes, when you drop things, they break. My mother taught me that.

It all started three summers ago. It all started when I met Luke.

Luke Anderson.

We were thrown together in this group that turned out to be something like a perfect circle. Addison was the leader. She was unquestionably the leader. Still is. Maybe it's the fact that she's the oldest of the group by six months. Maybe it's because she's the most mature. Maybe it's just her personality to take charge. Whatever it was, I knew from day one that Addison was the glue that held this group together.

That day more than one hundred Sundays ago, I walked into the singles class at Christ Community Church, dreading, dreading, *dreading* being there. Twenty-four years old and I felt like it was my first day of high school. I worried my outfit was too dressy, or not dressy enough. I worried the highlights in my shoulder-length light brown hair were too faint, or maybe too dark. I worried that I might sweat through my light gray blouse. I worried there was cat hair on the back of my black pants. I'm not really that much of an animal person, but people always seem to think I am because I have a cat. A cat that sheds like a pine tree in October. Long story.

Back to my point. I was nervous. I'd left a life full of friends in Austin, Texas when I'd moved back home to Houston. Framed in the doorway of the classroom at that moment, I'd never felt so alone.

The simple fact was that I'd moved back home. Now I needed people.

Addison Parker, tall with wavy auburn hair, stood at a table by an open box of doughnuts. She'd smiled at me and waved me over, and without a word, I knew I liked her. Who knows why? Maybe it was the pink-iced, sprinkled doughnut in her hand. Maybe it was how she hugged me before I could finish saying my name and then told me how glad she was to meet me.

Sam Spencer and Lily Morrison had walked in together, holding hands and arguing. They're still holding hands and arguing, come to think of it—Sam with his effortless nonchalance and messy brown hair, and petite Lily with her blonde pixie cut that fits her perfectly. Sam had nudged Addison over so he could grab a Styrofoam cup and fill it with coffee, while Lily, her eyes bright and exuberant, told her about the big sale happening at a nearby home décor store.

I could tell the three of them had been friends for a while. I was the newbie. Addison introduced me and I got another tight hug. Then from the back of the room came Jason Garcia, Hispanic, handsome, dark-haired, an immediate welcoming smile on his face. He beelined to me, introducing himself and asking me to sit with him and drawing me into conversation.

I could have loved him just for that, just for intentionally including me when I was feeling like a fish flopping on sand. The dark hair and dark eyes and olive skin were an added bonus to the stimulating conversation of *Is this your first time visiting Christ Community? Are you new to the area? Where do you work?* and so on. I sat sandwiched between Jason and Lily, who complimented my shoes and told me emphatically that I was joining her and Addison for lunch at Isabella's Deli after the class ended so they could learn everything about me. She couldn't have known how willing I was to say yes.

We sat in a circle, and Addison was just about to pray when the door opened, and my heart nearly stopped. Because the tall, blond, green-eyed guy who walked in elicited that response in me, just by walking through the door.

Very unfortunately, he still does.

A round of hellos greeted him, and I realized he was a regular. He took an open seat that just happened to be across from me. A golden tan and slight pink on his cheeks gave away the fact that he'd been in the sun a lot that summer. Right away I liked his short dark-blond hair and well-defined jaw. He wore khakis and sneakers and a brown T-shirt that fit those broad shoulders really well…

It was nearly impossible for me not to stare at him.

I should mention that I'd never, ever had that response to someone before. That sort of stolen-breath, heart-bursting reaction that feels so overwhelming your hands sweat and you try to swallow but can't.

He looked in my direction, and I was, of course, gazing at him (not drooling, thank heavens). And the smile on his face made everything oh-so-much worse.

Because it was undoubtedly the most beautiful smile I'd ever seen.

Addison started talking and I forced my attention back on her. About ten minutes later, the door opened and a girl with curly brown hair fluttered into the room.

I say *fluttered* because I learned that Debra Hart never just *walks* anywhere. The girl flutters and flies and invades and takes over and fills a room when she enters it. Her brown curls bounce when she moves. To me, that day, Luke walked in and sucked all the oxygen out of the room. Debra barreled in and infused the space with life. Everyone just seemed to smile at the sight of her. With apologies for being late, she came crashing in, carrying a coffee cup and a huge red purse and sat down next to Luke.

Close to Luke, I should add.

She settled back and his arm went around her. Well, his arm rested on the back of her chair, not exactly around *her*. But it was enough to make my heart sink. To make me instantly jealous. Then Debra was saying something funny—I can't even remember what—and we were all laughing, myself included. Because she's funny, and cute, and full of life—and that's just Debra.

Addison dived into the Bible study at that point, and I tried to concentrate, all while stealing glances at Luke ... and Debra (which really heightened that feeling of being back in high school, by the way). For some reason, the parable of Jesus raising Lazarus from the dead just wasn't enough to hold my attention, not with Luke sitting across from me.

The moment the class ended a few people left the room, but Addison, Lily, and Debra descended on me. Sam, Jason, and Luke took over the doughnut station, scrounging for leftovers. I didn't want to stay too long and seem desperate to be included; on the other hand, I obviously *was* desperate, so I ignored the panicky voice in my head telling me to hurry up and leave. The girls were talking—not necessarily *to* me, but I felt like I was at least part of the conversation, so I continued to stand there, hoping I looked interested while I was really trying to think of a way to get introduced to Luke. He glanced at me from the table, but Jason was saying something to him at that very moment, so he looked over at him.

"We're going to Isabella's," Lily had told Debra, who immediately swung that massive purse over her shoulder, curls bouncing in her excitement.

"I'm in."

"Where are we going?" Sam asked, before stuffing half a doughnut in his mouth.

"It's a girls' lunch, Samuel," Addison said. "No boys allowed."

"I heard someone say Isabella's," Jason said, putting an arm around Addison and an arm around Lily.

"Not invited to this conversation, Jase," Lily said bluntly.

"Isabella's has good chili. How about a guys' lunch at Isabella's?" Sam asked Luke and Jason, his voice all innocent. Both guys nodded. I remember looking at Luke (I couldn't help it) and the cool, collected, easy look on his face drew me in a little more—he was a mixture of everything that attracted me. A little James Dean. A little Brad Pitt. Self-assured. Confident. Comfortable. Strong. Reserved. Intense. We still hadn't been properly introduced.

Addison sighed. "Fine. But this lunch is about getting to know Sara. So no sports talk, fishing talk, work talk, annoying talk—got it?"

"Got it. Sara," Jason said smoothly, moving away from Addison and Lily and steering me toward the door. "So tell me, do you like chili?"

I laughed.

"Sara?" I nearly tripped turning around at the voice. Luke was standing behind us.

"We haven't really met yet. I'm Luke Anderson." He held out his hand, and I slid mine into his.

"Sara Witherspoon. I'm glad to meet you."

Please be my future husband.

It occurred to me I'd ridden to church with my parents, so I'd need a ride to Isabella's. The pleasant thought of riding with Luke gave me the boldness at that moment to say, "Hey, could I get a ride with someone to the restaurant? I didn't drive my car to church this morning."

I swear I remember Luke opening his mouth to speak, but next to me, Jason put his arm around my shoulders and directed me back toward the door.

"I'll give you a ride, Sara." I pushed aside the slight wave of disappointment I felt as I left with Jason.

Fifteen minutes later I was sitting between Addison and Jason at the table, trying to answer the onslaught of questions that were coming my way. Luke was seated across from me again, but diagonally this time and much closer. Close enough for me to notice he was more reserved than the other two guys, but that all three of them interacted like brothers—close, teasing each other, but loyal in an instant. He held himself well; I liked the maturity that came across in how he spoke and how he listened. I liked the fact that he smiled easily but didn't joke too much. I liked how he paid attention to each person at the table.

Honestly, this might sound strange—but looking back, I think I connected from the start to Luke's personality.

Because it was the same as mine. Quiet, a little introverted, but still willing to put himself out there and be friendly. His deep-green eyes and that make-me-melt smile were a bonus.

"Okay!" Addison had said loudly. "You guys! There's no way she can keep up with all these questions. Sara, you have the floor. Tell us your story."

And just like that, twelve eyes were glued to me. I took a deep breath.

"It's not a thrilling story, let me warn you. But here it is. You all know by this point that I'm Sara Witherspoon. I'm twenty-four and I graduated from A&M . . ." Sam groaned at that and Lily poked him hard. "... two years ago with a degree in design. I've been working at an art gallery in Austin since graduation, but the place closed down a couple of months ago, which, unfortunately, means that I just moved back in with my parents. They asked me to come to church with them, and I said yes because I hoped to meet some new people. So that's my life—living back in my old bedroom at my parents' house, currently job hunting, and it's really not that cool of an experience."

Sympathetic looks all around made me feel just a little better.

Addison reached over and squeezed my arm. "Do you get along with your parents?"

I shrugged. "Fairly well. Though I'm an only child, so I've always been my mother's favorite project. And from the looks of it, that hasn't changed despite the fact that I've been on my own for years. My dad is a family doctor and works at a practice near our home in Willow Heights."

Jason whistled at that and I flushed. I hated telling people where my family lived, but it was usually better to get it over with rather than face the questions later of *Why didn't you mention that you live in the affluent, illustrious Willow Heights area?*

"My mom volunteers with a lot of charities in the area, and she's really involved with her garden club and that sort of thing. She was a professional event planner for years. Living together would be easier if she and I weren't so alike in the fact that we love design yet have opposite style preferences. We learned this when I was ten years old and asked to be allowed to redecorate my room. It was war."

Everyone at the table laughed.

"I haven't lived in Houston on a permanent basis since before college. Now I'm back. In some ways ... I love it. I've always thought of Houston as home. I think I'd be a lot happier if this were happening on my own terms. But here I am. I'm hoping to find a job soon and get an apartment. Before my mother and I start driving each other past the point of crazy."

"Well, we're very glad you came to Christ Community today, Sara," Debra said, and everyone nodded their agreement. "I know it can be hard to feel like you're starting over. I moved out here because of a job, after growing up and going to college in Minnesota. Talk about a life change! I was desperate to know people too."

"And you know people now, Sara," Addison said firmly. "Welcome to the circle."

"Circle?" I repeated, my hands clenched together under the table.

Jason grinned. "Here's our story—Sam and Lily are the annoying ones who've been making out since high school."

"Jason!" Lily screeched. Sam just shrugged, unconcerned.

"Sam and I have known Addison and Luke since college. We all went to the University of Texas. Sam and Luke were roommates," Lily said, her face still beet red. "And yes, Sam and I have been dating since high school." She glared at Jason. Jason held up his hands as though he was asking *What?* A seemingly innocent grin spread across his face.

"There was that one year, Lil," Sam broke in. Lily's face turned more scarlet.

"Really? You're going to bring up the one year we weren't together?"

"Well, I mean, it's part of our story. And then there were those four months a couple of years ago."

"Sam, stop talking. Anyway, once we graduated from UT, Sam and Addison and I moved back to Houston. Luke's originally from Colorado, but he loved us all so much that he stayed in the great state of Texas and moved out here to Houston and got an apartment with Sam. We started going to Christ Community Church, which is where Addison has gone for years. So we're kind of like family at this point."

I broke in, worried I wouldn't get another chance. "So what made you choose UT?" I'd asked, looking directly at Luke. His eyebrows rose and he seemed surprised that I'd singled him out.

"Scholarship. I'd applied to several out-of-state schools. For a lot of reasons, I needed a break from Colorado. My parents had just divorced, and I was ready for a change from the scene I was used to, so I left the mountains and moved to the land-of-more-humidity-than-I'd-known-existed."

That brought a round of laughs and a smile to my face. He winked at me, and I wondered if and when I might get to hear more of his story—leaving Colorado; his parents breaking up. I wanted to know his history.

"Addison took over as the leader of the singles group at Christ Community about a year ago," Lily continued. "That's when we met Debra and Jason. Debra was an immediate fit to this group. Jason just started following us around, and we couldn't get rid of him."

"You needed me in this family, and you know it, Lily Morrison," Jason teased.

"He forced his way into the circle," Lily contradicted.

"He *belonged* in this circle, Lily," Addison said with a motherly sigh.

"And just like that, you guys want to let me in?" I said, raising my eyebrows.

They all exchanged looks around the table. I felt like they were having this private conversation and hoped the conclusion would be that they wanted me. Because there was something special about the people at this table. The way they kidded and joked and touched each other and moved like one breathing organism. The way they *did* seem like a family. Six people connected to each other. I wanted to be the seventh.

"I have a feeling, Sara Witherspoon," Addison said, tilting her head to the side and studying me as though she could see all the way to my heart, "you belong too."

I don't know how she knew, but she did. Like I said, Addison is the leader. She's the glue. Once she said those words, all tension melted away, and I was included. If Addison said I belonged, I did. She reminded me of Melanie Wilkes in *Gone with the Wind.* If Mrs. Wilkes was the cool-headed voice of reason that could settle the chaos around her, Addison was that same strong, trusted constant amid these six friends. Her word was law. And from that day forward, the six people around that table at Isabella's became like six extensions of myself.

We were a circle. Within a month, Jason asked me to go out to dinner with him. Luke hadn't shown any romantic interest in me, and there was Jason, with that thick dark hair and playful personality and handful of tattoos on his olive skin—how could I say no? We started dating. A year after that, we broke up. As much as I truly liked Jason and couldn't help feeling attracted to him, I hadn't fallen in love. I couldn't picture us married and having babies. We were better as friends. I know Jason didn't agree, but he and I both refused to let our break up damage the circle. Eventually, things between us returned to normal.

During my dating-Jason phase, Sam and Lily got married, which didn't really change anything since they were already such a unit. I realized early on that Luke and Debra were never an item. I'd mistaken Debra's warm and friendly demeanor and Luke's tendency to be protective and kind as the traits of a dating couple, but those endearing qualities of both of them extended to all of us. My crush on Luke diminished as Jason and I dated and then shifted to 'just friends.'

Sort of.

And somewhere along the way, painfully, Luke and I became best friends.

Chapter Two

Present Day

I tossed a swimsuit into my overnight bag and rummaged through my dresser for a pair of socks, since I can't seem to ever sleep without socks on, despite the hot and humid Texas weather. That probably had something to do with the fact that I usually ran the air conditioner until my apartment felt borderline frosty at night. I grabbed an ankle-length, yellow-striped pair and dropped them in my bag.

My phone buzzed for the tenth time, and I grabbed it. I'd been receiving texts from every member of the group for an hour and was ready to put the phone on silent mode so I could finally have some peace.

> RIDING TOGETHER? Luke texted me.
> NOPE. ADDISON ALREADY ASKED ME.

My phone rang seconds later.

"We have to ride together. I thought that was understood." I smiled at the sound of that voice that still stirred all sorts of feelings in me that I conveniently pretended didn't exist.

"Why would that be understood?" I asked, dropping two T-shirts into my bag.

"Because we're Luke and Sara and we ride together?"

I chuckled. "Was that a question? Anyway, you know I'd love for us to ride together so I can hear a detailed analysis about your latest architect project issues, but Addison asked me first, and I said yes. We'll all be at the same place tonight, and I can't wait. Dinner together at the lake house. Finally." I paused in front of the mirror to inspect my roots. The very subtle blonde highlights in my now long brown hair were growing out. Not attractive. I mentally told myself to make a hair appointment next week.

"I need to talk to you about something."

"Shoot," I said, my phone stuck between my shoulder and my ear as I plucked a suspiciously looking gray hair from the top of my head. He didn't answer. "I mean, 'shoot as in talk.' Come on, Luke. You speak Texan. What's up?"

"I wanted to talk in person."

I abandoned my gray-hair plucking for a moment, thinking of Luke's recent issues with his parents.

"Is it about your mom and dad? Is she still really upset that he's getting married again?"

In two weeks Luke's dad was remarrying. But it was bringing up all sorts of old heart-wounds because the woman he was marrying was the woman he'd cheated on Luke's mother with, resulting in their divorce. Extremely tough situation. And one Luke and I had been discussing a lot lately.

"No. I mean, yes, my mom is having a hard time with it. But, no, that's not what I wanted to talk about with you."

"Oh. So we talk tonight at the lake house. Are you planning to ski tomorrow?"

"Sara, I… What? Oh, yes. I'm skiing tomorrow. So are you."

"I don't know if I am. Definitely not if Sam's driving the boat and trying to kill all of us."

"I'll drive the boat. You'll ski. But this isn't what I was … I really wanted to have that two-hour drive to talk."

I plopped on my bed, his change in tone immediately registering with me. Over the course of more than three years, during at least half of that time, Luke had been my closest confidant. I knew that slight dip in his voice meant something was off.

"Talk to me now, Luke," I said, my words gentler. "What's going on with you?"

"I—" His words stopped as I heard him hold the phone away and talk to someone else. "Now's not a good time. I'm still at the office. We'll just have to talk tonight. You and Addison drive careful. What's on the menu?"

"Homemade lasagna."

"Excellent. Addison's specialty. Can't wait. I'll see you tonight."

He hung up and I just sat for a moment, puzzled by the conversation. Then I unzipped my bag to make sure I had everything I needed for two nights at Lake Shore Woods. Addison's parents had owned the house since she'd been in high school. During college, I suppose, Addison and the others used to go up there for weekends. But with demanding work schedules and the busyness of life, our group had made going to the lake house a bi-annual trip during the last three years.

We'd go out once during the summer and take Addison's parents' boat out on the water and ski. We'd eat at the worn table on the back deck, overlooking the south shore of the gorgeous lake, nestled by tall pine trees and a few houses, and catch up on life. The sound of rippling water and rustling tree leaves in our ears.

Sam liked to drag out Addison's dad's cornhole set from the garage and make us all play. After dark, we'd make s'mores. Debra never seemed able to toast a marshmallow without it catching fire. Jason would heroically swap her charcoaled marshmallows for his bubbly brown ones.

The guys would fish during the day and sometimes at night, usually depending on whether they'd caught enough to brag about. The girls would lay out and sip sweet tea. At even a hint of pink on her skin, Lily would flip out and put on her swimsuit cover-up. And always, at the end of a full day on the water, I loved the shine in Luke's eyes against his golden skin.

We'd talk and laugh, and every minute always seemed to feel like the perfection of a Southern summer weekend. And we'd go up once more during either winter or early spring. We'd play board games and pop big batches of popcorn. Luke and Sam and Jason would throw a football back and forth. Addison usually lit the fire pit, and we'd sit around, watching the flames. Sometimes we'd sing or play twenty questions. Lily would make her homemade cider, and we'd drink mugs of it while talking about anything and everything.

I loved summer best. The warmth, the beauty of the surrounding woods, the glorious feeling of escape, the ease that seemed to accompany summer in Texas.

I checked the clock.

One thirty.

Addison would be at my house in half an hour. I shook off worries about Luke's tone of voice and headed to the bathroom to pack shampoo, makeup, and everything else I might need.

I'd just finished filling Yoda's (my cat that still sheds like it's going out of style) food and water bowls and making sure her litter box was clean when Addison pulled her Subaru into one of the two guest spots in front of my apartment. Two o'clock on the dot—she was nothing if not precise. I waved from the window for Addison to stay where she was when I saw her open the car door, then grabbed my overnight bags and my purse, locked up my apartment, and headed out to where she was popping the trunk. I stowed my things and jumped into the passenger seat.

Addison slid on her sunglasses. "Can you believe this heat?"

I dug through my purse for my own sunglasses. "After a lifetime spent in Texas, unfortunately, yes, I can believe it. Where *are* my sunglasses? Grrr! And I just realized I forgot sunscreen. Someone better have some." I shook my purse.

Addison tsk-tsked. "How many Diet DPs have you had this morning?"

My addiction: Diet Dr Pepper. The gang liked to tease me about it. *As if* drinking Dr Pepper in Texas was a novelty. Sure, I might drink more soda than most—but we all have our vices. Thankfully, I've managed to keep my unnatural-for-anyone-older-than-ten-years-old appreciation for cherry Fruit Roll-Ups a secret to this point.

"What about Yoda?" Addison asked.

"She'll be fine. She'll love having complete run of the place for two days. I'll come home to so much fur everywhere that you'd think I lived with a gorilla." I found my sunglasses and calmed down, then sweet-talked Addison into pulling through a McDonald's drive-through so I could get a large Diet DP. It was Addison's fault really. She'd brought it up, and then I realized I'd forgotten to bring one for the road.

Summer in Texas was brutal. And even in early June … well, you learned to get used to it. The temperature on the car dial read ninety-eight degrees. We chit-chatted as we drove through the city; once we passed the Houston city limits, I turned down the radio.

"So tell me how things are with Glen," I told Addison, speaking of her boyfriend of the past nine months. She'd met the African American youth pastor from a nearby Bible church at a leadership conference.

"Good. Really good." Her tone sounded calm and even, but her grip on the steering wheel tightened.

"Are you sure?"

"Yes," she assured me. "I adore Glen."

"Well, what's not to adore?" I said, thinking of her attractive, outgoing, crazy-smart but kind-of-obsessed-with-bike-riding boyfriend. Addison smiled.

"So true."

"Are you doing that bike marathon with him this summer?" I asked and worked hard to keep my lips in a line to keep from laughing at the immediate frown on Addison's face.

"Hmm. I don't know. Probably. It's kind of a long marathon, and I'm not really … but, yeah, I mean, if I buy a new bike seat…" Her thoughts trailed off.

"Are you in love with Glen?"

"Without a doubt. I'm 100 percent in love with that man." She smiled, all thoughts of bike riding having vanished. A pang of longing shot through my heart. I could see the warm glow of love on Addi's face. Without warning, hope rose up in me that it would be my turn soon. I squashed it back down. To be honest, sometimes hope—amid waiting—hurt too much. Addison's grip on the wheel lessened, and she relaxed against the seat, subconscious, visible relief in the security of knowing she loved and was loved in return.

"How do you know?"

"When it's love, Sara, you know." She gave me a sideways glance, and her demeanor shifted again.

"How's Luke doing?"

It wasn't strange that she asked me. Everyone in our group knew that Luke and I were close.

"You know, he called me earlier, sounding a little distracted, saying we need to talk. Probably a work issue. Other than that, I think he's fine. He has a lot of pressure on him at his job. That promotion last year has been a mixed blessing. More money, way more responsibility. Still, he's so capable." I felt like I was rambling. The conversation with him earlier kept flashing back.

"Like you," Addison said, turning on her blinker and switching lanes.

"What?" I asked, my mind on that phone call.

"Capable like you," Addison said again. "It's like you two are the same person, Sara. You know that. We all know that. You finish each other's sentences. It's almost creepy how similar you and Luke are."

"It's not creepy!" I protested. But she was right. My friendship with Luke had started slow; conversations that ran long after hanging out with friends, running errands together because we always seem to take the same approach to shopping, about getting things done. Our taste in restaurants and entertainment, our views on spirituality and politics—everything clicked. Eventually, we just started spending more and more time together because our friendship was so easy.

Easy.

Easy for him.

"Do you think it's hard for girls and guys to be friends?" From her side profile, I watched Addison nod.

"Yes. But it's possible. Look at the seven of us. Our friendship is..."

"Unique," I answered after a moment.

"Right," she agreed, checking her blind spot before switching lanes again. "You and Jason are friends, but I was afraid you wouldn't be after you two broke up."

"I was afraid of that too. I'm incredibly thankful we've managed to stay friends, great friends. And Luke—well, Luke and I are BFFs, and he isn't even a girl."

Addison chuckled.

"He's your match, I guess," she said. I didn't answer. The words swirled in my head. For some reason, they didn't land, they just kept swirling.

"Could you tell from the beginning?" I asked. "Was that why you wanted me in the group, Addison? Because Luke and I were so much alike?"

Addison turned off the freeway. She shook her head without looking at me.

"Oh no, Sara. It was because of how Jason looked at you from the moment you walked in the room that day. I thought you were Jason's match."

I'm not sure why Addison's comment about Jason bothered me so much. Maybe because Addison was always so intuitive. Or maybe it was because no one ever seemed to expect more from Luke and me than friendship, including Luke. Or maybe it was concern that I'd been too indecisive to recognize that Jason *had* been my match.

Addison turned up the radio, and I rested my head back on the seat, listening to the sounds of her favorite country station. By the time we pulled down the woodsy Mulholland Lane, I'd just about convinced myself that Jason could not have been my match, and that just because Luke and I were really great at being friends didn't mean we couldn't be *even better* as a couple. A girl has to hold on to hope.

I prayed the prayer I'd prayed at least two thousand times: *God, could you please make Luke fall in love with me? I'm not talking Love Potion #9 or anything; I just wish the boy would see how great we would be together. But if that's not meant to be, help me be his best friend. And help me trust Your plan for my life.*

Having prayed "the prayer," I shook away my worries. Placing the situation in God's hands was all I ever seemed to be able to do when it came to Luke Anderson. Addison turned down a gravel road, and I sat up straight and took off my sunglasses to better appreciate the canopy of tall trees all around us.

In sync, Addison and I squealed with excitement.

"We're here!" she exclaimed, pulling into the driveway of the lake house. The gorgeous, two-story wood-framed house stirred delight in both of us. I saw Lily and Sam's Honda SUV parked in front of the garage, next to Jason's truck.

"Lily and Sam and Jase made it before us," I commented as I opened the door.

"I gave Lily the key yesterday. She told me they were going to leave early, and she offered to pick up groceries. I gave her a list and told her we'd all pitch in with the cost." Addison grabbed her phone and her purse.

The front door opened and Lily raced out to meet us, a huge grin on her face. You'd think we hadn't seen each other in years, rather than at Starbucks the morning before.

"Yay!" Lily cheered as we got out of the car. Sam came out from around the house. I assumed he'd been out on the back deck or down on the dock. He wore his signature green ball cap with his dad's landscape company's logo on the front. His striped board shorts and flip flops were a strong indicator that the guy was ready for the water. "Sam, help with the bags," Lily instructed, and Sam obediently sauntered over and helped grab a couple of our overnight bags. Lucky for him, both Addi and I traveled light.

"The water's perfect today," Sam said. "We should take the boat out later."

Addison slid her sunglasses up like a headband and nodded. "Go for it. The keys are in the cabinet by the fridge. Did you guys bring food?"

"Yes! We stopped on the way. Everything's ready. Jason started chopping veggies for a salad. For some reason, he's the *only* person who wants to help in the kitchen." Lily looked pointedly at Sam.

"There were only three of us here, Lily," he said with confusion.

"My point exactly."

"What point?" His cell phone rang and Sam stepped aside to take the call.

Lily looped her arms through mine and Addison's, and we headed slowly toward the front porch.

"I've been dreaming of this moment since May," I said.

"Me too," both girls echoed. We walked through the front door, and a breeze blew through the open windows in the living room. This being Texas, of course there was an air conditioner, but since the house was shut up for months at a time, Addison always wanted to air it out a bit at first. Pine trees separated the house from the water and created shade over the house. Myriad windows throughout provided a perfect view of the lake just beyond the trees. The large fan was spinning from the vaulted ceiling.

"Who's staying where?" I asked.

"Jason put his things in the loft. I think he'll take the pull-out sofa and Luke will take the other couch up there. Sam and I are staying in the master bedroom since we're the married couple."

Addison and I both rolled our eyes.

"So that leaves the blue room and the disturbing room with the deer head and the stuffed fox. And there's a new huge bass fish hanging on the wall, by the way."

"I call blue room," I piped up quickly.

Addison climbed the stairs in front of us. "Since it's my father who insists on keeping that deer head on the wall, I'll do the chivalrous thing and take the dead animal room. You and Debra can share the blue room, Sara."

"Excellent," Lily agreed.

We went our separate ways once we reached the second floor to get settled in our rooms. I put my purse and backpack on the chair, and Sam walked in and dropped my duffle bag on the bed. "You guys gave Addison the animal exhibit room? Nice," he said with a grin before heading down the hallway.

I walked to the bay window seat in the large room and looked out at the lake. We called it the blue room because of the blue-ringed quilt on the queen-sized bed. Drifting through the open windows, the sound of the wind rustling the trees nourished my soul.

There was just something about this place that felt like home. I knew it had a lot to do with the six other people who'd be filling the rooms later that evening. Lily yelled for me and Addison to come help with dinner, interrupting my reflective moment. I stopped at the antique vanity and spun my hair in a quick knot on my head, then skipped down the stairs to the kitchen.

I could hear Jason singing, as was his usual custom. The only guy in our group who liked to cook, Jason always helped Addison and Lily and I make the meals while Debra, the girl who hated to cook, usually disappeared outside with Sam and Luke. Addison was already washing her hands at the sink while Jason tossed a huge salad filled with greens, walnuts, vinaigrette, cucumber, and feta cheese.

"Has Luke arrived yet?" I asked, moving to the windows in front of the breakfast table and peering out to where Sam was milling about on the pier.

"He texted Sam and said that he and Debra would probably arrive right at dinner time. They were aiming for six."

I turned around, confused. "Was Debra riding with Luke?"

The thought didn't trouble me (much). I was just surprised since Luke had expected us to ride together. He'd said we'd needed to talk. The thought of him possibly confiding in Debra *did* trouble me, but I tried to shake off the feeling. Even if he'd offered Debra a ride, that didn't mean Luke was trusting her with whatever it was he wanted to tell me. They rarely, if ever, spent time alone together, and Luke wasn't one to share his innermost thoughts easily. Other than myself, if Luke really needed to talk to someone, he'd go to Sam.

"Sounds like it." Lily shrugged. "Makes sense to save gas money, don't you think? Plus, Debra hates driving long distances. She gets too bored."

"She also likes to blare the music and sing along. So that should be fun for Luke." Addison chuckled as she stirred tomato paste into the browned-meat mixture for the lasagna.

The more I thought about them listening to music and laughing and talking, the more bothered I became—and then annoyed at myself. Debra was Luke's friend too, but Luke and I were best friends. It wasn't a big deal. I needed a distraction. Lily told me to work on drinks, so I washed my hands before making one pitcher of iced tea and another of lemonade. Then I stopped in my tracks.

"Did anyone bring soda?" I asked suddenly. Jason grinned.

"Don't worry, Sara. I picked up a twelve-pack of Diet DPs for you."

I breathed a sigh of relief. But as I grabbed plates and napkins and headed outside to set the table on the deck, my mind started going a little haywire, worrying again that Jason could have been my match.

Because he brought me diet soda?

It was possible I was overreacting. I had a suspicion that Addison's statement that she'd thought Jason was my match, coupled with the notion of Luke and Deb riding together and my earlier moment of longing and loneliness, had my thoughts running wild. I took a deep breath and paused, taking a moment to look out over the still water and settle myself. In a few minutes, I'd sit here, surrounded by my favorite people in the world. I might not be in a loving relationship, but I *was* loved. And lucky to be part of this amazing circle of friends. My spirit calmed.

Sam joined me, lighting the tiki torch lamps that stood at every corner of the huge deck. The designer in me found candles to light at the table, along with flower petals to scatter.

"This isn't a romantic dinner for two," Sam reminded me. I ignored him. The table looked festive, not necessarily romantic. At six o'clock the sun was still shining, just dipping closer to the water. I went inside to help bring out the food, and I heard Debra burst in.

"We're here! It felt like the longest drive *ever*! Oh my gosh, that lasagna smells to-die-for good. I'm starving. Luke wouldn't stop for snacks!"

We all smiled at Debra's entrance. Her curly hair was longer than ever and flowed every which way. I loved her long navy summer dress that swept her ankles. She dropped her latest massive purse (orange) on the living room sofa and walked into the kitchen, pouring a glass of lemonade and distributing hugs to everyone. I turned to see Luke, the gentleman that he was, carrying *all* of their bags, and I might mention that Debra doesn't pack light—even for two days at the lake. He winked at me as he set down all the luggage. The wink sent flutters through my heart, and I had to take three-and-a-half seconds to scold myself for reacting that way.

We sat around the table outside, taking hands while Addison prayed over the meal. As conversation erupted and we passed platters around, I was quiet for a second and drank in the moment. The sun slipping behind the lake, the tiki lights flickering around us, the warm breeze blowing across my face, the scent of Addison's lasagna and toasted garlic bread wafting from my plate, the sound of my very closest friends talking and laughing and arguing.

Our perfect circle.

Chapter Three

Addison clapped her hands. We were all cleaning the kitchen (well, not all of us—just the usual kitchen-dwellers). Debra was making coffee, and Sam and Luke were setting up a game of Beatles-themed Monopoly.

"Family meeting in the living room," Addison yelled. Jason pulled out a cheesecake from the fridge.

"Did you make this?" I asked him, mouth salivating.

"Yeah. Last night. Help divvy out plates, will you?"

Makes incredible dessert. Another quality to add to Jason's list.

Once everyone had coffee and cheesecake and found seats on sofas or the floor in the living room, all eyes turned to Addison.

"Okay, we have something to discuss." She smoothed back her hair and folded her hands in her lap.

She's nervous.

I could see it in the way she moved. I couldn't imagine what would make Addison nervous.

"If this is about kicking me and Lily out of the singles class again and pushing us toward 'young marrieds,' it's not happening," Sam said immediately.

A small smile crept on Addison's face.

"No, Sam, as previously decided, you and Lily can go to whatever church class where you feel ministered to. Which seems to be the singles class, despite that you two are married."

I had a feeling I wasn't the only one trying not to laugh at this issue that Lily and Sam took very seriously.

"This *is* about the church class, but not related to Sam and Lily," Addison stated. "The fact is, I'm going to be leaving the class." Addison held up both hands at the protests rising from us. "I've loved leading; I've loved helping out once Derek took over for me; I've loved being part of Christ Community Church. But things are changing for me."

The room was completely silent. Addison opened her purse, which was next to her on the end table, and pulled out a diamond ring, then slipped it onto her ring finger.

"Glen asked me to marry him, and I've said yes. I'm going to be joining Westerfield Bible Church and leading the youth group with him, along with my job at the elementary school, of course. I'll keep teaching. The thing is … I love our group so much. I love you guys like family. We *are* family. I know this will change things a little, but not as much as you probably think. And change can be hard."

She stopped. I exhaled and noticed the tears in Addison's eyes.

"Glen is an incredibly lucky man, Addison. I'm so happy for you."

It was Luke who spoke. Luke—who always said just the right thing, who always stepped up when we needed him to. His comment segued into more of us crying and lots of congratulations and immediate wedding talk. Then Debra clapped her hands.

I saw Luke freeze.

"This is awesome, and while we will miss you at Christ Community so much, Addison, I want you to know that we're thrilled to see what God's doing for you and Glen. Sometimes change can be really good."

For some reason unknown to me, I felt my stomach drop as though I were at the top of a rollercoaster.

I hate rollercoasters.

"I have news as well," Debra continued. "Not as earth-shattering as Addison's—don't worry. But it's something that I—we—want all of you to know." The smile on Debra's face was eerily wide. "Luke and I are officially dating!"

Next to me, Lily's hand slid over mine and squeezed. There was noise in the room, but I was pretty sure I was having an out-of-body experience.

"Sara." Lily's low voice brought me back to earth. "Sara, honey." Her tone was soft, like she was speaking to a small child. In slow motion, I turned and took in the sight of Lily's wide eyes.

"You can't fall apart right now." I think she was just mouthing the words; either that or her whisper was barely audible. But she was right. In the far back of my mind the thought *Lily knows* registered, but I couldn't worry about that now. I made myself smile at Debra and somehow say, "Wow!" I couldn't look in Luke's direction.

My cheesecake went untouched and my hands started to shake. Lily took the plate and fork from me and disappeared into the kitchen.

Change was one thing.

Being hit by a bus was another.

I somehow managed to avoid speaking directly to Luke for the rest of the evening. I'm not sure how. Lily helped. Also, Debra and Luke disappeared for a moonlit stroll down to the pier after a while, at which point I said I had a headache and went to bed. I tried to think of a way to move into the taxidermy room. But I just couldn't come up with a believable reason for why I desperately needed a room to myself, especially one with a freaky dead deer head staring at me.

So I turned the lights off and pretended to be asleep when Debra finally came to bed. I heard her whisper my name a couple of times, but I didn't move so she gave up. Thankfully. If she wanted to stay up all night whispering to me about her new romance, that wasn't happening in this lifetime.

I woke up early after a restless night. Next to me, Debra was burrowed under the quilt, still sound asleep, only the top of her mass of brown curls peeking out from the blanket. I slipped from the bed and washed up in the adjoining bathroom, brushing my teeth and tying my hair into a braid. Then I pulled on some shorts and a T-shirt before padding downstairs for much-needed coffee. Jason was already in the kitchen, whipping up a breakfast casserole.

He took in my bloodshot eyes and inclination not to speak.

"Want to talk about it?"

"Talk about what?" I asked, going straight for the coffee. He slid a casserole dish in the oven.

"About last night. About Luke and Debra."

Does everyone know? Lord, this is getting worse.

I stirred cream into my coffee and dumped three spoonfuls of sugar in the mug.

"I'm happy for them."

So I lied. Sue me.

Jason folded his arms and just stared at me. "That's the story you're going with?"

I felt my pulse accelerate. "We're all happy for them. It's not a big deal. So they're dating, so what? What does that have to do with me?"

Jason walked over and stood directly in front of me. "You know you're a terrible liar, right?"

I gulped down a swig of coffee. "Jason, what do you want me to say? What am I supposed to say right now? You seem to be waiting for a specific response." I spat the words out, hating how angry I was growing. He didn't move.

"You can be mad, Sara. At least now you're being real."

I turned around and set my mug down, then placed both hands on the table.

"I know how you feel about Luke." From where he stood behind me, Jason's voice softened.

"You don't know what you're talking about," I told him.

"Try to believe that. It may help you get through this weekend. But you can't keep going back to that. I know you. All of us do. It's not that easy for you to pretend. You're not very good at being fake, Sara."

I turned around, still angry. "Luke and I are just friends. Obviously. Debra is one of my best friends too. And now they're dating."

He nodded calmly.

"I have to be okay with that. And I am. I'll be fine. Everything is fine."

I was breaking.

Jason pulled me to him, and I put my arms around his neck and held on for dear life, trying not to cry.

"It's okay, Sara," he said, his voice low and compassionate, seemingly unbothered by my crushing-bones grip around him.

"I need to go home," I said, my words muffled by his shirt. I let him go and wiped my eyes in case any stray tears had escaped.

He shook his head. "You can't. We're here. You can do this. Lily and Sam are leaving early tomorrow; he has to work in the afternoon. You could leave early with them," he suggested. I made an immediate decision to make that happen.

"How could you tell?" I asked him quietly. He laughed, but there wasn't any humor in it. Sadness maybe.

"I just could," he said after a moment. "Let's leave it at that."

I picked up my coffee cup and sat down at the table. Within seconds, Luke walked into the kitchen. I literally could not breathe.

"Good morning, Jason," he said, his tone short and abrupt. "Sara, walk down to the boat with me."

It wasn't a request, and as badly as I wanted to scream *No*, I figured we should get this over with. So I left the coffee cup and followed Luke outside. We were at the pier when he stopped and faced me.

"You avoided me last night."

"You were busy counting the stars with Debra."

Luke blinked in surprise at that response from me.

Take it down a notch.

I took a deep breath.

"Why didn't you tell me before?" I asked, working hard to keep my words even but not manic.

He ran his fingers through his hair. "Because it just happened! That's why I wanted us to drive down together. So I could tell you. Last Friday night I was helping Debra put together this bookcase she bought. Jason and Sam were busy, and it ended up taking forever, so we ordered takeout and just hung out. The next night I had that work dinner you couldn't make, so I figured I'd see if Deb could go with me. She could, so we went to the dinner together. Sunday after church she asked me to come over for lunch. Things just … well, I realized she liked me. And that maybe I liked her. She wanted to just talk about it and be open—so we decided we would start dating and see where it leads."

"And a week has gone by and you haven't told me."

"I'm not a girl, Sara." Luke's brow furrowed. "I wasn't going to call you that night and talk forever about how I have a girlfriend, and oh-my-gosh! She kissed me!" His tone rose at the end of his statement, and he shook his head in exasperation. His already sun-kissed cheeks flushed even further. The rest of my heart shattered at the mention of a kiss.

"I'm not like that," he continued. "I had every intention of telling you in person on the way here—I wanted to tell you. You're my best friend. Of course I was going to tell you."

I tried to talk but couldn't find anything to say.

Hold it together.

"Okay." I said it just to fill the silence. He leaned against the pier railing.

"You and I are best friends. Dating Debra doesn't change that."

"You're crazy if you think that," I said, my words so calm I wondered if I was actually the one saying them. He shook his head.

"Why? So I'm dating Debra. You dated Jason for a year."

"During which time you and I weren't … close friends." I took another breath and started speaking fast. "It's okay. It had to change sometime. One of us was bound to meet someone."

Except I always thought he'd wake up and realize he'd already met someone.

And now he had.

But she wasn't me.

At that point, my heart hurt so much I wished I could just feel numb.

Father, please help me.

"I'm not mad or anything—" Another lie. This wasn't my morning. "I'm just a little shocked, I guess. And sad this will change our friendship." At least *that* part was honest.

Luke's arms were tightly crossed at his chest, and he was looking downward, listening. I wanted him to say something.

"You know, I just want you to be happy. If Debra makes you happy, then that's … good."

Or catastrophic. Take your pick.

"Really, Luke, this is your decision, and I support you no matter what."

Still no response from the guy staring at the wooden beams beneath us.

Why on earth was I the one doing all the talking when I all I wanted was to throw myself into the lake?

He finally looked at me with an intense gaze that could make me shiver from across a crowded room.

"Is that how you really feel? Because I want to know. You've been the person closest to me for a long time now. I want you to tell me exactly how you feel."

The air left my lungs and my mouth went dry.

Now was my chance. Yell. Cry. Persuade. Be honest. Be real.

I tried to think through the haze of arguments darting around in my head.

Lord, I should be honest, right? Is this my moment? Where I tell him that I'm actually madly in love with him and seeing him with Debra will tear me into pieces? Where I finally just say what's on my heart and don't worry about how it will affect the group? I should just tell him, shouldn't I? He's asking. He deserves to know. I deserve to let go of this secret.

I thought of Lily and Jason. Apparently, I wasn't as good at hiding my feelings as I had thought. All the more reason to just blurt out the truth.

The words were on my tongue when several random thoughts invaded my heart.

Those who wait upon the Lord will renew their strength. They will mount up with wings as eagles. They will walk and not grow weary. They will run and not faint.

My grace is sufficient to meet your needs.

Trust in the Lord with all your heart and lean not unto your own understanding.

My heart broke.

Those weren't random thoughts after all. They were Scripture verses, flooding my heart. To be totally truthful, I couldn't know for sure if the push was from God or myself in that moment, but it was there. This quiet, tiny word landed.

Wait.

I can't, my heart replied. *Now's my chance. I need to tell him. I want to tell him. I can't leave this moment and truly support his relationship with Debra. There's no way I can do that.*

The Lord is my strength.

The sound of the water lapping against the boat docked next to the pier broke the silence between us. I met Luke's gaze and those green eyes almost cracked my resolve. But I steeled myself.

I didn't want to lie again and say that I was fine with him dating Debra. So I just didn't say anything. After a few more moments of listening to the water lap the boat, I had to say something.

"It's your choice," I reiterated. "I support you."

With God's help.

"You're still my best friend," he said, and I appreciated that his words were full of emotion.

"We'll always be friends," I said, my words soft but a little steadier.

But everything will change. Debra won't want to share you. I sure wouldn't.

"Hey, guys!" We both turned at the sound of Sam's voice yelling. He waved at us from the deck. "Breakfast is ready!"

We turned back to each other.

I wanted to tell him.

But I didn't. We walked back to the house, side by side. With every step that took us closer, dread rose in me. Once we entered the house, things would never be the same. Through the bay windows in the kitchen, I could see Jason and Lily laughing. Addison filling coffee cups. Sam sitting at the table, and Debra near the window, facing us.

"Luke." My voice cracked. He stopped and looked at me, patient as ever.

But I couldn't get the words out. He stepped closer, and all I wanted to do was touch him. But he wanted her, not me.

"We should go in." His words were gentle.

"I'll miss us."

His lips thinned out into a straight line. He stepped even closer, and I worried that Debra was watching from the window. His hand moved up, and I thought for a moment that he was going to touch me, but he moved back.

"You won't have to, Sara."

But I knew I would. And I think he knew it too.

Chapter Four

"Lily, please no more advice," I begged. The two of us had managed to escape going out onto the boat with the gang to ski and fish. That was thanks to Lily, really; she'd pulled Sam aside and told him that she and I wanted to stay behind and be left alone. When Luke started to object when I said I wanted to hang out at the house, Sam immediately steered him to the boat, and the group left us in peace to lay out on the deck.

A kind of peace.

But not really since Lily was giving me her mile-a-minute thought process on what we should do about my predicament. It had become a *we* situation somehow. I didn't mind, though. I needed someone to care about how tragic my life had become in the span of one night.

So we slathered ourselves in sunscreen; Lily wore her sunhat that covered half her body along with her sunglasses that left approximately one inch of her face visible (*She burned easily and rarely tanned,* she reminded me. Like I could forget.) and we laid out on the deck, sipping sodas and talking. Well, I was really only getting the opportunity to listen.

"I've known *forever*, of course," Lily told me. "Except when you were dating Jason." She paused to slurp down half her drink. "I really thought you two were perfect for each other."

Another sting to my heart—only adding to my self-doubt.

"The only person who's been loving Luke from afar longer than you is Debra."

I sat up from where I lay stretched out on the deck chair and lowered my sunglasses.

"Seriously?" I asked. Lily nodded.

"She's been crazy about Luke since before you joined the group. I mean, she's dated people now and then, but Debra's a lot more open than you, Sara," Lily said with pointed disapproval. "So she's told me and Addison how much she cares about Luke."

I laid back on my chair and put on my sunglasses without responding.

"What are you going to do?" she asked.

"What can I do? Nothing. Distance myself from the whole situation."

"You're not allowed to distance yourself from the group. We're a family."

"Not the group. Just Luke. It's only right anyway. He and I can't be the way we were now that he's got a girlfriend. I mean, we go grocery shopping together sometimes! It's not fair to Debra, and I won't do it. Oh, good grief!" I slapped my hand to my forehead.

"I told you to put on some insect repellant. The Off is by the door."

"It's not a mosquito, Lily. I've got the ladies' lunch thing with my mother next Sunday afternoon at my parents' house. I asked Luke to come with me and help, and he already said yes."

"I'll help you," Lily offered.

"Really? Do you have to work?" Lily worked part-time at a huge Barnes & Noble bookstore near where she and Sam lived.

"Not next Sunday. I can help."

"Thanks. I'll just tell Luke that you and I have it covered and he doesn't need to come."

"Okay."

"Do you think this is the real deal for Luke? He doesn't date casually. If he asked Debra out, it's because he's really interested."

Lily crossed her ankles. "She asked him."

I snorted.

"No, really," Lily continued. "She asked him over for lunch, then she told him that she really liked him and if he felt the same way, they should start dating."

Hmm.

"He's never seen me as anything but a friend," I said, to myself mostly.

"I don't think—" Lily stopped herself.

"What?" I pushed.

She twisted her mouth and shook her head. "It's not for me to say."

What wasn't she telling me? I hated being pushy, but the question was like a blinking lightbulb in my head.

"Lily—"

"Listen, Sara, you'll get through this." Lily sat up and leaned forward. "This is going to be a season of change. Think about it. Addison's getting married. We'll all be helping with wedding plans for months. She's leaving Christ Community. She's been trying to talk Sam and me into volunteering with the young marrieds' class for more than a year. Maybe now is the time for that. Sam's dad is finally making him the co-owner of the family construction business. I mean, really, it's past time. He'll have more say in the business, but he's going to be busier than ever."

"And Luke is dating Debra," I added to her list of changes.

"Yes." Lily nodded. "Luke is dating Debra. What if he were dating you? Debra would be going through the same thing that you are right now."

I hadn't thought of that before.

How would Debra have reacted if it had been me? Now knowing that she was just as crazy about Luke as I was, I couldn't help wondering. Would she have buried her feelings too? Would she have been supportive?

Probably. After all, she was my friend like I was hers.

But at the moment, I was the one feeling hurt and disappointed.

"I guess," I agreed, ready for a change of topic. "You should know that I'm going home early with you and Sam tomorrow. I know he's working in the afternoon."

Lily just nodded and shook the ice around in her glass. "Sure. But you have to make it through tonight."

Oh goody.

"What's for dinner tonight?" I asked.

"Jason's firing up the grill, and we're making shish kebabs. He's also making pineapple fried rice, which sounds delicious. Did you know he's going to take some culinary classes this summer?"

I shook my head, surprised. Jason worked as a computer programmer for a company in downtown Houston, a job he never seemed very excited about. Cooking was a hobby for him—maybe he wanted it to be more.

I closed my eyes behind my shades and soaked in the heat of the sun.

"You're lucky," I said after a moment.

"Why is that?"

"Because you've been with Sam since you were, like, ten."

Lily chuckled. "Slight exaggeration. Being together since high school can have its own set of challenges, believe me."

"But you've had someone who's been in love with you ever since it mattered."

"What do you mean?"

"I mean, we usually start dating in high school. Life is a series of relationships. And it's fun and dramatic and all that. Then you graduate from college and get a real job, and most of us are ready. We want a lasting relationship. We get tired of the rollercoaster relationships, and we want the real, steady, I'm-gonna-be-here-for-you-no-matter-what relationship. You've always had that."

"Like I said, there've been ups and downs, but I see your point."

"I feel ready for that. I haven't really dated anyone since Jason. But I'm settled; I love my job at the museum. I even hope to work my way up to museum manager, eventually. I like my apartment, but honestly, I'd love to get married and buy a house."

"Dreams of a woman," Lily said with compassion. "It'll happen for you, Sara."

"It might not be Luke, though," I said, disappointment seeping into my voice.

Next to me, Lily reached over a sunscreen-soaked hand and stroked my arm, leaving residue where she touched me.

"Honey, it's time to let go. Maybe it'll happen down the road for you two, maybe it won't. If that's what you've been waiting for this whole time, well, you've got to find a new dream."

A lump filled my throat.

Maybe it *had* all been just a dream. A hope that Luke would blink and realize he was in love with his best friend.

Lily was right. I needed a new dream. Preferably one with a gorgeous guy who could make me forget I ever loved Luke Anderson.

"I guess I have to give Luke over to God. Is that what you're saying?" I said with resignation. Lily slid down her sunglasses to the tip of her nose and peered at me over the rim.

"That's part of it, I guess. Sara, just give *yourself* over to God. He'll do the rest."

It occurred to me that sometimes, just sometimes, Lillian Spencer could say the exact thing I needed to hear. I looked at the girl next to me, complete with wide straw hat and all the Southern-belle charm I seemed to have missed out on.

"I love you, Lily," I told her. She slid her sunglasses back up and smiled.

"I love you, too, Sara."

The gang came back hours later, all pink-faced and exhausted but still exhilarated from time out on the lake. Lily and I made chocolate chip cookies while Jason and the guys grilled kebabs outside, and Debra and Addison took showers before dinner.

Once the kitchen smelled melted-chocolate heavenly and the cookies were cooling, Lily and I set the table outside. I'd found a random red tablecloth in one of the cabinets, so I flung it over the table. The tableware at the lake house was a hodgepodge of mixed-matched dinner plates, several with chipped edges, but it didn't matter. Chipped plates and white paper napkins, plastic cups and a couple of bottles of wine were all that were needed for an inviting dinner party.

I could hear laughter drifting over from the nearest neighbor's house. Lily lit more candles and made room for the platters of delicious chicken kebabs, colorfully layered with red and green peppers, and bright yellow squash and onion. An overflowing bowl of brown fried rice, complete with pineapple chunks and scrambled egg tidbits, sat in the center of the table. Addison brought a basket of warm, buttery dinner rolls, which I made sure was placed close to my seat. The shade by the house offered some relief from the still-grueling-at-six-o'clock heat.

Sandwiched between Lily and Addison, I ate my chicken kebab and listened to the recap of the day on the lake, trying not to notice (or care) that across the table Luke and Debra sat next to each other and their shoulders kept brushing each other. Apparently, the fish hadn't been biting all afternoon, and the guys were frustrated that they hadn't caught anything. Luke and Jason met Sam's suggestion of night fishing with immediate enthusiasm. Seemingly unwilling to be parted from Luke for more than ten minutes (okay, I might be a little bitter), Debra said she'd be going with them on the night excursion.

On one hand, this meant I'd be spared from being around the budding Luke-and-Debra romance. On the other hand, I'd be picturing them out on the water, under the full moon.

Lose, lose.

After dinner, we enjoyed cookies and ice cream out on the deck, watching a pink sunset over the water. I kept thinking that it had only been twenty-four hours since dinner the night before, when I'd sat at the table, reflecting on our perfect circle.

Not so perfect at the moment.

Debra brought out her acoustic guitar and started playing, humming quietly as she strummed chords. As a popular radio announcer for one of the local Christian radio stations and someone who gave private music lessons out of her home, Debra was known for her beautiful voice. Add musically gifted to her list of attractive qualities. From across the deck she started singing, and her melodic voice drifted through the air. I tried not to hear.

I could still enjoy the sunset, though. I watched the sun's last light spilling out onto the lake.

From the rising of the sun, to the going down of the same, the name of the Lord is to be praised.

The Bible verse came without warning, and I thought of my mom. For as long as I could remember, we'd had Psalm 113:3 printed somewhere in my family's home. On a canvas in my parents' room, on the chalkboard in the kitchen—somewhere.

I wondered why my mom loved it so much.

Thinking of it at that moment, as I watched the sun going down, the words took on new meaning for me. I didn't feel like praising. I felt like crying.

"Did you want coffee?"

Luke walked up to where I sat on the edge of the deck and handed me a cup. I took it from him, both surprised and pleased. I looked at the cup, which obviously already had my signature creamer and three sugars. (So I'm a sugar girl; there are worse things.)

He brings me coffee.

I reminded myself that Jason brought me Diet Dr Pepper and that was just as important, if not more so.

"Thanks," I said, sipping my perfectly made coffee by my ex-best-friend. Luke sat next to me.

"What were you thinking about?"

"My mother's favorite Bible verse. From the rising of the sun—"

"To the going down of the same, the name of the Lord is to be praised," Luke finished. He was looking out at the sunset; I was looking at him. He didn't ask me why I was thinking of the verse, and it reminded me of how well we fit together. We knew when to push for questions; we knew when to hold back. Besides, Luke's intentionality with his words was a quality I appreciated about him.

"We missed you out on the water, but Sam drove most of the time," he said, lowering his voice. "He did nearly kill all of us a time or two."

That brought a teeny smile to my face.

"So you're not up for night fishing?"

"No, thanks. You guys go and have fun," I told him, trying to sound as much like my regular old self as possible. The regular old self who usually loved every minute of time spent at the lake house, rather than the new me who was counting the minutes till I left with Sam and Lily in the morning.

Chapter Five

I didn't have to feign sleep when Debra came in that night. It must have been the middle of the night because I never heard a thing. I woke up again at the crack of dawn, slipped from the bed while Debra snored softly, and got ready as quickly as I could.

"They're not leaving this early," Jason yawned as he walked into the kitchen when I stood staring into the open refrigerator.

"I know," I told him. "I'm just ... hungry, and ready to go home."

He nodded and started the coffeemaker. "Let's make breakfast."

"What are we making?" I asked, washing my hands at the sink.

"Blueberry pancakes, bacon, and scrambled eggs. After the late-night fishing excursion, I have a feeling we'll have a group of hungry people pretty soon."

We worked together easily; I asked Jason about the culinary classes, which segued into conversation about both our jobs. The smell of bacon overtook the kitchen, and I kept snatching pieces until Jason made me take over at the scrambled egg station. I added a little green onion, Swiss cheese, and heavy cream to the egg mixture before pouring it onto the warm skillet. The sweet smell of bubbling blueberry pancakes roused the troops, and we heard footsteps above.

Lily came downstairs with her short hair wrapped in a towel. "Something smells really good."

"Why do you have a turban on your head?" Jason cocked his head in confusion, holding back laughter.

"You're not married yet, sweetheart. You'll get used to such things when you find the right girl," Lily said sweetly, pouring a cup of coffee and heading back upstairs. "I'll tell Sam breakfast is ready and be right back down without my turban, Jason," she called over her shoulder.

Addison came down and then Luke, and we started filling plates and crowding around the breakfast table. Debra was the last straggler to make her way, bleary eyed, to the table.

"Remind me next time that night fishing is when you sit on a boat when it's super dark outside and wait for fish to nibble at a line. Fish that are asleep, like you should be. Then I'll remember to stay here with the girls," Debra said, squeezing into a spot next to Luke. I'd already finished, and an early morning Luke-and-Debra cuddle fest appealed to me about as much as a run-in with fire ants, so I carried my plate to the sink.

The guys started protesting Debra's remarks, and I poured a half-cup of coffee, listening to the banter. When Lily brought over her plate, I leaned toward her.

"What time are we leaving?"

"Sam needs to be back in town by one. So I'm guessing we'll leave by ten."

Excellent news.

Everyone else seemed to be planning to stay till closer to evening. Addison was talking about grilling cheeseburgers for lunch, and Luke and Jason wanted to go back out on the water. But after breakfast, Sam and Lily and I packed up our things. I was zipping my duffle bag when Debra walked into the blue room and closed the door behind her.

Uh-oh.

"Sara, I want to say something to you."

My escape had been so close.

She sat down on the bed by my luggage.

"Sure, what's up?" I asked with all the nonchalance I could muster, unzipping my bag and pretending to look for something. It was all I could think to do. She placed a calm hand over mine and I stilled.

"Sit down for a sec, okay?"

I pushed over my bag and sat down on the bed.

"I know how close you and Luke are. He's told me multiple times that you guys are best friends, and I get that. I'm not trying to ruin your friendship with him."

I felt sick to my stomach, yet I forced myself to give Debra a tight smile and shrug. "Of course you're not trying to do that, Debra."

"I think he was worried about whether you'd be okay with him dating someone in our group. I think he was worried about you."

"Well"—I took a deep breath—"I'm fine. I'm happy for you." I know, lying again. What else could I say? Sitting before me was one of my sweetest, closest friends. I'd lost count of how many girls' nights she and I had spent with Addi and Lily—movies and cocktails and manicures and shopping, so many fun moments together. How many times had the girls and I shared prayer requests and talked about our hopes and dreams? I couldn't—wouldn't—dash her dreams now.

"I'm not going to freak out if you guys talk to each other. I don't want you to feel like you have to suddenly never contact him because he's dating me."

I bit my lip. "That's nice of you to say. But it changes things. He's your boyfriend. I respect that. I know if I were dating him—or anyone"—I cleared my throat, feeling like I just walked near a land mine—"I'd want everyone to, you know, be considerate of that."

She didn't respond for a second.

"I always thought he'd choose you."

I blinked rapidly to hold back the barrage of emotion that suddenly welled up behind my eyes. "Why would you say that?"

She shrugged. "Because it's true. I always thought Luke would ask you out, eventually. You guys have so much in common. But it never happened, so I figured—well, they really *are* just friends. So maybe that meant there was a chance for me."

Every word hurt.

"Then we had this moment ... and things shifted. He looked at me differently. And I thought, *finally*. I'm so happy." She couldn't keep the absolute giddiness from her voice, and her eyes lit up like it was Christmas.

"So happy." She sighed. "But I know your friendship is really special to him, and I'm fine with that."

I nodded. Then I dug deep and reached over and squeezed her hand.

"Don't forget that *your* friendship is important to me, Deb. Yes, Luke and I have been close friends. But so are we. Luke ... he's a great guy. I'm happy for you."

A necessary lie. Or so I told myself. There Debra sat, trying to be calm and grown up when I could tell she just wanted to jump up and squeal, "He loves me!"

Her smile stretched at my comment, and she threw her arms around me. "Thank you for saying that, Sara!" She hugged me tight and I reciprocated, wishing I wasn't so jealous. I'd liked Debra since that first day at Isabella's Deli when she'd immediately made me feel welcome. I liked her now. I even understood why Luke liked her. She was pretty and funny and the life of the party.

She was my friend too.

Which just made everything harder.

After that kill-me-with-kindness hug, I explained that I needed to get back home and so I was leaving soon with Sam and Lily. I re-zipped my bag and lugged everything downstairs.

The goodbyes were a little rough, honestly. Addison kept asking me to stay and drive back with her. Luke just kept frowning. And I kept thinking that everything had already changed; that getaways at the lake house were over as I knew them.

I'd realized within five minutes of our drive home that Lily and I were not keeping this "Luke problem" a secret from Sam since she'd talked to me about the situation as though Sam wasn't in the car with us. He looked at me through the rearview window and shrugged.

"Don't worry, Sara. For one thing, Lily tells me everything. Lucky for you, I'm a guy and I don't talk about this stuff like you girls do. So you can trust me."

I believed him but wasn't keen on having Sam be part of this experience. Too late, I supposed. Still, next to Luke, Lily had always been my closest friend in the group. I needed her support.

The fact that Sam had lived with Luke for years dawned on me.

"Were you surprised, Sam?" I wondered aloud. "About Luke and Debra? Or do they seem like a natural fit to you?"

From the backseat, I could see his neck stiffen. "Surprised? Um, yeah. As for a natural fit, I don't know. It could be that they end up complementing each other. You know, the opposites attract thing."

I didn't like the logic in his argument, but it was true. Debra could be over-the-top with her exuberance. Luke would probably temper that. Luke could be overly serious, like me. Debra would definitely liven up his life. Like Sam said, they might complement each other.

My heart sank a little further, if that was even possible at this point. Then again, everyone seemed to think Jason and I were a perfect match, and that hadn't worked out. I tried to find a way for that thought to encourage me, but it didn't work. For one thing, breaking up with Jason had been one of the hardest things I'd ever done. In my heart, I believed it to be the right choice, but at the current moment I couldn't keep from doubting all my choices—from deciding Jason wasn't the one for me, to not telling Luke how I felt about him. And what if Luke and Debra were a better fit together than Jason and I had been? Where did that leave me?

"What's your summer look like, Sara?" Lily asked.

I looked out at the trees we were passing. As a team leader for the Houston Museum of Natural Science, our most hectic season was about to begin. "Busy. Summer is always busy at the museum. We're doing a special watercolor exhibit later this month and giving some fun art classes for kids—we've got a bunch of special exhibits planned, actually. We're hosting three Friday night mixers and those are always popular.

"There are a slew of birthday parties on the schedule. And a couple of after-dark exhibits and special corporate events. Workshops, labs, behind-the-scenes tours . . . it's chaos, but I *really* love summer at the museum. Also, I'm volunteering with that nonprofit group I like, *Life as Art*, and they're doing a concert series and some cool outdoor activities, so I'll be working some weekends at the Miller Ampitheater."

"So you have a lot to look forward to," Lily surmised.

"That's true," I agreed.

But I won't be spending much time with Luke. He usually comes to the summer concerts with me. Not to mention barbecues with the gang, picnics, camping trips.

I grabbed my phone and sent Luke a text.

Lily's going to help out at the luncheon at my parents' house next Sunday. So you're off the hook.

I figured he would be out on the boat with Jason, and I wouldn't hear back from him for a while.

"We're going to look at wedding dresses with Addison soon! I can't wait! Addi wants a December wedding. How perfect!" Lily clapped her hands and squealed.

"You're all going to be bridesmaids, right?" Sam started scanning through radio stations.

"Yes, of course," Lily said. "Her first cousin is going to be her maid of honor, but we three girls will be her bridesmaids! I am so excited. Wedding plans are so fun. Did you hear Addison say she wants you to help a lot with the planning, Sara?"

I stared at the trees out the window. "Yes. She wants me to help her choose colors and design the wedding reception, but I think I'll just recommend a few wedding planners. My mom knows so many. My summer is booked."

"But we need your advice!"

"Don't worry. I'll help."

My phone buzzed and I looked at the incoming text.

Luke.

I'm still helping out on Sunday. Stop changing everything.

I felt like growling. *Me changing everything?*

> I'M NOT CHANGING EVERYTHING. IT'S JUST BETTER IF LILY HELPS ME. IT'S NOT A BIG DEAL.
>
> WE PLANNED THIS WEEKS AGO. I'M HELPING. I'VE ALREADY TOLD DEB. SEE YOU SUNDAY.

Already told Deb? Like he already needed her permission? Grrr.

"Luke's insisting he'll still help me Sunday, Lil." Her fingers tapped her phone as the bright colors and bubble shapes of Candy Crush flashed across the screen.

"Oh, okay," she said, her eyes glued to the game.

"No, not okay."

"Sara," Sam interjected. "Maybe it's a good thing. You can't cut Luke from your life because he's dating someone. If it were anyone but Debra, you'd let him help you without another thought."

"Doubtful," I answered.

"Sara, it's just this one little thing … unless you guys have a ton of things planned already for summer," Lily said, adding that last part as an afterthought.

"Not really."

"So let him help Sunday and try to be normal around him," Lily said, scowling at the phone in her hand.

I was less interesting than Candy Crush.

Disheartening.

I texted back.

> FINE. SEE YOU SUNDAY.

Chapter Six

"We need the banners hung higher!"

I nodded and wrote a notation on my clipboard as I followed Jeanie Young, the staff supervisor and my boss, through the lobby.

"And, good grief, is the air conditioning even *on*? I'm sweating like I just ate Indian food. Check the temperature and make it bearable."

Another nod. The ironic part of Jeanie's comment was her near obsession with Indian food. She had us order in lunch from Vatan Palace about once a week. I kept this observation to myself.

I clocked in Monday morning and shadowed Jeanie, making notes on the one million things that *had to be fixed* by Friday. After a working lunch, I spent most of the day at the concierge station. When I finally had a break, I grabbed a cup of coffee, stowed away in my cube, and checked the museum event calendar. Gosh, the days filled up quickly. With member-only events, family space day, finishing tours for the Buried Treasure exhibit, and Friday night movies hosted in the planetarium—the museum was, as usual, a hub for summer activity.

I'd be *way* too busy to hang out with the group.

Under normal circumstances, I'd make time to be with Addison and the others.

These were not normal circumstances.

The ping-pong noise from my computer signaled that an e-mail popped up in my inbox. I clicked on the message from Addison.

> Hey guys! Just FYI, I uploaded all the photos I took this weekend online. Check them out.

Oh dear. Addison was known for taking unintentionally awkward photos and posting them online for her seven hundred fifty-three friends to see. I figured I could take forty-five seconds to check the photos and then get back to work.

I pulled up our mutual social networking site and scrolled through Addison's many photo albums of our group. Christmas Party at Lily and Sam's; Memorial Day at the Lake House; Luke's Birthday Party; Volunteering at the Hope Soup Kitchen; Rodeo Days, and so on—*so* many memories together. I clicked on the newest album, titled Lake Shore Weekend, and looked at the pictures.

Okay, some of them were cute. Especially the ones taken pre-Debra-and-Luke-are-a-couple. I smiled at the pics of all of us girls admiring Addi's ring. I readied myself for the pictures past that night and bravely clicked to the next photo.

Everyone at the table, Luke and Debra next to each other.

Click.

The group on the boat, Debra and Luke holding hands.

Click.

A partial group photo of us on the deck. I groaned as I saw the picture. *Really, Addison? You thought that was a good idea?*

Luke with an arm around Debra. Then Sam on the other side of them. Then Lily. Then me, looking as though I've just been told I have three months to live.

My devastation—captured onscreen forever. I untagged myself from the photo immediately.

Then I logged off social networking. But the picture kept resurfacing in my mind. Addison's discernment (or lack thereof) with pictures really needed to be addressed.

Lily called me that night.

"What are you doing?"

I looked down at myself, sitting on the kitchen counter crisscross-applesauce style, wearing my pink-bunny pajamas for comfort, a Diet Dr Pepper right next to me and a jar in my hand, *Pride and Prejudice* muted on the TV.

"Eating Nutella with a spoon."

"I see." A few silent moments passed. "I saw the picture," Lily admitted.

"Ugh. I want you to have a talk with Addison."

"It's hopeless and you know it. At one time or another, we've all questioned her photography abilities. Don't worry, I don't think the guys ever even look at those photo albums."

"Luke does," I said glumly.

She sighed. "Sam does too."

We were both quiet.

"Want to come over?" Lily finally asked. "Sam's working in the garage on a project, and I'm just cleaning the kitchen. We could watch HGTV."

"No. Thanks, though. It's just a me-and-Nutella kind of night."

"Okay," Lily said, her voice soft. "Sara, it's going to get easier."

"You're probably right," I said. "Text me tomorrow."

"I will ... and don't eat the whole jar! You'll hate yourself tomorrow, and I refuse to go to the gym with you if you end up gaining weight as a result of your heartbreak. My face breaks out if I sweat too much."

"Thank you for your support, Lil. And this is Texas, love. We all sweat every day."

"Exactly. Adding sweat by working out is not in my future. So let's take it easy on the Nutella, honey."

"Fine."

I ended the call and then walked to my bedroom, flinging myself on the bed.

It will get easier, right? I began something of a hodge-podge prayer. *Because I've loved Luke for years. I'm not sure how to just "be okay" with him falling for Debra. Not when I've prayed for so long…*

It doesn't work that way.

I'm not sure where the thought came from. Maybe from God. Maybe from deep inside me. Maybe both. There it was either way. Not harsh or mean or uncaring. Just a whisper to my heart.

I closed my eyes for a moment and then pushed myself into a sitting position.

I think I need to move the sofa.

I went to the middle of the living room and stood, my arms crossed, envisioning a new layout, ignoring the mental reminders that I'm like my mother. I pushed and pulled and pushed and pulled until the small-ish sofa was now directly across from the TV. I moved the matching chair, then took twenty minutes to dig through my storage closet, looking for new accent pillows for the chair and sofa. But the new yellow pillows meant I needed to switch some of the artwork.

After spending so much time working for an art gallery, I had lots of art to choose from. I switched out a few pieces and then stood by the front door, taking the full room in view. Gray sofas and yellow pillows. Abstract art with yellow and orange and gray and black and white hues. A fluffy white rug underneath my coffee table, which had been an incredible find at a thrift store.

Satisfied and now exhausted, I turned off the lights and went to bed, groaning at the sight of Yoda sleeping in a pile of fur on my pillow.

By Thursday, I was desperate for a break. We'd had summer-school classes touring the museum all week, and since one of our employees was out sick, I had to lead tours every day. I'd woken up late that morning, too rushed to throw together a sack lunch, and hadn't had a chance to sit down in four hours.

I scarfed a cheeseburger from the museum café (also known as McDonald's), knowing I had only thirty minutes before I'd need to rejoin the tour. My phone buzzed and I clicked on the group text from Addison.

> Hey girls, wedding planning session at my house tonight? I'll order pizza.

I had a bad feeling that this was about to become my life—constant wedding planning for Addison while being forced to spend time with Debra and hear a perpetual rundown of her love life with my former best friend.

Hmm.

Before I could sniff and talk myself into the idea that my allergies were flaring up and I'd need to go to bed early … thoughts of Addison took over. The way she'd invited me into her life and shared all her friends with me. The way she'd drop everything for me if ever I needed her. The fact that I was so happy she'd found Glen and was about to begin her happily ever after.

I texted back that I'd be there.

The things we do for the people we love.

At six o'clock I walked into Addison's townhouse and kicked off my shoes by the front door.

"I'm here," I yelled, padding down the hallway and into the kitchen. The back door to the deck was open, and I could see Lily and Addison inspecting her growing tomatoes. Two large pizza boxes sat on the counter, along with a frosted pitcher of sweet tea.

Excellent.

I filled a glass then stepped out on the deck, barefoot.

"How are the tomatoes, Addison?"

Addison leaned down for a closer inspection. "I don't think I'm doing it right. Why is it taking forever for these things to grow?"

Lily smiled and patted her shoulder. "Give it time. My mother says that all Texas women should grow tomatoes in their backyard."

"So why aren't *you* planting a garden, Lily?" I asked. She glared at me.

"Come on, Addison. I worked all day at the bookstore, and I'm desperate for a piece of that Canadian bacon and pineapple."

In Lily language, all day is actually four hours.

I just smiled and stepped aside before following the girls back inside.

The front door opened, and we heard Debra come down the hallway.

"Is that iced tea?" she asked immediately. "Pour me a glass. All the way to the top, Addi. I'm beat. We're doing those gosh-awful donor things, where we answer phones and ask people for money. I ran out of perkiness at 10:00 a.m."

I doubted that. Debra was an unending well of perkiness. The pledge drives came twice a year at the listener-supported KKLE and always resulted in long hours with lots of talking for Deb. According to her, those weeks were the bane of her existence.

Addison quickly poured Debra a glass, and we sat down at the round antique table in her small but lovely kitchen. The townhouse had been new just a few years before when Addison had purchased it. Cream-and brown-flecked granite countertops lined the kitchen wall, and stainless-steel appliances gleamed. Light oak cabinets hung over a white-tiled backsplash. On the open opposite wall from the cabinets, a large painting of an old, beautiful wooden bridge with a still river underneath hung—a gift to Addison from myself.

The soft light of a hot summer evening spilled in through the windows, flanked by cream-colored curtains. Lily had moved the pizza boxes to the center of the table, and the four of us dove in. Pointing a piece of crust at Addison before biting off half, Lily got things started.

"So, a December wedding. What about venue?"

"We're going to have the wedding at Glen's church, but I'd like to have the reception at the Vineyard."

"Oooh."

The three of us gave a collective gasp. The Vineyard, also known as the coveted-reception-hall-for-all-brides-in-Houston. I'd helped my mother design at least three weddings at that very place. With elaborate crown molding, vaulted ceilings, deep mahogany floors, an intimate dining room, and gorgeous spots for photo-ops—the Vineyard was the ideal venue for Addison's romantic heart.

"Is it available?" I asked.

Addison nodded. "But I can't afford the deluxe wedding package. I can book the hall, but I need to have the food catered and bring my own decorations. They'll provide the tables and linens, though."

"We can work with that, Addison," I assured her. "You'll have a gorgeous reception. I can ask my mom for the names of a few wedding planners, and I know she can recommend an affordable deejay and caterer."

"I have a caterer," Addison told us.

"Oh. Who did you get?"

"His name is Jason Garcia. He's currently a student at the Cook-Stop downtown, but I think he'll do a great job." Addison grinned. All three of our jaws dropped.

"You're having *Jason* do the food? By himself?" I questioned, feeling very worried that Addison had just done something crazy like hire our friend to cater her wedding.

"He's getting two other guys from his culinary class to help, I think. It will be good experience for Jason. Catering a wedding will be great for his résumé. We're keeping the menu very simple. Salad to start with and a chicken with vegetables dish for the entrée, with gluten-free options too. We talked about the menu possibilities this week, and he said he'd make a few different meals for me to try. I was thinking you should all come with me. Jason will make three different dishes, and we'll decide which one we like best. He's not doing the cake, though."

Thank goodness for that.

"How many guests are you thinking?" I asked.

"Three hundred," Addison answered, followed by an *Eeek! I know that's a lot!* look on her face. "Glen has a huge family, and we have so many people we want to invite from both of our churches. Did I tell you my brother's coming to visit in August?"

Addison's twin brother, Everett, whom I'd met at least once during a Christmas holiday he spent in Texas a couple of years ago, lived in North Carolina and worked as a pilot for a small airline.

"How's Everett?" Debra asked.

"Good. He works a lot. But he wants to come out and get to know Glen a little better and be part of the wedding plans and all that. I'm thrilled."

"I hope we get to spend some time with him too." Debra refilled our glasses of tea. "We should all hang out while he's in town."

"Good thinking," Addison agreed. "Maybe I'll plan a get-together. He says he wants to be part of the wedding plans, but I doubt that extends to dresses and cakes and flowers." She grinned. "A barbecue with my friends will be much more fun for him."

"Well, I love hearing about dresses and cakes and flowers." Lily stood and grabbed the box of store-bought snickerdoodles on the counter. She popped one in her mouth before bringing the cookies to the table. "What are you thinking for bridesmaids' dresses? Just as a heads up, I don't look good in green."

"Since it's in December, I'm thinking I'd like to do something like a cranberry."

"That would be beautiful," I agreed.

"Can you recommend a baker for the cake?"

"I'll ask my mom to give you a few names."

"I'm so excited!" Addison suddenly burst out, clasping her hands together. Her enthusiasm spread to all of us, and we grinned with her.

"Oh, I can't wait until I get to plan my wedding." Debra sighed longingly. My grin vanished. I looked at Lily, who shook her head ever so slightly.

Code for *Keep calm and refrain from speech.*

"How are things with you and Luke?" Addison asked, not noticing Lily's disapproval.

"Excellent!" Debra beamed. "I never thought of Luke as very romantic, but he's really surprised me. He sent me flowers at work this week, so this morning, I went over to his apartment early and left him a card on his windshield. So fun! Tomorrow night we're going to have dinner at Duke's downtown. They have live music on Fridays." Debra's eyes sort of glazed over as she looked out the sliding door next to us.

Her eyes were in the general direction of the not-growing tomatoes, but I had a feeling all she saw was Luke.

Flowers. Cards. Dinner dates.

Oh, my.

Chapter Seven

I spent Saturday with my mother, preparing for the Sunday luncheon. We shopped all morning, prepped for the Sunday menu, then cleaned like crazy.

While I sorted through my mother's table linens, she tweaked the flower arrangements. She poured me a cup of green tea midafternoon, and we sat together at the kitchen island for a snack of cheese and crackers and fruit. My mother continued to pore over her lists for the following day.

"Luke will be here early, right? I want you two ready to serve as soon as guests arrive."

I popped a cheese cube in my mouth. "I told him to be here by ten forty-five since you said the guests will be arriving around eleven fifteen. Knowing Luke, he'll be early."

"Like you," my mother said, her eyes still on the notepad. She rested the tip of her pen on her bottom lip.

"You should keep the coffee containers full and the appetizer trays circulating. We'll have a buffet of food, but it would still be nice to have Luke carry around a tray. He's so adorable. The ladies will enjoy chatting with him."

I didn't roll my eyes even though I wanted to. She was right. He *was* adorable and every one of my mother's friends would probably end up trying to think of ways to set him up with their daughters.

"Luke is dating Debra," I told her. My mother's pen dropped to the marble island.

"Debra Hart? The loud one?"

I scowled. "She's not loud, Mother. She's outgoing."

"Hmm."

"They told us at the lake house they were dating. It's only been a few weeks. But she's crazy about him." I stared at the grapes on my plate.

"Well, he's certainly a great catch. But just a few weeks… They can't be very serious yet."

Here's the thing about my mother. She can make me nuts sometimes. My dad used to say that she and I clash because we're so similar. He stopped saying that, which was a wise decision on his part, but I know he kept thinking it.

As her only daughter, I had the undivided focus of my mother's attention, and at times that overwhelmed me. Since childhood, she would make assumptions about how I felt or what I wanted, and while she was often right, I wanted to make my own choices and do things my way. But in the end, I'd taken the long road to the same ending. Like her, I loved design and architecture and art. Like her, I loved making things beautiful. Like her, I breathed easiest in clean, organized, well-balanced spaces.

In some ways, our similarities resulted in making us closer; we enjoyed the same movies and books and hobbies. But her uncanny sense of who I was—or who she wanted me to be, or both—left me pushing against her at times.

But of all the close friends I have, my mother is the only person who has thought Luke was perfect for me from the first time she met him. It's maddening. I want to appreciate the fact that she thinks he and I are a match made in heaven. But since she's the *only one* who thinks that (apart from me), I doubt it's true. If I'm wrong, then she must be too.

For the record, my dad adored Jason and nearly cried when he and I broke up.

Such is my life.

"How are you doing with this?" My mother touched my hand. The thoughtful, focused look in her eyes was one I knew well—her mind turning this way and that, trying to find the solution to her daughter's pain.

I find it annoying she knows me so well.

"I'm okay. It was a shock, I'll be honest. But now that I'm used to the idea, it's fine. It changes things for me and Luke, though."

"He's still helping tomorrow," she pointed out. I shrugged. She went back to writing on her notepad, and I went back to eating cheese. After a few minutes, I broke the silence.

"Mom, why do you like that verse so much? The one about the Lord's name being praised from the rising of the sun until the going down of the same?"

She paused. "What do you mean?"

"You've always had that verse printed somewhere in our house. Remember when it was on that chalkboard we used to have? Now it's framed in the guest bedroom. You've never told me why you like it so much."

She looked back at her notepad. "It just speaks to me, I guess."

Her posture straightened and her grip on her pen tightened.

There's more to the story...

I didn't feel comfortable pressing the issue at that moment.

"I like it too," I offered instead. She added something to her list then stood up.

"We have all the ingredients for the chicken salad, along with croissant rolls. We'll serve a fresh green salad as well. We have the truffles, but we need to make the cheesecakes—one plain, one turtle—this afternoon."

"How many ladies are you having?"

"Twenty. We'll need to set both the dining table and the breakfast table for guests."

I nodded. My mother, the consummate hostess. Helping her host parties was second nature to me at this point. She put me to work creating the turtle cheesecake, but my mind was on anything but the dessert while I swirled the caramel and chocolate chips. The verse and my mother's subtle-but-obvious-to-me reaction to my mention of it wouldn't leave my thoughts.

Once the cheesecakes were cooling, the linens and silverware sat organized on the counter ready to be used, and the fresh flowers were arranged to perfection, I took off, deciding to go to the Saturday night church service.

I slipped in and sat in the back of the large, half-full sanctuary. Saturday nights usually drew a younger audience, including lots of couples with small children. I stood during worship, enjoying the acoustic set, while the dim lighting of the sanctuary lulled me toward sleep. One of the associate pastors began his message, and I tried to concentrate, but my mind kept drifting to thoughts of my mother and Luke and the upcoming luncheon. After church, I ran into Jason in the parking lot.

"What are you doing here?" I asked in surprise.

"I didn't have anything going on tonight, and I want to sleep in tomorrow," Jason explained. "Want to grab coffee?"

I nodded. "Okay. Let's go to Starbucks on Jasmine Street."

Ten minutes later, I was slurping down a caramel Frappuccino, peppering Jason with questions about how on earth he could agree to cater Addison's wedding.

"Have a little faith in me!" he laughed. "My buddy Chris and another student, Piper, are going to help me, and I'll split the paycheck with them. I'm psyched about it."

Certainly not lacking in self-confidence, that one.

I mentioned casually that Luke was helping me serve at my mother's luncheon tomorrow. The usual playfulness in Jason's dark-brown eyes vanished. His long, black lashes fluttered, and he tapped a finger to his lips for a moment.

"Is that a good idea?"

I wanted to flick my straw at him.

"I told him he didn't have to, but he insisted. He said he told Debra. Have you, um, seen him this week?"

Jason shook his head. "I think he had some big project he was working on. Sam and I hung out and played video games Wednesday, but Luke couldn't make it. And then last night he..." Jason paused.

"He went out with Debra. I know. It may help me feel more normal about it if you and Lily would actually *act* more normal."

Jason took off his red cap, tucked his curly black hair behind his ears, then put the cap back on. I could see half of his Celtic cross tattoo on his bicep peeking out beneath the sleeve of his T-shirt. One tanned hand lifted his coffee cup.

Sometimes I wished he weren't so cute. Then I wouldn't have those waves of conflicted feelings about breaking up with him.

"Do you want to know what I think, Sara?" He sipped his coffee again.

"About what?"

"About you and Luke."

"There is no me and Luke," I said, squirming uncomfortably. Despite the truth that Jason was one of my closest friends, there was still that fact that long ago he'd been my boyfriend. He'd kissed me and held my hand and held an umbrella for me when it rained.

"Jason, let's talk about something else."

"I need to say this. Sara, I don't think you should give up on him."

I looked at those black eyes of Jason's.

Gosh, he was a great guy.

But I couldn't create fireworks.

"Tell him how you feel," Jason whispered.

I shook my head. "I can't. I don't expect you to understand, but I just can't. I'll wait it out and see if things work out between him and Debra."

"And if they don't? Will you say something then?"

"I don't know. Maybe."

Jason pushed back in his chair and huffed. "You won't fight for what you want?"

That stung.

I didn't want to have this conversation with someone I cared so much about, about someone I couldn't stop loving.

"Don't you see, Jase? I don't want to *have* to fight for him. I want Luke to fight for me. But he doesn't"—my breath stopped short—"he doesn't feel that way about me. He never has. We've been best friends, but he's never shown interest deeper than that. Best friends. I was his *best friend.* I've got to support him through this."

Jason stared at me. "How long have you felt this way about him?"

Oh no.

"It's been off and on, okay? Please stop asking me questions. You *know*, but if you're my friend too, I need you to support me. Please." That last word barely made it out. Jason's warm hand covered my cold one.

"Sara, I'm sorry."

I peered up at him.

"You're right. That's none of my business. I just—"

"Not while we were dating," I said in a fast, hushed voice. "And he wasn't the reason I broke things off. It is and was because I adore you *as a friend.*"

"Okay," Jason said after a moment. He cracked his knuckles and looked out the window next to us. I had a feeling he didn't want to push further on that topic. Thank goodness. I took a breath, trying to slow my jumping heartbeat.

"And you're right. I want to support you," Jason said. "I'm here if you need me."

"I know you are." I struggled to get my voice back. "Promise me you won't say anything to him."

Jason coughed. "All right. I sort of feel like we're in high school." He raised both eyebrows and blushed before tugging his cap a bit lower.

A hollow laugh escaped me. "Me too."

I left in a hurry, thinking that coffee together had been a bad idea. The next time I talked about the Luke situation with someone, it might be easier if Lily were my confidant. I gripped the steering wheel, and for some reason, drove back to my parents' house.

"Sara?" I had let myself in. My mother poked her head around the corner of the hallway. "I didn't expect to see you again this evening."

"We've just had dinner," my dad said from his seat on the sofa, a warm smile filling his face at the sight of me. "Want leftovers?" From the living room, I could see my mother back in the kitchen, wiping down counters.

"What did you have?" I dropped my purse and made my way to my dad. The aroma of soy sauce, sugar, and chicken filled the living room. Dr. Witherspoon, with his short gray hair, crinkles at his eyes, and tan arms from his consistent morning run, accepted the hug I gave him. A few minutes later,

I sat on a barstool at the kitchen island next to my dad as my mother pushed a bowl of chicken teriyaki toward me.

"I wanted to check on my cheesecakes," I said, going back to her unasked question. Dad smiled and rested his chin on his fist, leaning over the island.

"I'm glad to see you for any reason."

With a mouthful of rice, the corners of my mouth lifted. My dad reached over and squeezed my shoulder.

"I'm going upstairs to change for bed, you two." Once Mom went up the stairs, I scraped the bottom of my bowl, filling my spoon.

"Dad, do you know why Mom likes that Bible verse about praising God from the rising of the sun?"

He stood up from his barstool. "That's been a favorite of hers for years, sweetheart. I suppose we all have Scripture passages that speak to us; I know I do. I'm going to go upstairs too—full day tomorrow. Why don't you stay the night? We could have breakfast together." He kissed the side of my head before heading for the stairs.

Alone in the kitchen, I rinsed out my bowl and stuck it in the dishwasher.

"Oh, Sara." My mother came back down the stairs and joined me in the kitchen. "Are you staying overnight, dear?"

I shook my head. "No, I just … I'm leaving soon."

"Well, you're welcome to stay. This is your home too." She joined me in the kitchen.

My home too. In some ways, I supposed. I looked around at the impeccably beautiful home. White couches and cream rugs. Cherry cabinets and planked hardwood floors. Straight lines and wood accents to bring texture. The faint smell of vanilla candles. Fresh flowers on the kitchen table. It was my mother's place. It felt and looked and breathed of her. She'd always made room for me, of course, but the space belonged to her.

"Mom, why do you like that verse?" I asked again. She stopped mid-step.

"We have a long day tomorrow, Sara."

"Please just tell me. It's only a Bible verse. I just want to know what it means to you."

She opened the cupboard and pulled out a glass.

"That verse was a comfort to me during a dark time." She put the glass under the tap and filled it with water. "It was a reminder to me—that even when things are difficult, even when things aren't going the way I would choose, from the moment I wake up until the time I go to sleep, God wants me to praise Him. I wasn't doing that very well. So I memorized the verse."

My mother shook back her hair.

With her house slippers, silk robe, and auburn-treated hair, even without her makeup on my mother looked beautiful. Like a movie star from a classic film.

We could drive each other crazy, my mother and me, but it occurred to me there was more to her than a polished exterior and an organized home.

"Maybe it's your turn to cling to that verse, Sara." Her words drifted over to me, softly, with understanding. I wondered where that understanding had come from. She walked to me and pulled me into a gentle hug. The smell of her favorite coconut-scented lotion comforted me but didn't detract from the unanswered questions lingering in the air.

My mother had secrets.

Chapter Eight

Luke! I'm thrilled to see you!"

"Suzanne, it's nice to see you again."

My mother's gushing could be heard from the front door to where I stood at the kitchen counter. Without looking at the clock, I knew Luke was early. He hated to be late. I kept sticking vegetables into tiny plastic cups filled with a third of a cup of blue cheese dressing.

"Hey, you."

My face tilted up at the sound of his voice. He stood there, tall, with his blond hair freshly cut, dressed in a white polo and khakis. (My mother's idea. She wanted us to match since we were basically her free servants for the luncheon.) The white polo hugged Luke, showing off his muscular frame and making his tan even more noticeable. The khakis fit in such a way that, to my embarrassment, I just wanted to keep looking him up and down every time he moved.

I, however, looked like a Cracker Barrel employee.

"Thanks for being here on time," I told him. He just lifted and dropped his shoulders, an easy smile on his face. The relaxed look in his eyes swept away some of the anxiety I'd been feeling about him helping out. He walked over to stand by me and gave me a quick side hug.

We were us again, just for a moment.

My mother immediately started giving him instructions, which I tuned out since I'd heard them yesterday and at least three times since 8:00 a.m. Undoubtedly, I'd hear them again before guests arrived. The timer on the oven beeped, and Mom abandoned her speech to rush to pull out a pan of soufflés. The warm, enticing smell of spinach and egg filled the kitchen. She set the pan on top of the stove, then reached for her buzzing cell phone on the counter and disappeared down the hallway.

"Are you hungry?" I pulled two plates from the cabinet next to the refrigerator. "We could eat a bite before everyone arrives."

Luke was already snagging a mini quiche. "Coffee?"

"I'll pour you a cup." I had this feeling I should ask how his date went. It seemed like the nice, friend-ish thing to do.

"How's work going?"

I went in another direction. Bringing up Debra and hearing a recap of their night together seemed like more than I wanted to take on at the moment.

"Good. I finished the Thompson project. I told you about that one, remember? The halfway house that's going up downtown?"

I nodded. A surge of pride welled up in me at the excitement in his voice and the light in his eyes as he talked about what I knew was a passion project for him. Luke loved his work like I loved art, and *this*—this sharing what we do and who we are—had been a source of connection for us for years.

"The plans are drawn and it should be a really nice facility. How are things at the museum?" Luke shifted his weight as he leaned against the counter. I kept my eyes on the soufflé on my plate, rather than again admire the man's quite attractive physique.

"Busy. Next weekend we start our outdoor concert series. I'll be working some weekends, but I don't mind. We've got this great local indie band coming for the first concert, and we're going to have a sidewalk display of chalk art. The kids and families always like that."

"Let me know the concert details ahead of time, okay? Debra and I might want to come."

I looked down at the blue-cheese cups. "Sure."

"We heard this band at Duke's last night. They were pretty good."

"Okay, you two."

Thank goodness for distractions. Luke and I turned our attention to my mom.

"Luke, I'd like you to walk around holding a tray with a variety of mini quiches, deviled eggs, sweets, and so on. Sara's already created that serving tray. I plan for everyone to just mingle and nibble on these snacks for the first fifteen minutes. Then you two will set aside the food and prepare for everyone to sit for luncheon around 11:30. Once we've seated and I've prayed, start serving lunch. Sara, keep an eye out for when people are finishing. Then Luke, you'll start to clear while Sara prepares the dessert plates."

She motioned to the tables, which she and I had spent over an hour putting together. The white-on-silver table settings were all my mother and looked like they belonged in a design magazine. Starched white linens, silver napkin rings, white wooden candle holders, centerpieces of bouquets of white flowers in short glass vases—the tables were decorated to perfection. Rather than having just a buffet for the luncheon, Luke and I were now full-service participants in this affair.

Luke finished his coffee and stuck the mug in the dishwasher. He washed his hands and turned to me.

"Am I allowed to accept tips?" he whispered, his green eyes twinkling with humor. With a laugh, I reached up and smoothed the collar of his shirt.

"Absolutely. Feel free to be as charming as possible with my mother's friends. They'll love you."

He winked at me, and for a moment we just stood there. Me looking up at him. Him looking down at me. If we'd been a couple, I would have traced his jaw with my finger before planting a kiss on his cheek.

Instead, I handed him the tray and reminded him to tell the ladies that coffee and tea were available.

An hour and a half later, Luke and I were clearing away dessert plates and refilling coffee cups while my mother and her friends sat and chatted around the tables.

Running the coffee station and keeping the food coming had kept me busy. Still, I'd stolen a few glances at Luke, smiling at the sight of him trapped in conversation with one woman after another. They gathered around him, complimenting the food and the service. He handled it as I knew he would, kindly serving the ladies and giving them his full attention. He came over twice to refill the platter. At one point, I pretended to scold him.

"I think you were flirting with Mrs. Ramirez!" He shook his head.

"No! She's the one who asked me if I have plans later tonight!"

I laughed and he winked at me as he went back into the den of lions—I mean, Christian women.

Soft, instrumental music played over the surround sound, and the faint aroma of bacon and eggs floated throughout the first floor. After all the dishes were stacked in the kitchen, and the women were content for the moment, Luke and I sat at the island together and snacked on leftovers.

"Your mother is great at hosting parties." We could hear the laughter and conversation drifting all through the first floor of the house.

"I know. She creates spaces that look and feel inviting, and then she brings people together. She seems to know just the words to say to make people feel welcome."

"You have that gift too."

I shook my head at Luke's statement. "Oh no. I'm much more introverted."

Luke popped open a water bottle and took a swig. "You like your space, and you need time alone. That doesn't mean you don't have the gift of hospitality, Sara. Remember that time you hosted Addison's birthday party? The platters were so nice that no one wanted to touch them and mess up the food! And then you hosted Lily and Sam's couple's shower…" Luke pointed his water bottle at me. "By the way, I don't support a couple's shower for Addison and Glen. Those aren't my favorite. Try to talk her into just doing one with the girls. We had to watch Lily open about two hundred presents. Then you hosted that birthday party for me, which was amazing, considering how small my apartment is. You served those really good spicy stuffed peppers. You love hosting parties. You're just good at keeping a healthy balance for yourself. You don't spread yourself too thin, but you're quick to be open to the people around you."

A smile had crept up on my face as I listened to Luke talk. "Well, it's impossible to be too introverted with our group," I said. "Lily doesn't tolerate much 'alone time.'"

Luke chuckled. We took a walk through the dining areas to make sure everyone had what they needed. Women seemed to be dispersing, so we cleared away the tea and coffee cups while they congregated in the living room and foyer, saying goodbyes, all of them thanking my mother—Luke and myself as well—for the wonderful afternoon and the delicious food.

Once the house was empty of guests, my mother shooed Luke and I out to the deck. We offered to wash dishes, but she assured us she had a cleaning service coming first thing Monday. Luke and I sat on the deck swing together, snacking on watermelon slices while looking out over the golf course.

"Have you talked to your dad lately?" I waited for him to speak, knowing his dad's upcoming marriage was a sore subject.

Luke's jaw tightened. "He called last night again, asking if I would come to the wedding."

I winced.

"He doesn't seem to get it. Even if I wanted to go, I could never hurt my mom that way."

"I know."

"I wish I knew how to help my mom get through this. I wish he understood how much he's hurt all of us by doing this, but there's nothing I can do."

We drifted back and forth under the pergola. Flanking the glossy redwood deck, pink azalea bushes rustled with the warm breeze that snaked through the air. The soothing sound pierced the quiet between us. Not that I minded; I could be quiet with Luke for as long as he wanted.

"My mom says that when things are out of her control, she clings to that verse that you and I were talking about at the lake house. From the rising of the sun, until the going down of the same, the name of the Lord is to be praised. When she can't do anything else, she says she praises the Lord."

Luke didn't speak.

Finally, he broke the silence. "I figure eventually I'll get used to him being married to Tanya. It'll become our new normal. It's not like he was ever a very impressive father or husband, if I'm honest, but my mother loved him. She stayed with him. With all he put her through, it's hard to see her being the one left by him."

I pushed off from the deck, and we swung a bit higher.

"You never know, maybe God's going to do something great in your mom's life. She's free to do whatever she wants now. After a while, I think she's going to begin to enjoy that freedom."

Luke folded his arms over his chest and nodded slowly. "That's true. She's been held back by my dad for a long time. Maybe this will be her season to thrive."

I nudged his shoulder. "You should go see her sometime this summer."

Luke rested his head on the back of the swing. "I know. I've gone over my schedule again and again. There's just so much work to do in the next few weeks."

I drew my knees up to my chin. "She needs you, Luke."

"I'll make it work somehow. I'll find the time. Debra may want to go with me."

I traced an imaginary circle around the freckle I knew was on my right knee. Luke taking Debra to Colorado with him to meet his family sounded ... well, like words I'd never thought I'd have to hear.

"I'm going to try, Sara," he said in a decisive voice.

Try? Try what? Try to make his relationship with Debra one that will last?

"I'm going to try to praise the name of the Lord, like your mom says. When things are out of my control."

Oh.

You and me both.

My mother came outside, drying her hands on a dishtowel.

"Mom, did you seriously wash dishes? After we offered?" I said with annoyance. She shrugged.

"I couldn't wait. You know that a sink full of dishes makes me crazy."

Yes, I did know that.

"It'll take more than one load anyway, and like I told you, I have help coming tomorrow. Luke, Dr. Witherspoon will be home soon. He decided to play golf this afternoon. We're going to grill salmon. Would you like to stay for an early dinner?"

"Oh, I'm sure Luke can't stay, Mom," I said quickly, my eyes trying to convey to her to back off.

"Well, Debra's working tonight, actually. It's the last night of that telethon thing at the radio station, so they needed extra people." He looked at me and raised his eyebrows.

Normally, the two of us having an impromptu dinner at my parents' house wouldn't be a big deal.

I couldn't help wondering what Debra would think, though.

"Well, then, it's settled. The least I can do is feed you after you waited tables at my house today!" My mother laughed at her own joke, and my lips thinned out in a line. She avoided eye contact with me.

"Backing off" has never been her strong suit.

She disappeared back into the house, and Luke and I kept swinging and talking for another hour. Other than the few times Luke mentioned Debra, conversation between us flowed like nothing had changed. We laughed and teased each other with the ease we'd had before. But as much as I wished I could rewind time back to before that weekend at the lake house, I couldn't. Maybe I held on to every moment more because we both knew he was with Debra. I knew these moments together would now be few and far between.

As we sat next to each other on that swing, I was painfully aware of every move of his body. His laugh brought a smile to my face and an ache to my chest.

Once my dad came home, he was eager to catch up with Luke, so I helped my mother inside, preparing sides for dinner.

"Mom, I told you he's dating Debra!" The measuring cup of rice I held in my hand shook and rice grains spilled everywhere. With a huff, I poured the rest of the rice into the cooker and cleaned up the mess.

"Oh, Sara. You two have been friends for years. Dinner over here is not a big deal. Don't get so riled up." (Texas, y'all.)

"She may think so!"

"Let him worry about that. He said yes. Make some iced tea, will you?"

I sighed.

So dinner commenced. With the four of us eating grilled salmon, wild rice, and salad, seated at the outdoor table under an orange umbrella. Afterward, we sipped cappuccinos and laughed as my dad told us about his latest antics on the golf course.

An otherwise perfect evening.

If my date didn't already have a girlfriend.

Chapter Nine

I started my workday the following morning by strolling through the Butterfly Center. Something about that area always transported me to someplace else, someplace much more exotic than downtown Houston. I walked through the center alone, taking a few minutes to focus and breathe before diving into yet another busy day at the museum. So far, summer had proven to be even more hectic than we thought. Today I knew that several groups of Boy Scouts and Girl Scouts were coming to enjoy the *Under the Sea* film at the planetarium before touring multiple exhibits.

However, my day would be spent manning the customer service desk, which meant I'd be answering a million questions—from whether we had Band-Aids to where were the dinosaurs.

Moms and dads and kids and strollers filled every corner of the building. Screeches and scolding and baby cries echoed through the hallways. I had to work past noon because of the steady stream of guests stopping at my station. Finally, I disappeared into my cubicle for a break.

At 1:00, my friend Wendy popped her head into my office.

"I picked up tacos from Bodegas."

The smell of spicy ground sirloin inundated my senses, and I reached for the bag. "You are truly a great person."

Wendy laughed. She plopped into the extra chair stuck in the corner of my cubicle and opened her own Styrofoam box.

"How much do I owe you?" I opened the desk drawer that held my purse. Wendy waved her napkin at me.

"You buy next week and we're even. I knew you'd skipped lunch."

"Customer service," I said by way of explanation as I opened the small, plastic container of pineapple salsa and sprinkled it on top of my taco.

"I'm excited about the new artwork. Don't get me wrong, I love dinosaurs and space and mummies, but the special art exhibits are my favorite," Wendy said before biting into a soft vegetarian taco, which I knew to be her favorite. We went to Bodegas at least once a week.

Another art history major and just two years younger than myself, Wendy was a kindred spirit when it came to loving fine arts. "I'm really looking forward to having a few minutes to actually walk through the new exhibit and see the paintings. And I can't wait for the new IMAX showing next month. *Tales from Egypt*. Are we going to get an early showing?"

I finished another bite of my delicious taco and took a swig from my water bottle. "Definitely. Jeanie said the staff can view it as soon as it comes in."

We chit-chatted about the schedule before Wendy left for a tour. I went through the paperwork stacked neatly on my small desk, and in the semi-privacy of my cubicle, I slipped off my heels and checked my e-mail.

Once I'd responded to a few urgent e-mails, I turned my attention to the calendar in front of me. One activity after another, one special exhibit after another—the museum would be packed for the next several weeks. Our floor staff often rotated positions, so I'd most likely move around everywhere from the planetarium to the parking garage if we were desperate. More often than not, Jeanie seemed to want me at customer service, which was fine by me.

After closing that night, I went to the store on my way home to get more litter for my precious Yoda. Then I came home to an upchucked fur ball on my living room floor.

Nice.

Here's the thing about me and animals. My mom never let me have a pet while I was growing up. She's supposedly allergic, though I'm pretty sure that was a self-diagnosis to avoid arguments from me. She can't handle animal fur or animal food or animal anything in the house.

My childhood dreams of having a pet never went away. When I got my own place in Austin, I promptly went to the animal shelter, where I met Yoda. A tiny little ball of black fur, with green eyes and a light pink tongue—she hooked me. Yet for all of her cuteness, not one person at the shelter mentioned how much Persian cats, even mixed Persian cats, shed as they get older.

At the time, I was dating a guy whose obsession with Star Wars probably bordered on unhealthy. I sat through every Star Wars movie multiple times with him.

Hence, my kitten was named Yoda.

The relationship did not last, but my knowledge of Star Wars remains with me to this day.

So, as darling Yoda grew, I was again, unfortunately, reminded that I'm like my mother. I'm not crazy about fur or litter or cat vomit.

Yet, I made a commitment to Yoda and I hold to that. For the most part, she holds up her end of the bargain. She's cute. She likes to be petted but not too much. And she sleeps at the foot of my bed (or on my pillow when I'm not home). Occasionally she kills spiders. If she can muster the motivation.

We have a solid relationship.

I'd just finished cleaning up the cat vomit when someone knocked on the door. Lily was standing on my front porch.

"Hey!" I said, giving her a quick hug. "What are you doing here?"

"Sam has to work late. I'm bored. I want to hang out. I was fix'n to text you, then decided to just show up." (Texas, y'all.)

I pushed the door open even further and motioned for her to follow me. "Come in then."

Lily chopped lettuce and tomatoes while I put together a simple dressing for a Southwest chicken salad, and we discussed Addison's wedding plans.

"Addison and Glen just seem so perfect for each other, don't you think?" Lily asked.

"I do. Remember when we first met him?"

Lily laughed. "Um, yes. He was wearing spandex."

"It was a bike ride, Lily!" I couldn't help chuckling. Glen and Addison had been dating for a month when he'd asked her to attend a bike race. Lily and Addison and I had sat together in the stands and waited … and waited for the race to end. Debra had needed to work that day. Once Glen passed the finish line, we'd met up with him at the water and snack station. He had, indeed, been wearing spandex.

Glen had the build of a bike rider, lean and strong. His head was completely shaved, which took both me and Lily by surprise since Addi had never mentioned it. He had us laughing right away at some joke, and his passion for his faith came through as he'd talked about the youth group kids he loved so much.

"I mostly recall how he kept looking over at Addison every second." Lily wiped her hands on a dishtowel and then tossed it on the counter.

"He was smitten all right." I pulled up a barstool next to Lily, and we began to eat.

"Thank you for feeding me, by the way," she said as an afterthought.

"What are friends for?"

"What's for dessert? Nutella?" she teased. I nudged her.

"Ha ha. Lily," I said, after downing half a Diet Dr Pepper. "Why did you think Jason and I were perfect for each other?"

She took another generous bite, and I waited while she chewed. Finally, she swallowed.

"I don't know. You look great together. You always got along so well. He basically fell in love with you the moment he saw you."

My chest tightened at that comment.

"He's moved on," I said, mostly to comfort myself.

"Yeah, I think so," Lily agreed, which also comforted me. "And if you weren't crazy about him, which you weren't, then you guys obviously weren't perfect for each other. Just because things add up on paper doesn't mean they work out in real life."

"Are you still crazy about Sam?" She took a sip of her soda.

"Ninety percent of the time. That's enough. I do start to twitch a little when he absentmindedly plays with that cowlick above his right ear. Seriously. I've been watching him mess with that piece of hair for more than ten years. And the reality that I'll be watching him mess with it for the rest of my life..."

I nodded with empathy. "That would make anyone twitch." I could see Lily getting annoyed just thinking about it, so a change of topic felt necessary.

"You should start dating again, Sara," Lily informed me. Well, that took care of the subject change.

"I think so too," I agreed. "Don't try to set me up, though," I instantly stated.

"I don't have anyone in mind," Lily told me. "Jason and Luke are Sam's best friends. I can't think of anyone else."

"Maybe I'll try online dating."

Lily shuddered. "Really? What if you get creepy stalkers?"

"Then I'll stop online dating."

"Let's ask Addison to see if there are any cute single guys at Glen's church."

"No."

"I'll ask, but I won't mention you."

"No."

"I'll let you know what she says."

After dinner, Lily and I watched HGTV until Sam texted her that he was on his way home. Yoda took over her spot on the sofa just as my phone buzzed.

Luke.

> Hey. I had fun at your parents' house yesterday. Have a good week.

I read the message three times before punching in my response.

Thanks for your help. I hope you have a good week too.

I supposed I should be relieved he hadn't completely dropped me from his life upon getting a girlfriend, but my heart couldn't seem to move past the realization that I got polite, short texts while Debra got flowers and kisses and romance.

My mind jumped over the kisses thought, because if I dwelled on that too long, I started to feel like a crazy woman. The temptation to call Luke and ramble on about how I loved him and wished he'd stop kissing Debra might be too strong.

I turned off the TV and tidied up my apartment before taking a hot bath and then climbing in bed. Thoughts of my mother's "dark time" came back to me as I continued to think about the mystery surrounding the Bible verse. I had wracked my memory and couldn't think of anything. Unless she'd meant her battle with infertility before and after I was born. But she'd been open about that with me, and I still didn't understand her reluctance to share whatever else could have caused her such heartache.

I reached for my iPad on the nightstand and pulled up Psalm 113:3. I read the short chapter, stopping suddenly at verse nine.

He settles the childless woman in her home as a happy mother of children.

Praise the Lord.

I'd never ever read the whole chapter before, but those last few lines leapt out at me.

The dark time must have been associated with her infertility. It seemed fitting. Maybe she memorized the verse before she got pregnant with me. Or maybe not.

I wanted to know.

A crew of us stayed after closing at the museum a few days later, including Jeanie, which surprised me. Our manager normally left early. She lived far outside the city and hated to drive through five o'clock traffic.

The watercolor paintings were unveiled and lined up on display. The display opened Saturday, and I was on the schedule to stand at the concierge desk. We knew from past experience that our special summer exhibits tended to bring in large crowds.

By Saturday night I was exhausted from working such long hours. After I woke up on the sofa to the feeling of Yoda pawing through my hair, I shuffled to the bedroom and collapsed on my bed. Sunday I dragged myself to church with every intention of going straight home for a nap, but it just so happened that our whole gang, except for Addison, went to the same service. Lily and Debra came up with the great idea that we should all go to lunch together at the Dumpling House. I couldn't say no. Everyone knew it was my favorite Chinese restaurant in the city.

Without Addison, and now with the coupling of Debra and Luke, the six of us felt too much like a triple date. Jason and I ended up across from each other at the end of the table, the odd people out. I sat next to Lily and Sam, and Jason sat next to Luke and Debra.

At least the sweet-and-sour chicken was delicious.

I'd finished half my plate when my phone buzzed. I flipped it over to see the incoming text.

ARE YOU GOING TO CONTRIBUTE TO THIS CONVERSATION?

Lily. I hadn't even seen her hold her phone. Sneaky, that girl. I punched in my reply.

I'M EATING.

That warranted a poke in the leg from her.

"So, it sounds like Addison's found a bridesmaid's dress she likes for us," Debra said. Even her voice held the trepidation that followed every bridesmaid as she waited in fear of the horrific dress the bride has chosen.

Lily, Debra, and I had a moment of silence.

"I'm sure it'll be fine," Jason said after a moment, with a roll of his eyes.

"How's cooking school going?" I asked him. Jason's face lit up.

"So great! I love it. Really, I'm happier peeling potatoes than I have been in the three years I've worked as a programmer. Last week we had a whole class just about seasoning. There's so much to learn!"

That made me again worried about Jason's role as head chef of Addison's wedding.

"How did the grand opening of the exhibit go, Sara?"

I appreciated that Luke remembered.

"Really well. We were packed all day. The paintings are gorgeous. You guys should all come out and walk through the gallery. We usually have photography on display, so I'm thrilled that we have watercolor artwork right now!"

"It's running for the next six weeks, right?" Lily scrunched her nose; I knew from experience that she was trying to pull up her mental calendar.

Just a note about Lily—she's not good at remembering things.

"Right," I confirmed. "We've got some great art on loan from Sugar Land and Dallas. Starting Wednesday, we have a local artist coming to do classes on watercolor for kids. It should be fun. We're doing two classes a day for three days, and we're completely booked."

"When does the concert series begin? You're volunteering, right?" Debra asked. "Luke told me about it."

"Next Saturday evening at the amphitheater."

"We'll be there," Luke told me with an enthusiastic nod from Debra.

How wonderful.

I poked Lily this time.

"Sam's grandmother's birthday is next Saturday. We're driving up to Lufkin for a big barbecue that day, and we're staying overnight," she said apologetically.

"I'll come if I can. You should invite Addison and Glen, Sara," Jason piped up.

"Good idea." I nodded. "I'll let her know."

"Yes! Then we could all go out for drinks downtown afterward!" Debra's voice had reached the point of giddy, as though this was the best idea of all time. Her long brown curly hair bounced around her face as she moved, and black feather earrings swished back and forth. Her sleeveless turquoise blouse looked striking against her dark hair. Luke put his arm around her, and she beamed and moved even closer to him.

They shared a moment.

I concentrated on eating every last grain of fried rice on my plate and then waved at the waiter to bring the checks.

Once the group had dispersed, I fully intended to head back to my apartment for that nap. A phone call from my mother telling me to meet her at our favorite flea market changed those plans. I drove over to San Jacinto and met her at the entrance of the San Jac Flea Market. She stood by the entrance, wearing large dark sunglasses and heeled sandals, a black sleeveless top with a wide collar, and white capris. Somehow my mother managed to look elegant even in one-hundred-degree Texas heat.

"I was here last week," she explained as I approached her. "There was an antique end table that I loved, but they were asking too much for it. I want to see it again."

"Lead the way." We walked slowly through the aisles. Shopping with my mother—another thing that was second nature to me.

She showed me the end table and then argued with the dealer until he knocked off twenty dollars. Then I had the job of carrying the small table to her SUV.

"Want to grab an iced coffee?" she asked, rather shyly. Her tone confused me. Especially when it came to me, my mother was never shy. Over-opinionated and direct, yes. Shy, no. I nodded and we stopped at a mom-and-pop coffee shop a few paces down from the market.

We sat at a round table for two in the window of Pat's Coffee and Cakes, both sipping iced vanilla coffees, my mother's obvious nerves growing.

"Mom, what is going on?" She pushed aside her drink.

"All right, I keep thinking about your questions regarding that Bible verse."

My stomach knotted. Suddenly, I wasn't sure I wanted to know more.

"You don't have to tell me," I finally offered. "If it's private for you, I understand." And I did. The mystery might kill me, but I understood the need for privacy.

We were similar in that way.

"I don't like keeping things from you. And while it *is* private, I think you're old enough to know."

Good grief. I had a feeling I'd opened a can of worms. (Texas, y'all.)

Chapter Ten

I sipped my drink, now feeling just as nervous as my mother.

"We'd tried for five years to get pregnant, Sara. You can't understand what that's like, and I hope you never do. Month after month of disappointment. Doctor's appointments with no solutions. Blaming each other. Blaming ourselves. Stressed. Frustrated. Heartbroken. And the whole terrible experience started over again every twenty-eight days."

I flinched. Pain-filled memories laced my mother's words.

"We'd given up about six months before. Though we'd discussed adoption at times, we just needed to take a break from all 'baby' talk. We went to four counseling sessions together because by that point, we were broken. We planned a trip and went on a cruise, trying to have fun and reconnect and start the healing process from all the things we'd said that had hurt each other."

My mother looked at her manicured hands, quiet for a moment. I wondered if she was trying to decide how much to tell me.

"It didn't work. We fought on the cruise. Things were tense when we came home, and we decided that we needed some space. So your father moved out."

I nodded as though hearing that was normal, but the story sounded like it must be about another couple. Not my parents. Not Dr. and Mrs. Witherspoon—they loved each other too much. They complemented each other in so many ways—my mother, the consummate partner to my father's endeavors, and my father, the steady constant to help channel my mom's boundless energy. He moved and she moved. She stopped and he stopped. A partnership that I admired. The thought of him moving out and leaving her rattled me. I worked hard to keep my breathing even so my mother would feel comfortable sharing with me.

"We were separated for about a year. It was a mutual separation. We both needed it. I was grieving the loss of my dreams of what family looked like. He was grieving as well. I was fairly certain we would divorce, eventually."

My parents nearly divorced?

"I threw myself into my work. My days as an event planner were full and long."

She looked worried. I tried to keep my face void of emotion.

"Your father was seeing someone else—by that I mean that they were in a relationship. I knew it. I wasn't angry, Sara. I'd had a few casual coffee dates with men who were friends too. You have to understand that by that point, neither of us saw a future together. We were moving on."

I took a deep breath and felt my eyes water.

"He was seeing someone else? You guys were still married … you both were Christians—"

A sad look filled my mother's eyes. "Oh, Sara. We all make choices that hurt us sometimes. We're a broken people, honey. That's why the story of redemption reaches us at our core."

That pricked my heart. I nodded after a moment, still reeling.

"Is that when you came across the verse?" I asked. She sipped her iced coffee and then shook back her thick hair.

"Well, like I said, I was working a lot, and I'd heard from friends that your father was in a rather serious relationship. We'd been separated about ten months. I figured it was time we made the decision to end things permanently. So I called him and asked him to come over. I'd already met with a divorce attorney, though no paperwork had been filed. He came over to the house."

Her line of view drifted to the window, and I could see the weight of the memory.

"It was a difficult discussion, but even as we sat there, talking about ending our marriage, I kept feeling this voice inside me say that it wasn't over. That this was wrong. That even broken things could be fixed."

She sipped her drink again, then looked at me. "So instead of asking for a divorce, I asked for more time."

I leaned forward, needing to absorb every word. "What about Dad? And the other woman?"

"Well, he was shocked by my request. Like me, he'd assumed we were ready to divorce. He told me he'd think about it and call me the next day." My mother clasped her hands together on the table. "I didn't sleep all night, Sara. For ten months I'd worked and stayed busy with friends. I hadn't gone to church. I'd prayed so much for those five years—prayed for a baby, you see. *So* many prayers. When your dad moved out, I didn't feel like praying anymore.

"But that night, I prayed. For hours. I cried. At seven the next morning, your dad called. He said that he'd ended the relationship he'd been in, and he was willing to try. We agreed to take things slowly. We started dating again. Dinner and a movie. Coffee and conversation. Slow. One Friday night at a time. We started visiting a new church together. We were still living apart, but we met with the pastor and explained our situation. He made us feel so welcome. He and his wife started meeting with us every other week. To talk. To process. To rebuild.

"The first time we met with Miguel and Anna—the pastor and his wife—she gave me a framed picture with the words of Psalm 113:3. She told me that when everything feels hopeless, praise the Lord. And when the healing comes, praise the Lord. Be steady. Lean into my faith. Honestly, I didn't have enough faith for anything right then, but I memorized the verse."

I inhaled deeply.

"When I woke up alone every morning, I'd say the verse. When I went to bed alone every night, I said it again. When I saw my best friends taking their children to kindergarten and first grade, and I felt as though I was held together by nothing more than Scotch tape, I still clung to the words. When I worried about whether your father missed his girlfriend, whether he wanted someone else who could give him children—I just repeated the verse."

My mother's voice scratched just above a whisper, hurt saturating the retelling of her story. Emotion welled up in my throat, and I had to take a sip of coffee to try to get it under control.

"Now, I don't want this to change your relationship with your dad, Sara," my mother insisted. "This all happened a long time ago. I have forgiven him. He's forgiven me. God's forgiven both of us and restored our marriage in such a way that has changed us forever. But you started asking questions, and I could tell you knew there was a deeper story, and I think it's okay for you to know that your parents are human too."

But still. My dad … I couldn't help wondering about the other woman. I managed a nod to appease my mom.

"What about me?" I asked. "When did I show up?"

That brought a smile to her face.

"Eventually, your dad asked if he could move back home. I wanted him to. God had given me back my love for him, and I was ready to be married again in every way. So he moved back home, but we avoided the 'b' word. *Baby.* Neither of us brought that up again. We both accepted that children weren't part of our future, though it was still a deep desire in our hearts. If we were going to make it, we needed to concentrate on rebuilding *us* for a time, not hoping for more than we had. And then, six months after he moved back home, I missed my period."

I gasped. Her eyes shone.

"I waited until I was sure, then I told your dad. That was such a good day." My mother wiped her eyes and chuckled at herself with embarrassment.

"Still makes me emotional after all this time," she said. Both of our cups sat empty on the table.

"Mom." I reached across the table and took her hand in mine. She held it tight and took a breath.

"We thought we'd have no trouble having more children after you, but it didn't happen. When I started to feel discouraged about that, Psalm 113:3 came back to me. It wasn't easy, but I kept giving the disappointment over to God and finally chose to simply praise him for my healed marriage and my precious daughter. You were enough, Sara," she assured me. "When I called Anna and told her the news, she told me to read all of Psalm 113."

"He settles the childless woman in her home as a happy mother of children. Praise the Lord," I finished for her. My mother's eyebrows rose a notch.

"Praise the Lord," she agreed, reaching over and squeezing my hand.

Alone in my apartment that night, I replayed the story in my mind. My parents fighting, my dad moving out and dating someone, my mother working all hours to distract herself from the heartache.

I needed to talk about it with someone. Really, I wanted to talk about it with Luke. I knew Luke would listen, he would sympathize, he would say whatever it was I needed to hear.

I just couldn't bring myself to call him. Confiding in Luke, sharing my innermost thoughts with him … it seemed like a privilege that wasn't mine anymore.

I considered calling Lily—I knew she would care. She would listen, but she would for sure tell Sam. Her telling Sam wouldn't normally bother me, but for some reason, I just felt like keeping this a little more private. I thought about Jason and quickly changed my mind. The last thing I needed was a heartfelt conversation where I confided in him. I thought about Addison. I knew she'd help me process, but she was so busy with wedding plans and Glen.

In the end, I just sat alone, absentmindedly stroking Yoda's head.

"Saturday night, Addison," I said into my phone, my eyes stuck on the fourth grader to my left and her watercolor painting. The little girl with brown hair in a ponytail moved her brush carefully, leaving a line of bright pink on her canvas. She focused intently, biting her lower lip as she painted.

"Sure, that sounds fun. Glen's taking the youth group on a bike ride Saturday afternoon. I'm supposed to go too, but—"

I grinned.

"Well, I should probably join you at the concert. Especially if Lily and Sam are out of town."

"My thoughts exactly," I told her, perking up at the thought of Addison saving me and Jason from going on a double date with Debra and Luke after the concert.

"Are you working all day Saturday? Or do you want to get together and talk wedding stuff?" Since I was pretty sure Addison hadn't called any of the wedding planners I'd recommended, I had a strong feeling I was the pseudo planner.

"Sure. I don't have to be at the amphitheater until four o'clock. We can get together and go over wedding details and make lists and stuff."

Addison heaved a loud sigh of relief. "Great. Thanks, Sara. I have lots of questions about etiquette—what my parents are responsible for and what Glen's family is responsible for. How to involve my mother-in-law without giving my mother a heart attack, and so on. You've helped your mother with so many weddings; I know you're practically an expert."

It occurred to me that Addison's view of "expert" was rather loose. According to her, Jason was now an expert on catering and I was now an expert on wedding etiquette.

"I'll help however I can," I promised her. I tucked my phone in my pocket and leaned over the shoulder of the little girl.

"Why did you choose the pink?" I asked. She put her brush in the water and stirred.

"Pink's my favorite."

"I like pink too." Together we admired the painting. Swirls of bubblegum pink, hot pink, and magenta filled the canvas before us, not to mention the splatters on the little girl's arms and a few drops that had made it to her shoes.

"You're a very good artist," I told her. She looked at me, seemingly deciding whether my opinion mattered.

"Are you an artist?" I smiled and shook my head.

"Not really. I like to paint every now and then. Mostly I like to study art."

She nodded with approval. "That sounds like a good job."

"It is." I left the ponytail-haired girl to her work and strolled through the room, making sure all the children had enough paint as they followed the instructor's teaching.

When I swung my purse over my shoulder that night, I decided to do one last walk through the gallery, itching to see one of the paintings that had come in from Sugar Land. When I'd first seen it, I'd known instantly that I'd need more time with the piece. In the silence and stillness of the empty hallway, I stood in front of the large watercolor.

The title over the frame read *The Undoing*.

I took in the watery image of a woman standing alone on a pier, a sunset of orange, pink, and yellow spilling over the rippled water. My eyes focused on the large straw hat she wore, a red ribbon falling from it. She faced the water, her arms held tightly around her.

The picture evoked so many feelings in me. I *was* that woman. Holding myself together.

I stared at the blues and greens and grays that made the water appear so fluid. The yellow in her dress that matched the yellow on the water. Then the deep, striking colors of the sunset. The bright red in the falling ribbon. The movement of the painting.

The movement in me.

"Sara?"

I turned quickly, wiping a runaway tear from my eyes. There stood Wendy, understanding in her face.

"We're locking up."

With a final look at *The Undoing*, and feeling utterly undone myself, I left.

Chapter Eleven

A week later I sat crushed between Lily and Addison on the small sofa in the bridal shop. The door opened and Debra rushed in to the sound of a bell chiming.

"I've got exactly forty minutes. Does anyone have a granola bar or something? I'm starving!" She started digging through her huge purse, and I was reminded of Mary Poppins pulling everything but the kitchen sink from her carpet bag.

"There's a sandwich shop right next door," Addison said. "Run over and grab a bag of chips."

Debra's head bobbed. "Excellent idea. I'll be right back."

Addison's phone rang, and she stood up and walked over to the window to take the call. Lily stared intently at the Candy Crush game she was playing. My eyes wandered around the cute shop, complete with crystal chandeliers and stuffed to the brim with white poufy dresses.

"All right. Here we are. This is the bridesmaid's dress you chose, Addison." The attendant came in carrying several sizes of the same style dress. She hung up several on a portable rack and held one up for us to see. You could hear a collective exhale of relief from myself and Lily. The cranberry-colored, off-the-shoulders, ankle-length gown looked lovely. Simple and classic and doable.

Debra walked back in and squealed. "Is that the bridesmaid's dress? Oh, I love it!"

Addison smiled. "Really?"

Lily and I echoed Debra's sentiments. We dutifully tried on our respective sizes and twirled in front of the multiple mirrors. While we waited for Debra to come out of the dressing room, Lily leaned close to me and whispered, "So how did the other night go? Did y'all go for drinks after the concert?"

A mental movie reel flashed through my mind. Luke and Debra sitting on a blanket at the amphitheater, his arm around her and her head on his shoulder as they listened to the band. Luke and Debra holding hands every second of the evening. Sharing a tender kiss at the table across from where I was sitting. Debra telling all of us that she and Luke would be taking a trip to Colorado in July to see his family.

I'd grown a little accustomed to the hurt by this point, but the jealousy had hit me full force on Saturday night. I'm sure my face was a deep shade of green by the time I left for home.

"Yeah, we went to Duke's for drinks and appetizers after the concert. It went fine." I said the words, knowing this was my life and these were my friends and I had to get over it. "Addison and I spent most of Saturday morning working on wedding plans. I gave her this great planner that my mom recommends for brides. We went through it, making lists of everything we—I mean she—"

Lily and I exchanged a look. "You mean you," she said.

"I mean *we*," I insisted, "need to do every week until December. I found out Jason's cooking the trial food for Addison next weekend, so there's an official girls' night in at her place in two weeks for us to sample the food. Saturday after next."

"Ooooh! Yum! I can't wait for that. Can't the guys come? Sam would love to, if there's food."

I shook my head. "Addison doesn't want the guys there. She's afraid they'll joke around too much and make Jason nervous. If the food doesn't turn out great, Jason will come up with other recipe ideas and we'll do another trial run in a couple of weeks. We're to take this very seriously, Lily," I informed her.

"Okay, okay."

Debra came out in her bridesmaid's dress at that moment, and we all complimented her.

"I'll have to stop eating today if this thing is going to fit by December," Debra said, gasping dramatically for breath and eliciting giggles from us.

"They run a little small," the attendant said. "We can alter them to your specific size, of course." Debra was still gasping, now waddling like a penguin, and we were still giggling.

"Addison," the attendant continued, drawing our attention back to her. "I've got your top three on the rack. Do you want to try them on?"

We immediately pushed for her to show us, so Addison disappeared into the dressing room with the attendant. A few minutes later, she emerged and stood on the small platform, surrounded by mirrors.

"Oh, Addi," Debra breathed. I sniffled and Lily started fanning herself to keep from crying.

"You look so beautiful," I told her. With a poufy tulle skirt and a beaded bodice, Addison looked like a fairy.

"I don't know. I like it, especially the skirt, but I sort of feel like I'm the good witch in the *Wizard of Oz*. Remember how she looked? I feel like I should be flying around, holding a wand or something," Addison said doubtfully. "I'll go try on the next one."

When Addison stepped onto the platform a second time, I cocked my head and studied her. The simple white A-line gown looked beautiful, but it didn't seem to match her personality. While I'd never considered Addison to be flashy or divaesque whatsoever, I had a feeling that the hopeless romantic in her needed to feel like a modern-day princess on her wedding day. That simple, almost plain dress wasn't cutting it.

"That one's pretty too, Addison. Let's see the last one," Debra suggested.

When Addison stepped out a third time, a smile immediately filled my face. From the sofa where we sat, Lily, Debra, and I broke out into applause.

"Love it," I said.

"It's so you." Debra grinned.

"I want to get married all over again," Lily stated.

A sleeveless lace bodice with a scoop neck accentuated Addison's trim waist; the lace drifted down over the wide white skirt. The bridal gown looked as though it had been made for her.

The attendant stepped up and attached a long, simple veil to Addison's twisted bun. We were up out of our seats, *oohing* and *aahing* and examining every detail of the dress.

"This was my mom's favorite too." Addison twirled in front of the mirror. "The lace is gorgeous."

We had just found *the* dress.

After Addison changed out of her dress and we all made reservations for dress alterations, we had just enough time to pick up sandwiches-to-go next door before heading back to our respective jobs.

Debra gave me a quick hug before dashing to her car.

"Luke told me to tell you to call him. He said you guys haven't talked in forever. I think he wants to update you on how his mom is doing," she said, squeezing me tight before we went our separate ways.

Apparently, I now received messages from Luke through Debra.

Highly depressing.

Why hadn't he just texted me or called me himself?

I wanted to just ignore the whole thing, but honestly, I also wanted to know how his mom was doing. Once I got back to the museum, I sent him a quick text.

Hey, how are you? Let's chat soon.

Five minutes later his response came through. From where I sat at my desk, I grabbed the phone sitting on top of my calendar.

Sounds good. Lunch Friday?

Really, I was thinking a phone call would work, or even an extended text session. But Luke liked connecting in person—something that now complicated matters for me. From a distance, I could be a silent, supportive friend. But together at a restaurant—well, I had to be a convincingly happy and supportive friend. And what about Debra? Would she care that we were having lunch alone together? I supposed not, or he wouldn't have asked me.

Okay. California Pizza Kitchen at noon?

I'll be there.

Friday I left the museum, walking past a long line of summer-school students eating sack lunches outside. I was sweating by the time I got to the car. The temperature on my car dial read 104.

Seriously.

The heat had rendered my hair lifeless during the time it took me to get to my car. Sheesh. I pulled it back into a knot and drove to CPK, blasting the air conditioner on my face.

A line of people reached all the way outside, but Luke had texted that he'd gotten us a table. I squeezed through the masses and stood on tiptoes, scanning the restaurant. There in the back, that blond-haired guy.

I had to smile.

It was Luke after all. His dress-shirt sleeves were rolled up slightly, and he wore a dark-green-and-blue paisley tie and gray slacks. The color of his tie highlighted the sharp green of his eyes. His blond hair had grown out a little.

It looked as though he'd run his fingers through it to the side, and there it stayed. I'd always loved how Luke seemed just as comfortable in a suit and tie as he did in shorts and a T-shirt, which was lucky really, since he looked gorgeous in both.

I slid into the booth across from him.

"Hey, you," I said.

"Hey. I already ordered since the place is so busy. Thai Crunch okay?"

I nodded. "Presentation today?"

Confusion clouded his eyes. "How'd you know?"

I grinned. "Because you only wear ties on the days you have presentations."

He looked at his paisley tie, then back up at me. The right corner of his mouth tilted upward.

"Yeah. I had a presentation."

"How'd it go?"

"Fine."

We just smiled at each other for a moment. All right, I'd missed him. A lot.

The waiter came and deposited two sodas for us.

"So, I heard Addison picked a dress."

"Oh, it's beautiful, Luke," I told him. I grabbed a piece of bread from the plate between us and slathered some butter on it. "We're in full-on wedding mode now. Very exciting."

"I'm sure."

"Debra mentioned you guys were going to Colorado." My voice didn't reach the level of interest I'd been aiming for. I could barely manage indifferent, which, I supposed, was better than sounding distraught.

"Yeah. Second weekend in July. My mom cried when I told her, Sara. You were right. She needs me to come see her."

"I'm glad you're going."

"It'll be fun. It's just for a long weekend, but I'm going to take Deb kayaking while we're out there. Maybe we'll go on a hike or two. The heat in Colorado isn't like here. It's a dry heat, so we won't pass out if we're outside for more than twenty minutes. And my mom will be so excited to cook for us."

I took another bite of bread to avoid having to reply.

Luke's mom lived in a small trailer park up in the mountains. He and I had talked about driving up there together several times but had never seemed to make it work. Now he and Debra were flying to Colorado together, going on the adventure I had dreamed of for years.

I pushed the salad around on my plate. "That's great, Luke. It sounds like so much fun."

He paused for a moment, and I wondered if he was remembering that we'd talked about taking that same trip.

"How are you?" He changed the subject as our lunch was served.

"I'm good." I cut my salad counterclockwise. "The museum has been full of energy this summer. The kids' classes were a total success."

"How're your parents?"

The simple question brought to mind my conversation with my mother. Sitting there across from Luke, I felt an almost desperate need to tell him. I'd come close to telling Lily, or even Addison, but just hadn't reached out. When it came to Luke, I'd had to *avoid* calling him. For so long, he'd been my person, my secret keeper. But it had been mutual back then. He'd confided in me too. Now he shared his thoughts and feelings with Debra, which left me with the sad realization that even grown-up girls can feel left out among friends.

I stared at my salad. "They're fine."

"Sara?"

I looked up.

"Whatever it is, tell me."

He was just like my mom sometimes, reading me like a book.

I inhaled for a second, held it, and then released the breath, my shoulders falling. He'd asked. And in truth, I needed to talk about it in order to process my feelings.

"Okay. I had coffee with Mom the other day, and I was really thrown after the conversation."

Luke didn't speak, he just kept listening—his way of telling me to continue. I plunged forward and told him the whole story. He interjected a couple of times with questions, and thirty minutes later his plate was nearly empty, but mine was still half full since I'd been doing all the talking.

"Wow," he said, wiping his mouth. "That's pretty intense, Sara. How are you doing with all that?"

"I've been thinking about it for days! It just weighs on my mind."

He frowned. "Why didn't you call me?"

Oops.

Because you have a girlfriend.

I shrugged. "I keep wondering how I'll feel when I see my dad. I wonder if my mom told him that I know the story."

"He's the same dad today that he was last week, Sara," Luke said gently. "Like your mom said, it happened a long time ago. Before you were even born."

"I know. It's just hard to picture my parents—my age, fighting and nearly divorcing, my dad dating another woman while he was still married to my mom. I never ever would have imagined that from them."

"It sounds like it was a part of their journey that made them who they are today. They've always seemed to have such a great marriage to me. Maybe it's because they realize how important it is. Your parents have the kind of marriage that I wished my mom and dad had. The kind I'd like to have myself."

I wanted to reach over and touch him, but I didn't. Still, his words reached my heart. I knew from dozens of conversations the difficult family life that had been Luke's childhood. Volatile parents with a lot of fighting. Verbal and sometimes physical abuse from his father.

My dad seemed like a saint in comparison.

Except he wasn't.

"My mom told me that it's okay for me to know that she and my dad are only human." I ate a forkful of salad, mulling over my mother's words.

"We all need grace," Luke said after a moment. He looked past me, out the nearby window, for a second. "My dad included. I have to keep reminding myself of that. As believers, it's our privilege to give grace."

At that, I did reach over and rest my hand on Luke's. "We give it because we've received it," I said softly. His hand shook ever so slightly under mine.

"Addison used to say that if we cover people in grace, love will follow," he said, his eyes meeting mine again.

"Grace givers, she called us. I remember." I looked at Luke. The thoughtful look in his eyes that let me know I had his full attention. That sincere compassion in his voice and challenge to himself that was just so *Luke*. If he could extend grace to his dad, heaven knows I could give it to mine.

"You know, I've made mistakes that I wouldn't want to share with my mom," Luke told me. "It's pretty impressive that Suzanne was brave enough to share her experience with you, Sara."

"She's a brave woman." And I meant it.

My mom was, is, human—just like me. Scratching to praise God when it didn't come easy.

"Brave like you," Luke said with a small smile.

I didn't answer. Part of me felt that if I were truly brave, I'd just confess my feelings to Luke then and there, but it was too late for that.

The waitress boxed up my salad for me, and then Luke walked me to my car. He gave me a quick hug.

I looked at the box in my hands. “I really hope you and Deb have a great time in Colorado.”

“Thanks. Hey, next time, don’t wait so long to tell me what’s going on with you. I’ve missed hearing from you.”

A dagger to my heart.

I looked up at those beautiful green eyes that always seemed to see the real me.

“I’ve missed you too.”

Chapter Twelve

"What do you see?" I asked. It was midmorning on Monday—and one of the few "free admission" days at the museum—and I'd just finished a behind-the-scenes tour of the watercolor paintings for a ladies' group that had come in. "Behind-the-scenes" meant I had just walked them through the hallway and they asked me two million questions about the artwork.

Two teenage girls turned around in surprise at my voice. I smiled. They looked at my nametag, realized I worked for the museum, and then one of them pointed at the painting in front of them.

"You mean this? It's a painting," the girl said, then chuckled. I moved to stand next to them. The other girl tucked her phone in her back pocket and smoothed back her black-streaked-with-bright-blue hair.

"What do *you* see?" she asked me. I stepped closer and looked at the painting before us.

"Hmm. Let me think. Well, I see really good technique and form, for one thing. This tells me the artist knew what he was doing and every stroke was intentional. I see beauty and talent. I see vision. You have to wonder what the inspiration was with a painting like this."

Both girls directed their view to the framed portrait of five women laughing and telling secrets around a well.

"I see history, a moment of time captured. Incredible detail and color. I see secrets and friendship. This painting makes me smile," I continued.

"Me too," the non-black-with-blue-streaked-hair girl said shyly. "I wonder what they're whispering about."

"I like how the painting looks so real," the other girl chimed in.

"I wonder about the shape of the women," the other one said, regarding the women's frames. "They're so curvy. You know, it seems like all the girls in magazines today are really skinny. I think the artist had a different idea about beauty."

"I think the women are really beautiful. I like how that one's hair is piled up high on her head." The other girl's eyes were still on the painting as she spoke. "I like this picture a lot."

I smiled again. "Me too," I murmured. "Take a look at that one, girls." I pointed to another portrait near the end of the hall. "See what you think about how the artist treated light in the painting."

This time, they nodded with interest, smiling at me before they walked down the hallway.

Art is made so much better by conversation.

There was a tap on my shoulder—one of the other team leaders letting me know there was a problem at the ticket counter and Jeanie had asked for me to go help. I rushed up front and spent the next hour assisting one of the new guys with the onslaught of guests. Congested lines trickled from the ticket counters located inside by the entrance to outside the building, with most of our guests looking annoyed. Free days always resulted in a deluge of families at the museum, lots of little kids and strollers and groups visiting together, and an overall long day for the staff.

My cell rang as I walked to my car at five that evening.

"Hey, Lil. What's up?"

I heard her sniff, and I stopped walking.

"Sam's dad, Richard, was in an accident. We're at Hermann. Can you come?" Her voice trembled.

"I'm on my way. E.R.?"

"I don't know. We just got here." Lily sounded as though she were already crying.

"I'm coming, love."

"Send out a text for me and ask everybody to pray."

"Will do."

I hung up and ran the rest of the way to my car, my heart pounding. I took fifteen seconds to send a group text to Addison, Luke, Debra, and Jason. My phone hummed with a steady flow of incoming texts, but I concentrated on getting to Hermann Hospital as soon as possible. The tremble in Lily's voice played like a broken record in my head, resulting in a white-knuckled grip on the steering wheel and a loud groan emanating from me every time I hit a red light.

Thankfully, the hospital was only a short distance from the museum. Once there, I parked and ran into the emergency area. The woman behind the counter directed me down the hallway to where Lily, Sam, and Sam's mother, Macy, stood together.

"Sara," Lily said. I walked straight over and hugged her. She gripped me tight, and I held her until she finally relaxed in my arms and stepped back.

"Thanks for coming, Sara." I looked at Sam over Lily's shoulder. Just like Lily, his voice shook.

"Of course. How is he?"

"They're taking him upstairs now and evaluating him. We don't know the extent of the damage yet, but they're pretty sure he's about to go into emergency surgery. The person driving the car that hit Sam's dad is already in the operating room. His situation looks even worse."

Macy Spencer wiped a fast tear from her face. Sam noticed and put one arm around his mother; she stood rigid.

"Mom, there's a little more paperwork we need to fill out. We arrived in a rush. Let me help you with that, then we'll head upstairs. Lil, you and Sara go on up to the third floor. We'll meet you there." Solemn fear had replaced his normally jovial smile.

Lily and I took the elevator upstairs. Once the doors closed and we were inside, I turned to her.

"What happened?"

She gripped the railing that circled the perimeter of the elevator's interior. "They'd worked all day on a job. Sam was with him. They'd left the property to head home, and Sam was driving behind Richard. The light turned green and his dad drove forward, but the SUV from the left didn't stop. He plowed right into Sam's dad's truck on the driver's side. Sam saw everything. He held his dad until the ambulance arrived and rode with him here. After he called me, I picked up his mom. He didn't want her driving after she heard what had happened."

Lily's white skin seemed paler than usual, and she kept fidgeting with her purse. I reached out and took her hand in mine. "This hospital is one of the best, Lily. They'll do everything they can."

"Sam's terrified. I can tell. He adores his dad. The police have already talked to us."

The elevator doors opened, and we walked to the administration desk to find out more information. They sent us to the waiting room for the moment. A few minutes later, when the elevator doors opened again, we could see Sam, his mom, and Luke walk through them. Palpable relief washed over me at the sight of Luke. In Dockers and a dress shirt, he'd obviously come straight from work. I could see the tension in his jaw and the concern in his eyes.

Sam and his mom went to find the doctor, and Luke joined me and Lily. After about five minutes, Lily left to find out where they were.

"How do you think Sam's holding up?" I asked, keeping my voice low.

"He'll be strong for his mother. His brother's driving down from Dallas."

"I'm glad you're here."

Luke put his arm around me. "I'm glad you're here too." Without thinking, I leaned into Luke, thankful for the comfort I felt being close to him. Just sitting together, the faint scent of his cologne in the air, provided a moment of normalcy for me.

The elevator opened again a few minutes later, and Addison and Glen walked in. "How is he?" she asked immediately. Luke stood up and shook hands with Glen. The air conditioning hit me without Luke's warmth, and my heart twinged at the abrupt end of my brief feeling of solace.

Lily came back to give us an update.

"They're prepping for surgery. For sure one of his legs and one of his arms are broken, and he's lost a lot of blood. We won't know the extent of all the damage until after surgery." She rubbed her temples. "Y'all can go home. We'll probably be here all night."

"Then we should find some coffee. We're not going anywhere, Lily," Luke said firmly. She went back to join Sam and his mom, and the rest of us sat down on the sofas. I rubbed my arms in an attempt to fight the freezing temperature and wished I'd worn a sweater. I sat as close to Addison as possible, but neither of us seemed up for talking. I mindlessly scrolled through news articles on my phone while Addi checked her e-mail. Luke and Glen spoke in hushed voices. The cold, stark-white atmosphere did nothing to help with the fear drifting around all of us. About half an hour later, after Richard was taken into surgery, Sam, Lily, and his mom joined us in the waiting room. Jason came in at the same time.

Debra arrived about ten minutes later with reinforcements in the way of food. Most of us had missed dinner. We all reached for the sacks of Whataburger (Texas, y'all.) meals she dropped on the coffee table in the waiting room. The warm aroma of cheeseburgers, fries, and onion rings filled the area and was a welcome contrast to the smell of disinfectant cleaner. My stomach growled and I bit into a burger, thankful for Debra's thoughtfulness. She and I sat silently next to each other, sharing French fries and watching Sam's mother pace in the hallway.

I looked at our group. Debra and I sharing snacks. Addison on her phone. Luke and Jason and Glen watching ESPN on the mounted TV. Lily and Sam holding hands.

I felt it all over again.

Family.

These were my people.

Over the next two hours, more visitors stopped by, namely the pastor of the church Sam's parents attended and two of his mother's close friends.

Around 9:30 the doctor came out, and the Spencers all walked down the hallway with him for an update. We all perked up and Luke jumped out of his seat. After a few minutes, they came back to the waiting room.

"Thank you all for coming," Macy said, obviously on the verge of tears.

"He's out of surgery and stable for now, for the most part. They've stopped the bleeding and set the arm and leg. The doctor removed his spleen. I think Dad will be moving to the ICU." Sam paused, taking a deep breath, his eyes red with restrained tears. "I'm going to be here overnight. My brother should be here in an hour. My aunt and uncle are coming from Shreveport tomorrow. Lily's going to take my mom home now, though. They'll be back first thing in the morning."

"What can I do, bro?" Luke asked, placing a hand on Sam's shoulder.

That simple gesture seemed to evoke all the emotion Sam tried to hold back; he just stared at the floor, unable to speak. We were all up at this point. Luke pulled him into a hug, and my eyes filled with tears. Jason moved close to put his arms around both of the guys. Then all of us were closing in, reaching out to touch Sam, reaching out to touch each other. The circle tightening.

Addison held Sam's mother as she cried.

"Lord, we praise you in this moment," Glen prayed aloud. My eyes squeezed shut.

We praise you when there's nothing else we can do.

Teach me how, God.

Chapter Thirteen

Tuesday afternoon I left work early to join Lily at the hospital. She was sitting in the ICU waiting room, and I handed her a white mocha latte before sitting down next to her.

"Did you get any sleep last night?"

She yawned. "Not much. I got here at seven this morning and found Luke and Sam eating breakfast in the cafeteria."

"Luke was here at seven?"

She nodded and warmed both hands around the cup. "He was here all night. I think he slept for a couple of hours on one of the waiting room sofas, but he wouldn't leave Sam here alone."

I smoothed my black cropped pants and crossed my legs. My heart squeezed at the thought of Luke sleeping here, to be near Sam. That was just how supportive of a friend Luke was.

"Sam and Macy are with Richard now. He's sleeping. He looks terrible, Sara." Dark circles ringed her eyes, and Lily's normally coiffed short blonde hair hung lifeless and dry around her face.

"Oh, Lily." Weight settled on my chest and my throat tightened.

"We're just thankful he's alive, of course. The driver of the other car died this morning."

I gasped.

"His family was here earlier. That was devastating." Lily closed her eyes. "They're watching Richard closely. He's had a fever today. They said they may have to do another surgery when he's a little stronger. I have to try not to cringe when I see him. There are stitches across his forehead. He's bruised badly. The arm and leg are in casts."

"But he's alive, like you said," I told her. "That's what matters. He's alive."

Lily sipped her coffee. "I'm glad they'd already begun the transition for Sam to take over more of the business responsibilities. He'll need to handle everything for a long time to come."

"How long do they think his dad will be in the hospital?"

"They haven't said. With the fever and an additional surgery, I expect him to be here for a while."

"How can we help Macy? Do you want the gang to bring over meals?"

"Their church has stepped in to help, and they're taking care of that. Sam's brother and sister-in-law, and his aunt and uncle are all staying at Macy's house, which is good because she's not alone. Sam will have a couple of guys from the business take care of the yard for her, but if I think of anything, don't worry, I'll call on the group. I know you guys are there for us."

"We are. You guys are never alone in this. Not for one minute," I promised.

"You know what the scariest part was, Sara? It was just a regular day. We weren't ready—the thought of Sam never seeing his dad again, it would never have occurred to us. You're just going about your life, and then suddenly something happens and the world stops for you."

I placed my hand on her arm. "I know." My heart ached for Sam, Lily, and Macy. "But he's going to make it through. We have to keep believing that." He'd come so far already. I shot up another frantic prayer that God would bring healing and comfort for Richard and the rest of the family.

"I know. At least, we think so. He's weak from the surgery. That's why they're watching him so closely for infection, for more bleeding." Lily looked at me. "I've never seen Sam really afraid before now," she said. "We haven't gone through anything like this together. This is new ground for us."

"You're the strongest couple I know," I told her. "He needs you now, Lily."

She nodded her agreement.

Jason showed up an hour later with dinner for Macy, Sam, Lily, and myself. We ate, and he and I sat and talked with Lily and Sam for a while. Macy rarely left Richard's room, but Lily and Sam needed a break. While Jason and Sam watched TV in the waiting room, Lily and I went for some fresh air outside. A couple of hours later, Jason walked me to my car when it was time to go.

"I wish there were more we could do," he said with obvious frustration.

"I think it helps just knowing how much we all care. Knowing we'll be here if they call on us. Knowing that when we say we're praying for them, we really mean it."

Jason and I walked together slowly through the parking lot, passing row after row of cars. The muscles in my shoulders throbbed from a long day at the museum and now hours spent at the hospital, and Jason seemed quiet, lost in his thoughts. I pulled out my keys as we reached my car.

Jason stuck his hands in his pockets. "Sam is my best friend," he said, staring out at the night sky. "He and Luke are the brothers I never had. I'd do anything I could for him." I paused and turned to him.

"I know," I said. "He knows." Neither of us spoke for a moment. The parking lot was silent.

"The night we met, we were at the church gym, playing basketball with a bunch of people. Sam dunked on me and nearly broke my nose. Afterward, he and Luke took me out to that little hole-in-the-wall Mexican restaurant we used to go to—Guadalupe's—for tamales. We've been best friends ever since."

It was a story I'd heard many times. The guys loved to tell it—eating tamales with Jason, bonding over bloody noses. I stepped forward and gave Jason a hug. He patted my back before releasing me.

"Good night then, Sara." Jason took off toward his car, and I got into mine. I sat for a moment, wanting to pray. No words came to me, but love for my friends flooded my heart. And that felt like a prayer somehow.

As fate would have it, I was the only one available to take Debra and Luke to the airport the following Saturday morning at 6:30. The irony of this was not lost on me. That love that had flooded my heart days earlier was waning a bit. Deb sat in the backseat, chattering away on a work-related call. In the front seats, Luke and I spoke in quiet voices.

"No word on Sam's dad being released from the hospital yet?" he asked me. I shook my head.

"Lily said they'll do the other surgery Monday morning. Probably at least another week and a half in the hospital, if not more. He's also going to need physical therapy after the bones heal."

"Call me if anything happens, okay?"

"Okay," I agreed.

"Jason's picking us up Tuesday night, so don't worry about that."

Excellent.

I swerved into the departures lanes at Bush Intercontinental Airport. Cars filled nearly every spot.

"Looks like a busy travel day," I commented.

"What?" Debra said, clicking off her phone and looking out her window in the back.

"See, Debra. I told you," Luke said.

"Yeah, yeah. I still think we didn't need to get here two hours early," she grumbled. Luke's insistence to be cautiously early to airports and Debra's tendency to be late to every event she attended had me suppressing a laugh. Luke hauled their luggage from the trunk to the sidewalk. Then we stood awkwardly, saying goodbye. I felt like I was their mother or something. *Goodbye, children! Please don't do anything inappropriate, like make out on the plane!*

After dutifully hugging them both and saying to have a great time, I left.

Working for *Art as Life* that Saturday turned out to be a godsend. The crowds and activities at the park and amphitheater kept my mind off Colorado and the lovebirds. Chalk artists drew colorful art on the sidewalks near the amphitheater. Families and couples and groups of teenagers visited vendor booths selling everything from artwork to popcorn. A lively bluegrass band played onstage. Since the park was so close to the hospital, Lily came over later to get a break. She and I walked around, looking at chalk art and eating peppermint fudge.

"I wonder how it's going for Luke and Deb," Lily mused.

Really? When I'm pretending they aren't on a weekend trip together?

"I'm trying not to think about it." We paused to see what the man in front of us was drawing.

"How's that going for you?" She knew me too well.

I glanced over my shoulder at the band as the tempo picked up. "I'm all right. There are worse things in life than losing the man you love to one of your closest friends."

Lily chuckled. "Such as?"

I didn't answer, though Sam's dad came to mind. "I keep thinking—and maybe this is wrong—but I just can't help wondering if Luke's going to realize that they are so different, that maybe it's not the match he was thinking it would be."

"That could happen," Lily allowed. "But you need to prepare yourself, honey, if it doesn't. Lots of couples are very different, and they make it work. Look at me and Sam. I mean, this morning the boy went to do a job wearing the same clothes he worked and sweated in yesterday."

She wrinkled her nose. "I just looked at him and thought, *Lord, who is this man I married?* When I mentioned to him I thought that was gross, he told me he's just going to get dirty and sweaty again today."

I nodded with understanding.

"So, Addison pushed out the trial food service date since Debra's out of town and you have so much going on with Sam's family," I told Lily. "I think it's next Sunday night, and if you can't make it even then, don't hesitate to say so. She understands. We all know how much stress your family is under right now."

Lily didn't respond for a moment.

"Lily?"

"I'm trying to be extra patient with Sam right now. He's really the one under all the stress. Between spending as much time at the hospital as he can and managing all the jobs they had lined up, he's running on fumes at the moment. But I have to go back to work at the bookstore next week. I know he thinks it's not as important, but we need that extra money every month. He wants me ferrying his mom back and forth to the hospital. But she's perfectly capable of driving. She's much better now that they feel Richard's going to pull through. And Macy has friends from church helping her. I can't spend every day glued to her hip."

I just listened.

"The rest of the family who came from Dallas and Louisiana have to leave by Tuesday. Maybe that will help us get back to some kind of normalcy. Of course, we'll keep going to the hospital as long as he's there. It's when he's home that I'm thinking about. Macy will need help moving Richard around. He can't do anything with the casts on, and he's really weak. She's going to need Sam to help maneuver him. Everyone else will be gone."

We came upon a bench, and I sat down and pulled Lily next to me.

"Don't get me wrong. All of this is doable. We're a family. We pull together. Sam's just already hanging on by a thread. He's running low on patience and energy. I'm running low on those things too."

I scooted close enough so that our shoulders pressed up against each other. It hit me at that moment that we'd mostly been thinking of ways to help Macy and Richard, but Lily and Sam needed us to serve them while they served their parents.

"When do you want to go back to work?"

"I'll need to be at the hospital with Sam on Monday during the surgery. And I need to be around Tuesday to say goodbye to our extended family. But I was thinking I should try to get back on the schedule on Wednesday."

"Okay then. I've got your garage door code. I'm bringing dinner on Wednesday. I'll let myself in. Don't argue," I insisted when Lily opened her mouth to object. "And Addison and Jason will want to bring meals over the next couple of weeks too. Zip it." I stopped her again. "This is what friendship is, Lily. When we say we're a family—this is what that looks like."

She nodded finally.

"I'll be at the hospital as soon as I get off work Monday."

"Thank you, Sara."

Nudging her shoulder, I put on my best imitation of Lily's southern drawl. "Sure thing, honey." She chuckled and relief washed over me. While the heaviness of the situation had not lessened, it felt good to hear Lily get her laugh back, even if just for a moment.

When I showed up at the hospital Monday, I found a weary group of people. The surgery had taken some unexpected turns, but overall, Richard had pulled through. Lily, Sam, and Macy wouldn't be able to see him for at least another half hour, so Lily had asked me to take a bunch of the flowers they'd received to her house. At that point, Richard's room resembled a florist shop, and they needed more space.

So I packed my little car with bouquets of flowers and headed to Lily's house. I let myself in through the garage and drew in my breath sharply as I walked in the kitchen.

Let me explain that Lily is from a *Better Homes and Gardens* era. The kind where everything has a place and better be in it, y'all. So to see her sink full of dishes, garbage filled to the brim of the stainless-steel trash can, and clothes spilling out of the laundry room—I was in shock.

It took three trips to the car to unload all the flowers. I glanced at the clock. 6:30 p.m. I cracked my neck, rolled up my sleeves, and started a load of clothes before I tackled the dishes in the sink.

Two hours later I headed home, dead tired, but Lily's house sparkled. I'd just changed into my pj's when my phone buzzed. I checked the text.

> We just walked through the door. I'd call you, but I'm bawling. You cleaned my house.

I smiled.

> Love you too.

The next day I called Addison at lunchtime to explain the situation with Lily and Sam. She immediately said she'd take over a meal Friday. She also said she'd call Jason. With his need for culinary practice, we could probably get a whole slew of meals that Lily and Sam could freeze.

Mission accomplished.

Well, first mission.

I knew Luke and Debra arrived back in town that night, and I was wondering how long I could put off hearing about their no-doubt glorious trip.

I actually did manage to avoid this inevitability until Sunday night, the night Jason was cooking for me and Addison and Debra and Lily. Addison had told Lily she absolutely didn't have to come, but according to Lily, she desperately needed a fun night away from the hospital.

Fun night is not how I would describe the evening.

We all sat in the living room while Chef Jason cooked in Addison's kitchen. Sipping on white wine and munching on appetizers, we waited for Jason to impress us. I'd had one stuffed mushroom when Debra squealed and clapped.

"Okay! I just *have* to tell you guys about the trip! Oh my gosh. I love Colorado."

I pasted what I hoped was a pleasant look on my face and prepared myself for another play-by-play of the Debra-and-Luke romance.

We listened to a minute-by-minute retelling of Debra meeting Luke's mom. Debra and Luke hiking up in the mountains and kayaking down the river, then fishing for trout. Luke's mom cooking dinner and the three of them eating outside on the deck in the non-humid fresh air.

By this time, Jason called us into the kitchen. The four of us sat at Addison's breakfast table while Jason described what he'd made and provided sampler plates for us to taste test.

"First we have coconut-crusted jumbo stuffed shrimp, with my own style of lemon-based dipping sauce, a light salad, and a fresh fruit cocktail."

There was silence around the table while we tasted the sampler entrée.

Okay.

So Jason's a pretty good cook.

We basically scarfed down every bite he put in front of us. He just leaned against the counter and grinned, a cat-that-caught-the-canary look on his face, his Houston Astros cap taming down that mess of dark hair, and a plain white T-shirt emphasizing his olive skin. I could easily picture him as a chef—long white apron and backward cap, singing and joking around in the kitchen.

Next, we had an herb-marinated roast chicken with fresh vegetables and seasoned red potatoes.

I now wanted Jason to cater my wedding.

I've noticed that when people really enjoy food, they don't want to leave the table. The four of us just sat there, talking and laughing and drinking more wine. While Jason cleaned up and we discussed in detail our favorite flavors, I began to relax and feel as though I'd heard all about Debra's trip and still survived the night.

That was a mistake.

"So back to my trip—" Debra interjected after a moment. I poured another glass of wine.

"I haven't told you the most important thing yet." Her eyes glimmered. I took another gulp of wine.

"Luke and I went for a walk one evening, down by the river near where his mom lives. The setting was gorgeous. This wide rushing river right by us, crashing over rocks and logs. Evergreen trees climbing up the side of the mountain in the distance. The moment felt so perfect ... I told Luke that I love him."

Chapter Fourteen

Maybe it was the wine, but the whole room looked fuzzy at that moment. In slow motion, Jason turned around from where he stood at the sink, his eyes wide and directly on me. I saw Lily take the wine glass from my hand and move it out of reach. I saw Debra smiling like the Cheshire Cat.

The whole thing felt funny.

Lily pinched me.

I looked at her.

"Not a funny moment," she whispered through her teeth. Oh, I must have giggled. Next thing I knew, Jason put a cup of coffee in front of me.

"Coffee's ready!" he announced. I sipped the coffee, feeling less fuzzy and more sad.

"You told Luke you loved him first?" I clarified. Lily shook her head ever so briefly. I pretended not to see it.

Debra frowned. "Sure. What does that matter?"

I shrugged. "It doesn't. Luke just … he seems like the kind of guy who'd want to say that first in a relationship."

You could hear the crickets singing outside. Jason was standing behind Debra's chair motioning for me to stop talking. Addison's brow was creased, and Lily was shooting laser beams at me through her eyes.

Debra stared at me, her eyes squinting as she bit her lower lip.

The fuzziness had all evaporated now, and I realized that I'd just said the wrong thing.

Really wrong.

"Well, *Sara*," Debra said, her voice past the point of even. "I know you know my boyfriend, but I think I know him on a different level. Since he immediately said that he loves me too and then hugged me, I think maybe it didn't matter who said it first."

Kill me.

I nodded. "You're right, Deb. I'm sorry I said that."

The apology seemed to diffuse the rising anger in Debra. She literally deflated in front of me. What I saw in her eyes next looked a whole lot like pity.

Which really did kill me.

"I'm completely in love with Luke, and he's in love with me." She said the words gently but firmly.

My eyes were swimming, and I was dangerously close to losing it.

"All right!" Jason interrupted. "So, I know I'm not making the wedding cake, but I did make dessert for you girls. Why don't you head into the living room, and I'll bring out dessert plates."

Lily and Addison were out of their seats like someone lit a fire under them, chattering on with Debra to fill the awkward silence. I was left alone in the kitchen with Jason.

"What was that? Are you crazy?" he whispered. I shook my head and wiped stubborn tears away. The tears seemed to soften Jason. He pulled me into a hug.

"You've got to pull it together, Sara. It sounds to me like Luke and Deb are on their way toward happily ever after."

"I know … it was probably the wine. I feel so emotional."

He nodded. "I'll pour you another cup of coffee. Try not to talk anymore."

I spent the rest of the evening (the longest half hour ever) completely silent, mechanically taking bites of chocolate cream pie and sipping coffee. Lily saved me by saying she needed to head home and get some rest, which provided me the perfect opportunity to tell Addison that I had to be at work early the next day, so I needed to leave too. I had my purse on my shoulder within twenty seconds of that comment and was out the door and in my car.

My phone kept buzzing.

> Tonight seemed a little tense. Are you okay? Addison texted me.
>
> That was awful. I'm worried about you. Lily texted right after.
>
> It'll be okay. Hang in there. From Jason.

I turned off my phone and went to bed, laying there and staring at the ceiling once my eyes adjusted to the darkness.

I wanted to pray but couldn't think of anything to say. My heart was too heavy.

Was Luke in love with Debra? It sure sounded like it.

"What can I do, God?" I whispered.

My mother came to mind. Praising God didn't seem possible. I had a picture of her in my mind—not that much older than me, experiencing devastation in her marriage, brokenhearted and longing for a baby. Still trying to praise God through tears.

Then the picture of our gang at the hospital, clinging to each other in a moment of pain came to mind. Glen's strong voice praising God amid our fear and worry.

One tear fell from my eye and drifted down the side of my face and into my hair. The first of many. I rolled onto my side and cried.

Luke loved Debra.

You must have a different plan from the one I wanted, God. My eyes closed from exhaustion. *I do want Your plan, not my own. Even if it's not Luke. I need You more than I need him.*

Nothing can separate you from My love.

The words came from somewhere within me. The reminder that I was loved. The grace I craved even after a night of blunders. I finally relaxed.

Loved in the middle of my messy life. Wrapped in God's grace even when I felt jealous and hurt.

My breathing slowed and my tears subsided.

Halfway through August, Addison called me and asked if I'd go with her to meet with a florist and talk flowers for the wedding. We picked a Friday afternoon when I had some extra time and went to four different florists. By five o'clock we were worn out. I climbed into the passenger side of Addison's Volvo.

"You're staying for dinner at my house tonight, you know. Non-negotiable," Addison told me.

I leaned my head back on the seat. While I really just wanted to go home and take a hot bath, dinner with Addison sounded better than takeout.

"Sure. What are you making?"

"Glen's grilling steak."

"Oh, Addison. I don't like being the third wheel. If you and Glen are having dinner tonight, I'd rather sit this one out."

She chuckled. "You won't be the third wheel. Glen picked up Everett from the airport this morning."

I coughed. "Everett? Your brother? You're just now telling me?'

"Well, I wasn't really expecting him till tomorrow, but he was flying standby with his airline and got a seat today, so he decided to come early. Honestly, I've had wedding stuff on the brain for days."

That was definitely true. "Are you sure you want company for dinner? Seems like kind of a family night to me."

"You *are* family. I want you to join us. Glen's grilling steaks and fresh corn on the cob. It's going to be fun. You remember Everett, don't you?"

Eating corn on the cob in front of Addison's brother didn't sound very cool to me. I'd need to run to the bathroom after dinner to check my teeth.

"Vaguely. I met him at the Christmas Eve candlelight service a couple of years ago."

"Right! I haven't seen him since New Year's. I wish we lived closer to each other."

Addison pulled into the driveway of her townhouse, and we went inside. From the entry hallway, we could hear voices through the screen door leading to the backyard. Addison rushed outside with me right behind her.

"Everett!" she hollered. (Texas, y'all.) He turned around and grinned as Addison flew into his arms.

"Hey, sis!" Once he released her, Addison gave Glen a quick peck on the cheek and thanked him for picking Everett up at the airport. In the middle of that exchange, Everett noticed me. I was wishing Addison would remember that I was awkwardly standing there, but Everett stepped closer to me and stuck out his hand for me to shake.

"Have we met?" He scrunched his brow and looked as though he were trying to remember.

"It was a few years back," I told him. "I'm Sara."

"Right! Addison talks about you all the time."

I smiled. "It's nice to see you again. How was your flight?"

He shrugged. "Uneventful. It's nice to be back in Texas. I always forget how humid it is out here, though."

I nodded sympathetically. "I bet you were reminded before you even got off the plane."

He laughed. "Yeah. It hits you like a wave."

Everett seemed different from what I remembered. Then again, we'd only met briefly. Like Addison, he was tall, with chocolate-colored eyes. His hair was dark brown, though, unlike Addi's wavy auburn locks. Still, it was almost uncanny how they had such similar ways of speaking. Even their mannerisms seemed to mimic each other. Everett moved his right hand a lot when he talked, just like Addi. And the two of them laughed in perfect unison throughout the conversation.

They stood side by side, Everett's arm around Addison's shoulders and her arm around his waist. To me, Everett's height and build seemed comparable to Jason's. I liked his straight, bright smile and his easy laugh. I liked the smattering of freckles across his face and the way his short brown hair looked a little messy.

"Oh good! You two got reacquainted. I'm going to set the table inside. It's too hot to eat out here. Sara, can I get you a drink?"

"I'll get it," I said.

"No, no. Keep Everett entertained while I fix the table, okay?" She disappeared into the house. Everett and I sat down on the patio chairs, talking about his job and my job, with Glen piping up every now and then into the conversation.

I was so engrossed in one of Everett's stories of flying to Shanghai that I jumped when Addison touched my shoulder and told us that dinner was ready. The four of us sat around the table, and Glen prayed before we started eating.

Between dinner and dessert, I dashed to the bathroom to do a teeth check. The corn had been so delicious that we'd all had seconds. Since Addison and I had been on-the-go since noon, I felt the need to at least finger-brush my hair and reapply lipstick. Plus, even ten minutes outside in the heat meant that my makeup had melted off and my hair had gone flat.

I stared at myself in the mirror for a moment.

Everett's cute, I admitted. *And super nice.*

Without warning, a smile spread across my face.

Chapter Fifteen

Addison passed around root-beer floats on the back patio. Everett and I sat next to each other on the swing attached to the pergola, drifting back and forth under a canopy of lights. On the patio table, candles gave off a soft glow and kept insects away from our circle. As we all laughed at one of Glen's early-ministry disaster stories, I couldn't help thinking of how much fun I was having.

Since we'd sat down to dinner, conversation had flowed nonstop. I hated for the evening to end. Glen and Addison excused themselves to clean up inside after a while, refusing offers of help from myself and Everett. So we just kept swinging and talking.

"Do you ever get tired of traveling?" I asked him. "Travel wears me out."

He shrugged. "Not really. It's just part of my life. I've got my route that I fly on a regular basis. Now, travel that includes hotels and overnights and sightseeing—yeah, I can see how that wears you out. For myself, it seems like a good time to see the world. I don't have a family or even a steady girlfriend. So my schedule's my own. For now."

I confess my heart picked up speed when he mentioned that he didn't have a girlfriend.

"Have you traveled much?" he asked.

"Well, my parents took me to London the summer before college. Sort of a graduation gift. During my high school years I went on two missions trips to Mexico. And during college I went to Europe for about six weeks. I took an art history course while I was in France. We were mostly in Paris, but we took several daytrips to places like Versailles and Giverny, and I'd take the Euro rail whenever we had a few days off to travel to other places. I fell in love with Paris, though."

"The Louvre," he said knowingly. "I'm guessing for an art lover like yourself, that was a little piece of heaven."

"Oh gosh, yes. I spent days at the Louvre. I also have an appreciation for architecture. Which is another reason to love Paris. And I love history! So Europe in general was just a wonderful experience."

"I minored in history," Everett said. "That's part of why I love to travel. It brings history to life. Seeing places—touching them—you feel connected to the past. You learn so much."

I enjoyed our conversation to the extent that I ignored the mosquito bite on my ankle that was itching like crazy.

"Have you ever been to Virginia or the Carolinas? There's so much American history in that part of the country."

I shook my head.

"Well, if you're ever up my way, I hope you'll let me show you around." The smile that reached his eyes sent flutters through my stomach.

"How long will you be in town?" I asked, trying not to sound timid. "If you have any extra time, you could always take a tour of the museum, as my guest, of course."

He just looked at me for a moment, and I hoped I didn't blush because he seemed to be studying me. I also hoped I hadn't overlooked any stray corn when checking my teeth.

"That sounds really fun, Sara. I'd love to do that. I'll be here with Addison for about two weeks, so I'll have plenty of time. Let me know what works for you, and we'll make it happen. In fact, I'd love to take you out to dinner sometime while I'm here. You pick the place since you know the area, but dinner is on me."

I bit my lip but couldn't keep from grinning. "I am totally up for that, Everett," I said, unable to mask the ridiculous eagerness in my voice.

"I have a feeling this is going to be a really memorable trip." Everett leaned just a little closer to me.

There under the twinkle lights, the flutters in my stomach turned into full-fledged chemistry with the handsome pilot sitting next to me.

Sunday afternoon I sat in the driveway of my parents' house. Lunch with my parents. My keys were in my hand, but every time I thought about getting out, I stalled. I should've asked my mom if she'd told my dad about our conversation.

I didn't want things to be weird between the two of us.

Finally, I gritted my teeth and got out of the car, noticing that Mom's poor perennials looked sadly wilted in the front flower garden. The stifling warm weather had me sweating just from the short walk up the driveway to the house. I let myself inside the house, slid off my sandals by the front door, and walked through the entry hallway, my short, flowered dress swishing. I paused at the hall mirror to pull my hair into a ponytail.

"Mom?"

"In here," she answered. I followed her voice to the kitchen.

There stood my mother, still dressed in her navy pants suit and heels from church, flipping through a design magazine.

"Oh, good. I made the ham salad before we left for church this morning. Could you pull it out and slice the croissant rolls, Sara? I'm going to go change into something more comfortable."

"Sure. Where's Dad?"

"I sent him to the grocery store. We needed a few things. He'll be right back."

"Mom, wait." She stopped mid-step. "I was just wondering, did you tell Dad that you told me about … you know?"

She nodded. "I told you, Sara, that was years ago. It's ancient history."

"I know. Is he—was he okay with you telling me?"

"He asked me how you reacted. I suppose he may have been a little worried about how it would make you feel. Don't bring it up, all right? If he brings it up, that's different. But I doubt he will."

"Okay." She disappeared upstairs, and I set to work slicing croissant rolls. Then I chopped some lettuce and tomato to go with the sandwiches, all the while thinking about how much I loved my mother's ham salad. The first time I made it for the gang, Lily and Addison sat at the island in my apartment and watched me throw ham and mayo and sweet relish and Dijon mustard in the food processor. Lily wrinkled her nose. I told her that I knew it didn't look all that appealing, but to trust me. An hour later when people were still asking for thirds and fourths, I'd sold everyone on ham salad.

It's one of my mother's best recipes.

I filled a glass bowl with baked chips, then put all the food on the table. My mom came downstairs right as my dad walked through the door. He set bags on the counter, and I started to put away the groceries.

"I got some of those cookies from the bakery that your mother likes. And there's milk that needs to go in the fridge, Sara."

So far, so good. Everything seemed normal.

The three of us sat down at the table and ate our light lunch. My mother wanted a full report on Lily's father and how the family was doing. I mentioned the dinner at Addison's house with Everett. As I spoke, her eyes widened, and she scooted her chair forward. I could see that my mother's interest had just been piqued. An interrogation of all-things-Everett followed.

My dad, of course, found this amusing.

"You should bring him over while he's in town," he suggested. I rolled my eyes.

"Yes. Sure. *So, Everett, I know we barely know each other, but would you like to meet my parents?*"

"What's wrong with that?" my mom asked, confused. I started clearing the table. My dad opened the package of cookies and stuffed a whole one in his mouth. My mother frowned at him. I wanted to laugh. The entire scene had been my life for so many years that every detail felt familiar. Luckily, my dad's cookie eating distracted my mom from more talk about my nonexistent love life.

"I'll clean up." Mom reached for the package of cookies, but not before Dad snagged one more. He then turned on a golf tournament on TV (which went right above "reading Leviticus" in my level of interest), so I decided to head to the study. I wanted to look through our old family albums. Specifically, the one in which all my baby pictures were located.

Thanks to my mother's near-superhuman organization skills, I found the album in no time and plopped down in my father's desk chair to look through it. I studied pictures of my parents when my mother was pregnant with me.

They seemed happy.

"What are you looking at?" I nearly jumped out of my skin at my dad's voice.

"Oh, um, pictures from the year I was born."

"Let me take a look." He slid on his glasses and came over behind the desk to where I was sitting. He chuckled at one where my mother was clearly nearing the end of her pregnancy. "When your mom was pregnant, she wanted fruit popsicles from the time she woke up until the time she went to sleep. I've never known her to eat them before or after her pregnancy, but I should have bought stock in popsicles that year."

I smiled, glad he'd shared that tidbit with me.

"So." My dad carried the album with him to the brown leather chair in front of his desk and sat down; he flipped to the next page. "Your mom told me that she had a conversation with you about some problems we had before you were born."

Eek.

I nodded. "I kept asking her about Psalm 113:3, so she finally told me the story."

"It was years ago, Sara. We were different back then."

"I know," I told him.

"I was different back then." He looked back down at the album. His voice wavered, and he kept fidgeting with the album. Maybe it was just the uncomfortableness of the topic. I admit I felt a bit uncomfortable myself.

Honestly, I wished I could ask if he'd ever really loved that other woman, if they'd ever kept in touch after he and my mom got back together.

But I knew I didn't need to hear every part of my dad's story. There were pieces that he and my mom should keep to themselves. That pain—that season of hurt—was between the two of them.

"I'm glad you and Mom got back together," I said, my words soft.

He looked up, and I could be wrong, but his eyes looked watery. "There hasn't been one day since that I haven't thanked God for that same thing. I wish I could say that I'd fought harder for our marriage back in the beginning. But God used your mother. She was stronger than I was back then." He closed the album and set it on the desk. "Now—I'd fight to the death before I'd let my family fall apart."

Emotion welled up in me, and I could hardly breathe as I listened to my dad's words.

"That's what I want for you, Sara. Someone who will fight for you." Now there were definite tears in his eyes, which immediately brought about tears in my own.

"That's what I want too," I managed to say, looking at my dad, with his gray hair and tan skin, with his quick wit and strong hands that helped so many people. "I want someone like you." And the words were true. Not someone who never made mistakes—someone who learned from them.

My dad shook his head and looked down. He wiped his eyes as he cried. Covered in grace, right in front of me.

Chapter Sixteen

BBQ AT ADDISON'S TONIGHT. 5:30.

The group text came Monday afternoon. I read it then tucked my phone in my pocket. My tour group looked ready to move again. I pointed out artwork and talked about trends and styles and history—but my mind kept wandering to Everett and the fact that I'd be seeing him in approximately four hours.

There was just enough time for me to rush home and change clothes before heading to Addison's house. I stood in front of my closet, completely unsure of what to wear. A bright, multi-colored, sleeveless, ankle-length sundress shoved in the back (the tags still on), jumped out at me. It was the kind of dress Debra might wear, to be honest. And for that reason, it just didn't feel like me. Too loud. Too bold. Too noticeable. But the day I'd seen it on the rack at the store, I couldn't keep my eyes off it. I'd loved the colors and the flowy look of it.

Staring at that dress now, for once, I decided, Debra Hart wouldn't be the only girl to be bold.

I ripped the tags off, slipped into the dress, put on my favorite gold dangly earrings and sandals, and drove over to Addison's before I could talk myself out of it.

Lily and Sam parked on the street in front of me. After giving Lily a big hug, we linked arms and walked toward the front door.

"Sara, you look gorgeous!" Lily eyed my outfit as if she almost didn't recognize me.

"Thanks."

"No, you're always pretty, Sara. But honestly, that dress is stunning on you. Is it new?"

I shook my head. "I got it ages ago and just haven't worn it."

"Well, honey, you need to wear it more often 'cause it looks amazing on you, and I like your earrings too! And you're wearing that gold eyeliner I love! Goodness, Sara Witherspoon, you went all out tonight."

Oh, good grief. My face felt on fire. Wait till Lily saw Everett. She would definitely put two and two together fast enough.

I followed her into the house, my nerves doing a Zumba dance in my stomach. Jason, Debra, and Glen were in the kitchen, pouring drinks and chatting. Sam and Lily stopped to talk, and I waved and kept going out to the backyard. There on the deck stood Addison, Luke, and Everett. All three looked in my direction as I stepped outside. My eyes went straight for Everett.

By the way his eyes did a double-take, and the moment it took for his smile to register, I had a feeling he liked the dress. I hoped I wasn't blushing!

"Sara!" Addison came over and squeezed my arm. "You look beautiful! I want that dress."

I chuckled nervously, still looking in Everett's direction. Through my peripheral, I could see Addison follow my gaze to Everett, then Everett's to me. Surprised pleasure filled her face.

"Sara, um…" Everett stepped closer to me. "You really do. I mean, Addi's right, you're … that is, you look great."

I smiled. "Thanks, Everett. It's nice to see you again."

Luke stepped to the side and caught my attention.

"Hey you," I said in his direction. "How are you?"

I couldn't quite put my finger on Luke's expression, which was odd, considering I had almost every one of his expressions memorized, but sometimes he could be a little hard to read.

"Good."

Ohhhkay. Luke was obviously not feeling very verbose at the moment.

Glen came outside to fire up the grill, and Debra was right on his heels. She attached herself to Luke, and for once, I didn't feel so despondent. Not with the way Everett was looking at me.

"How about something to drink?" Everett said, and we walked inside together. Lily was in the kitchen, and her mouth fell open when she saw me and Everett walk in together. To her credit, she quickly recovered.

"Everett! I completely forgot you were in town!" Lily exclaimed. Sam walked over and shook hands with him.

"It's great to see you again, Everett. How are you?"

He chatted for a moment with Sam and Jason while I poured myself a glass of iced tea. Lily was on me like white on rice within two seconds.

"What's going on with you two?" she whispered. I shrugged innocently.

"Nothing, of course."

"Nothing? Now I know why you pulled out this long-forgotten dress, Miss Temptress!"

I couldn't help laughing out loud, then quickly turned the laughter into a cough.

"I had dinner here Friday and happened to get reacquainted with Everett. No big deal. We're also possibly going out while he's in town," I whispered back to her.

I'll admit it. I enjoyed the utter shock on Lily's face.

"I can't think of a word to say," she said, which was a feat in itself.

"Sara, I want you to try this appetizer." Jason broke up our whispered conversation.

"Oh, sure. Did you make these?" I asked, taking one of the meatballs on the small plate he held out to me.

"Yeah. I'm thinking we should have a few appetizer dishes at Addison's wedding, so I've been playing with recipes."

I bit into the meatball and closed my eyes.

"Jason, this is impressive."

"Good." He smiled. "By the way, you look incredible tonight." He winked at me as he took the tray of meatballs outside.

So basically, the dress was a man magnet.

"Temptress," Lily teased again. I poked her.

"Shh!"

Lily, Sam, Everett, and I joined the others out back. Addison turned on some music, and soon the smell of grilled hot dogs and hamburgers wafted through the air. Everett and I ended up sitting side by side on two lawn chairs in the backyard, eating cheeseburgers.

Unlike me, Everett's quick conversation and hilarious stories proved how comfortable he felt even with a group of people he didn't know well. I liked hearing him talk, and I liked how every time I spoke, he gave me his undivided attention.

"So," Everett said and lowered his voice, only speaking to me this time. "When are we having a date? And I won't be mad if you wear that dress again," he said with mock seriousness. I giggled. I'm serious! Ridiculous, I know, but the guy made me giggle.

"Well, since I get to pick the place, I was thinking we should go to the Spaghetti Warehouse. Do you like Italian?"

He nodded. "Sure. That sounds great."

"Okay, would Wednesday night work? I can pick you up after I get off work."

"I'm available, Sara, whenever you are."

Sheesh. If my face wasn't already flushed from the heat, my cheeks were tomatoes by that point. I tried to temper my huge grin as he smiled at me. That messy brown hair and those playful chocolate eyes were a dangerous combination. My heart skipped.

"So what are you guys talking about?" Debra's sing-song voice broke in. She and Luke pulled up two chairs across from us.

"Oh, well," I stammered.

"Sara and I are going to dinner Wednesday, so we were just talking about where to go," Everett said easily.

Not that it was a secret, but I wasn't planning on telling the entire group! What if the date was a complete flop? Best not to tell the world ahead of time. Apparently, Everett didn't know this piece of dating etiquette.

Debra's eyes rounded like saucers.

"Oh, that's great! How fun. Where are you going?"

"Where did you say, Sara?" Everett looked at me. "The Spaghetti—"

"Warehouse," Luke finished. "That's Sara's favorite Italian restaurant."

Yes. Okay. The moment was beginning to feel awkward for me.

"Why is it your favorite?" Debra cocked her head to the side. "I don't think I've been there." She glanced at Everett, then back at me.

I felt all six eyes staring at me. Where was Lily when I needed her?

"For one thing, they have the best spaghetti ever. And it's a really old restaurant. In fact, my parents went there when they were dating."

"Wow! That's really special," Debra said. My mouth felt as dry as concrete during a Texas heat wave. Everett reached over and took the empty glass from my hand, and we made eye contact. My breath stopped short at the image of the soft, pleased look on his face.

"Well, I can't wait to try it, Sara," he said in a gentle tone. "I'm going to get you a refill." He stood up and walked toward the deck. My gaze followed him.

"Are you guys dating?" Debra squealed.

"No, we just met! I mean, we met a few years ago, but barely. He's just really nice. I told him I could show him around the museum while he's in town, and he ended up saying we should have dinner. Not a big deal at all."

"Well, I think it's so exciting!" Debra seemed thrilled for me. I looked at Luke, sitting in the lawn chair directly across from me. Again with the mysterious facial expression I couldn't quite place.

"How's work, Luke?" I hoped to draw him out of whatever was making him so sullen.

"Fine. Kind of—well, things are a little stressful with one of my projects right now."

"Debra said your trip to see your mom went well." Luke nodded at my comment.

"We had a great time. My mom was really glad to see us. I think our visit lifted her spirits."

"I'm so glad." I studied him. "Are you—is everything okay?"

Luke's gaze didn't meet mine. "I'm tired, I guess. Sam, Jason, and I met at the gym for basketball at six this morning."

Everett rejoined us, handing me another iced tea and inching his chair slightly closer to mine before he sat down. Debra joined in, asking him tons of questions about life as a pilot. I sipped my iced tea and looked up, glancing over at Luke, who was staring straight at me.

Something seemed off. I wished we could talk alone for a minute. Was he really tired or was something else wrong? He suddenly stood up and Debra stopped midsentence.

"I'm just going to get another burger. Anyone need anything?"

I fought the urge to jump up and follow him. If something was wrong, he had Debra to talk to at any time.

My stomach twisted in knots. A familiar sense of loneliness rushed through me at the sight of Luke leaving our group, but I pushed it away as soon as it surfaced. Next to me, Everett touched my arm lightly and asked if I knew where Glen and Addison were going on their honeymoon. Wedding conversation ensued, but Luke never returned. Eventually, Debra hopped off to find him. When I noticed Everett, no longer used to our sweltering humidity, wipe his brow, I suggested we go inside to cool off.

Lily and Sam left before dusk. I knew they were both still more than a bit overwhelmed with Sam's father's recovery, juggling the family business, and all Lily was doing to be a help to Sam's mother. She and I walked together out to her car.

"He's adorable, Sara. Really. I could eat him up," Lily said with a grin.

Sam rolled his eyes. "Try to control yourself, wife." Lily and I laughed.

"So you're going out with him Wednesday?" she clarified. I nodded. "Good. I want to hear every detail, so text me when you get home, even if it's scandalously late. In fact, I hope it's scandalously late."

"Let's not get carried away. He's only in town for two weeks, Lil. Then what?"

"He flies planes for a living. I think he can make it down here to see you, sugar," she said, her drawl thicker than ever.

"I know. It's just…"

Sam got in the car and Lily put both hands on my shoulders. "This isn't about Luke. This is about you. You're allowed to have a life. He's taken, honey." Her voice softened. "Go have a good time with Everett. Keep your heart open."

My mouth tightened but I nodded. She was right.

"I'll text you Wednesday night," I promised.

Chapter Seventeen

The thing about having such a close-knit group of friends is that it's impossible to keep anything to yourself. By Wednesday morning, Addison was texting me that she was doing cartwheels because she was so excited I was dating her brother. Then, since Everett had so kindly told Luke and Deb about the date, Deb started texting me that she was itching to know the details first thing Thursday. Lily called midmorning and told me to text her what I planned to wear so she could let me know if she approved.

By the time my shift ended, I wanted to throw my phone into a river somewhere.

I tried to shake off nerves compounded by the girls hounding me as I rushed home to change. Since it was about one hundred degrees outside and the restaurant wasn't all that fancy, I stuck with my favorite jean capris, my strappy healed black sandals, and my favorite loose black top. I swept my hair to the side, stuck in some silver hoop earrings, and touched up my makeup before heading to Addi's house.

Everett stepped outside the minute I pulled up, and I breathed a sigh of relief. I'd been contemplating my situation of that as high school boy, walking up the sidewalk to get my date and having to say hello to the family before we were allowed to leave.

He slid into the passenger seat, and I could smell the subtle fragrance of his cologne. Honestly, Lily was right. He was adorable. In jeans and a short sleeved navy collared shirt, he seemed completely comfortable with himself.

I still felt nervous.

"I had to force Addi to stay in the house. Seriously, you'd think we were going to the prom or something. I think she wanted to take our picture for Facebook."

Laughter escaped me, and my racing pulse slowed a bit.

"How was work today?" he asked. We hit traffic but conversation flowed so easily between us that it didn't seem to matter. We pulled up at the restaurant right at 7:00 and were seated immediately since I had made a reservation. I sat across from Everett at the small table for two, one flickering candle between us, and I couldn't help feeling incredibly lucky to be on a date with this guy. His beautiful brown eyes stayed right on me as we talked and laughed over salad and spaghetti.

Our empty plates had been cleared away, and we were having coffee and brownies when Everett cleared his throat.

"So, what's the story with you and Luke?"

I'm not kidding when I say I choked.

After drinking half a glass of water, I managed to stop sounding like there was a hamster wedged in my throat.

"Um, what do you mean?"

Everett gave me a look. "I mean, did you guys used to date or something?"

Or something.

I shook my head. "Oh no. We're just really good friends. You saw that he was with our friend Debra, right? They're dating."

"Right. I noticed that. But I just thought … it seemed like you guys have history."

I looked at the remnants of my brownie. "Well, we're close friends. We have a lot in common, I guess. But there's never been anything romantic between us."

He raised his eyebrows, and I hoped my cheeks didn't flush. Everett leaned closer.

"Never?"

I sipped my coffee, not quite sure how to get out of this conversation without turning myself into a liar.

"We've always just been friends," I answered. "I dated Jason for a while several years ago." I threw that out there, hoping it might change the questioning.

Everett nodded. "Addison told me."

What else had she told him?

"So there's nothing between you and Luke?" I looked up in response to his lowered, unconvinced tone, curious as to the effect Everett was having on me. Was I just tired of lying about my feelings? Was it the knowing look in Everett's gaze?

Moisture burned behind my eyes.

"He's never wanted more than friendship." I'm pretty sure my voice squeaked.

The restaurant buzzed with conversations, but at our little table, everything went silent. Everett's hand covered mine.

"Have you?"

"Why are you asking me?" I said just above a whisper.

"Because I like you, Sara. I'd like to continue getting to know you. I think you're beautiful, and smart, and I like talking to you. I think we both value our faith. Did I mention you're beautiful?"

I did blush at that and a small smile worked its way to my face. He smiled back but it faded quickly.

"The thing is, long distance relationships hardly ever work. At least, from my experience. Do you hope we stay in touch after I leave?"

"Yes," I answered immediately. He nodded.

"I'm very happy to hear that. I want that too. That's why I'm asking … is there anything I should know about your friendship with Luke? And just so you know—you can be totally honest with me. You can trust me, Sara."

Could I?

"Okay, fine. Yes, there was a time I'd hoped Luke might be interested in me as more than a friend. But he never has. I've accepted that—" My words stopped. "Of course, I respect and care about him. But I want him to be happy, and Debra makes him happy. He chose her." I couldn't keep my voice from shaking at that point.

Talk about humiliating.

Everett squeezed my hand.

"I couldn't tell him—we were best friends. I kept thinking one day he'd see how I felt. Maybe I just hoped his feelings would change. Then he started dating Deb, and I realized it was never going to happen. So I just…" I tried to stop rambling, but my thoughts were racing now. About Luke. About Everett. About Debra. I shook my head and closed my eyes.

"Hey." Everett's soft response pushed me to open my eyes. "It's okay."

"It's not," I said, trying to regain control of my crazy emotions.

"It is," Everett told me, his tone casual but firm. "I'm glad you told me, Sara. But I have to wonder if…" Everett's voice trailed off.

"What?" He shrugged at my insistence.

"I can see you were disappointed that things didn't happen with Luke. I can also see that you're open to moving on from that." Everett laced our fingers together across the table. "You are here with me after all."

"I am." Even if I'd made the gravest dating mistake possible—talking about your feelings for someone else while sitting across from a prospective partner.

"I like you too, Everett." I just went ahead and said it. Why not? I'd already said more than I should have. I needed to at least *attempt* to turn this back into a date.

"So you're saying I have a chance?" he asked, that boyish grin returning.

"Definitely." My mood lifted, maybe as a result of the honesty between us. "Now, we have to get going. I have a surprise for you."

Everett's brown eyes lit up, confirming my instinct that he really liked surprises. We arrived at the museum just in time. Everett reached for my hand as we walked through the dark parking lot filled with a smattering of cars. I led him to the planetarium, and we found spots together near the front.

"This is the IMAX, right? What is it tonight? Underwater sea creatures or the rainforest?" he whispered. I smiled.

"Neither."

The lights went out and pulsating music came through the speakers. Different colored light beams filled the screen, in tune with the pounding music.

"What is this?" Everett leaned over and asked.

"Pink Floyd laser light show." I said the words into his ear so he could hear me above the music, and I will readily admit that being that close to him sent butterflies all through me.

I settled back next to him, and we watched the lights that pulsed to the sound of Pink Floyd music, our hands still connected. Afterward, we walked back to my car slowly, stopping under a streetlight.

"Sara, that was without a doubt the coolest date I've ever been on."

I smiled. "I'm so glad you liked it."

"I can't believe I've never been to one of those before! It was awesome. Do you think they'd have them at the museum near where I live?"

"Hey," I complained. "You better not be thinking about taking anyone else on a laser light show date."

He took both of my hands in his. "Don't worry."

I stood frozen, not breathing.

"Thank you, Sara. This was a good surprise," he said, staring down at me. For some reason, I felt a little lighter knowing I'd told him about Luke. Everything felt honest between us. A tad awkward maybe, but honest at least.

"I should warn you," Everett said, pulling me a step closer to him. "It's our first date…"

"I know," I said, my heart pounding as he leaned down.

"And I'm about to kiss you."

I stared into the refrigerator and could hear the buzzing of my cell phone on the kitchen counter. Lily had been texting me her interrogation of my date. When my answers were too vague, the phone finally rang. I grabbed a water bottle, then answered the phone.

"Yes, Lily?"

"What the heck does 'It went fine' mean?"

I laughed. "It went fine! We had a great time. Dinner was delicious. The laser light show was a big hit. He's a fun person to go out with."

"You like him," she surmised. I sipped my water bottle and turned off lights as I made my way to my room.

"I do."

"More than Luke?" I set the water bottle on my nightstand and climbed into bed.

"That's a ridiculous question, Lily. I barely know him in comparison to Luke."

"Did you feel fireworks?"

I clicked off the lamp by my bed and leaned back against the headboard in the darkness.

"Like it was the fourth of July."

"Lord, have mercy," Lily groaned. "Tell me now. Did the boy kiss you?"

I ran my hand across the soft blanket. "It was our first date!"

"Stop stalling. Answer the question."

Lily was too smart for her own good.

"All right. He kissed me."

Lily was quiet for a split-second—shocking, I know.

"Impressive," she finally murmured, and I felt the corners of my mouth lift at her response.

"I thought so."

After I promised to go into more detail tomorrow, Lily let me hang up. I pulled the covers up to my chin and thought about that kiss.

Alone in the dark, I tried to slow down the rollercoaster of thoughts going through my mind and focus enough to pray but just couldn't seem to do it. I figured God probably kept up with my random thoughts regardless.

My mind kept reliving the moment in the parking lot. Everett's spicy, woodsy cologne, his playful brown eyes, his self-assured confidence—

everything swirled in my mind, colliding with the moment he pulled me close and pressed his lips to mine—firm, tender, fueled by attraction—without hesitation. His mouth tasted of spearmint. His strong hands circled my waist.

The truth was that, before tonight, I hadn't been kissed in a really long time, and now, right out of the blue, I'd been kissed. And kissed well, if I would admit it. I'd missed that physical aspect of being in a relationship. This time, rather than feeling lonely at that thought, I let myself revel in the hope that was sparked by my unexpected foray into romance.

I touched my lips and smiled in the dark. Maybe, just maybe, my love story was about to begin.

Chapter Eighteen

"Deb wants to work on her tan," Addison told me Thursday morning. I tried to concentrate both on the computer screen in front of me and the conversation on speakerphone. I scrolled down the screen.

"Sara? Are you listening?"

"I'm working!" I argued, pausing for a moment. "What were you saying?"

"I'm saying that Deb wants to work on her tan. Me too. Lily, well … she wants to hang out with us regardless. We were wondering if you could get us into your parents' clubhouse Saturday. What do you think? All of us could go to the pool for a couple of hours, before dinner that night at La Velita Blanca? You haven't forgotten we're going out for Mexican with Everett Saturday night, right?"

"I haven't forgotten. Saturday. The pool. My parents' neighborhood. Sure. That works."

"I know he kissed you," Addison said slyly. My fingers halted in midair over my keyboard.

"What? Why did he tell you?"

"Because I'm his twin sister and you're one of my best friends! I should know these things!"

I didn't answer for a moment. This could get tricky. "Addison," I began, feeling again like a teenage boy who is trying to get the family to like him. "You know, it just happened and I—"

"How do you feel about Everett?" she asked, her tone softer.

"I really like him," I assured her.

"Good. That's all I'm saying. You guys are adults. What you do is your business."

"Hmph." In our circle of friends, *my business* was only an illusion. I hung up the phone, now distracted again by the not-so-distant memory of kissing Everett. Still, I had tours to run and museum guests to interact with. Thoughts of romance would have to wait. But when Everett texted me at four o'clock, wondering if I wanted to go see a movie that night, the kiss came back to my mind in full force.

Yes, I texted back.

Once I actually had a few minutes to check movie times, I realized that there wasn't anything all that great at the theater. I invited him to watch a movie at my apartment instead, and I enticed him with dinner.

No judgment, please. A girl has to do what a girl has to do.

At five o'clock, I raced to the grocery store, picked up everything I needed to make my mother's best chicken casserole recipe, along with bread and the makings of a simple salad, and rushed home. I figured we could rent a movie on demand or just watch something I already owned. Thankfully, my apartment was already spic-and-span clean, so I could concentrate on cooking and setting a nice table (two of my favorite things).

Everett ended up borrowing Addison's car since she had a church thing to attend with Glen. He walked through my door at six thirty, wearing knee-length gray shorts and a black T-shirt.

"Your hair is wet."

He handed me a bouquet of pink roses. "I just took a shower. I've been bike riding with Glen for … I'm not sure. It feels like my whole life."

I laughed to the point that my eyes watered. His face broke into a smile. I took the flowers, thanked him once I managed to stop laughing, and found a vase. Everett helped himself to a glass of Chardonnay, then sat at a barstool while I finished putting together the salad.

"Bonding over bikes, huh? I suspect Addison will be doing more than her fair share of bike marathons in the near future," I said, keeping my tone light.

We shared a look of near hilarity, both knowing Addison so well.

"Well, please tell me you have some Tylenol because I have a feeling every muscle in my body will kill me tomorrow."

I looked up from the salad, and we just smiled at each other for a moment.

Gosh, it was nice having him in my apartment, sitting at my counter, about to have dinner together. I could get used to seeing him shake back that cute, slightly unkempt hair and hearing his laughter fill the space across from me.

I don't think I'd realized, until that moment, just how lonely I'd been feeling. And here was a living, breathing, adorable pilot—about to eat my chicken casserole. He took a look around the apartment before we sat down to dinner.

"Sara, you realize your apartment looks like something out of a magazine, right?"

I chuckled, setting the casserole pan on the table and going back to the kitchen for salad tongs. "One of those magazines featuring the smallest living spaces imaginable, maybe."

"At least you have two bedrooms. I've got a studio apartment. It serves its purpose but it's not spacious. But really, this is beautiful. How do you make everything … you know, go together?"

I poured a glass of wine for myself before we sat down. "My mother's an interior designer, Everett. Making things go together has been ingrained in me since childhood."

"Even the table!" Everett said. "If we were eating at my place, well, I don't even have plates that match." He met my eyes, wanting me to know he appreciated the effort I'd taken. My heart filled, and I smiled back at him. How many guys were so intent on showing gratitude?

Well, Luke, of course. Before he became Debra's Casanova, I'd always found him to be observant and gracious when we spent time together.

And Jason … despite his fun-loving and joking personality, I'd never known him not to be sweet and appreciative.

So, there was that. I pushed away thoughts of the other men in my life and passed Everett the salad bowl. Our hands brushed as he took it from me and tingles shot up my neck.

"Thanks, Sara. Everything looks delicious."

Good heavens.

"Everett." I tore a piece of bread in half. "I enjoy this kind of thing, and I wanted to set a special table for a special guest."

Over chicken casserole, warm French bread, salad, and two glasses of wine, Everett told me in detail about his day of bike riding with Glen. By the time we moved to the living room to turn on a movie, darkness had fallen, and we'd covered every topic from Glen and Addison's engagement to the time Everett broke his arm as a sixth grader.

Everett went through my movies. I bit back a smile as he moved quickly past the many romantic comedies.

"Finding anything?" I asked, setting two espressos on the coffee table.

"One that seems acceptable," he said at last, holding up *Star Wars*.

Oh dear.

From where she sat on the couch, Yoda just yawned.

I stretched out on the deck chair and wiggled my toes in the Saturday sunshine. It was ten forty-five in the morning but still hot as blazes. The four of us girls were nearly alone at the pool in my parents' neighborhood.

"This was actually a really good idea, Addison," I said. Lily just huffed from under the umbrella.

"Maybe for those of us not concerned with skin cancer," she said.

"We're all wearing sunscreen, and we won't be out for too long," Deb said soothingly while she piled that mass of hair of hers up in a topknot. "I've got the cutest white dress to wear to dinner with Luke next week, and I don't want to look pale."

For a few minutes the four of us relaxed in silence. The only sound was that of Addison turning the pages of the bridal magazine she was reading.

Lily broke the silence. "So, we all know he kissed you Wednesday. Has it happened again?"

"We ALL know?" I glared at her. Addison and Debra shrugged.

"You can't leave me out of things like that, Sara," Debra scolded. "If Lily and Addison know, I need to know too."

"She asked me point-blank, Sara," Addison said as if that made all the difference.

"So, did he kiss you Thursday when he had dinner at your place?"

I thought back over the way the night had ended—me watching the familiar Han Solo, with Everett passed out from bike-riding exhaustion on my sofa.

"No. Well, he kissed my cheek before he left. The truth is that he fell asleep on the couch during the movie. I woke him up after and he left, still tired. But I *will* say that he looked adorable sleeping," I said, thinking back to the way his brown hair looked a bit crazy when he finally woke up.

"Sam sleeps with his mouth wide open, and he flails about like a catfish out of water. Not adorable," Lily said, adjusting her hat. I choked back a laugh. Lily's gaze drifted off to the pool. "But, when he comes home from working all day—usually bone-tired and covered in grass stains, with his face pink and flushed from the sun—he looks so … I don't even like sweat and dirt! Maybe it's something about how manly he seems right then. But when he comes home like that, I…" Lily shivered visibly and grinned.

"Good grief, Lil," I said.

Addison chuckled. "Tone it down, girlfriend."

"Someone take a sledgehammer to the visual in my mind." Debra groaned.

Lily shrugged. "He's my match. What can I say? You girls should be so lucky."

I had to smile at that. Lily and Sam were a match, indeed. Everett invaded my thoughts again. Could he be my match? With that bedhead brown hair and the way his hand felt so warm against mine? The secret thought of more spearmint-flavored kisses in my future brought a flush to my face.

"Glen is my match," Addison said wistfully. "Every morning I wake up thinking it's one more day closer until I get to be his wife."

Debra leaned forward and took off her sunglasses. "I want Luke to be my match. I don't think he's sure yet. But I think he's getting closer."

My whole body stiffened. Thoughts of Everett faded, and images of Luke and Debra came front and center in my mind.

"Well, he's told you he loves you, Deb. He took you to meet his mom. You know Luke. We all do. If he's going to do something, he's going to take his time and be cautious about it," Addison said. I could practically see Lily's eyes on me behind those huge sunglasses on her face.

"I know," Deb said with resignation. "I also know it's only been a few months, but I can't imagine being with anyone else. He knows how I feel."

"Have you guys argued yet?" Lily asked. Debra smiled.

"Not really. Just little spats, I suppose. I can get all worked up over the smallest things. Luke is the calmest person I've ever met. Sometimes I *wish* he'd argue with me, but nothing ruffles him. He's so logical about everything. When I'm annoyed with him about something, he always says that I'm not being logical." She slid her shades back on.

We went back to relaxing in comfortable silence. Addison returned to her magazine. The sun only barely touched Lily's toes, the rest of her body safe and secure under the umbrella.

"What do you think, Sara?" Debra said after a minute, in a quiet voice next to me.

"Hmm?" I looked over at her.

"About me and Luke. Do you think we're a good match?"

My lips felt dry and chapped at that moment. I reached down for my water bottle.

"Of course I do," I answered. Really, what else was there to say? And in truth, thinking of Sam's assessment of how they might balance each other, I had to agree that it could be possible.

"Have you told him that?"

Gulp.

"We haven't talked about it, Deb. I mean, you know Luke's very private about things."

A pinched look crossed her face. "Not usually with you."

Cold condensation dripped from my water bottle to my leg. "Well, things change."

"I'm going to get a soda from the machine," Lily said. She lightly touched my shoulder as she walked past us. "Sara, want one?"

I jumped up. "A soda would be great."

We walked together, barefoot, down to the soda machine near the restrooms, neither of us saying anything at first. Lily stuck a dollar bill and some change into the machine and handed me the Dr Pepper that rolled out.

"What are you thinking, Lily?" I finally asked. She reached down for the Coke that thundered down the machine next.

"Not a thing. It just seemed like a good time to take a walk."

I leaned against the building. "The truth is that Luke and I don't talk that much anymore. Not like we used to."

"You miss him." It wasn't a question.

"Of course. I'd miss you if suddenly we didn't talk very much."

"I'd miss you too," Lily said with a sad sort of smile. "But you like Everett, right?"

I nodded. "Very much. He's romantic. He's straight to the point. He's fun."

"Not to mention good-looking and totally into you."

Lily gulped her soda.

"Addison's thrilled that you guys are dating. Be careful with that."

I chuckled. "You don't want me to break her heart?"

"I'm being serious! She's probably already thinking that it would be wonderful for you two to be sisters."

"It's way too soon to think that way."

Lily poked me. "You know us girls. We can't seem to help getting ahead of ourselves."

"True," I agreed. We walked back to our chairs, but I wasn't eager to reengage in conversation with Debra so I eased into the water to swim a few laps. The water chilled my skin, but I dove under anyway. Finally breathless, I pulled myself up to the side of the pool and sat down, keeping my legs in the water.

"Stop making us look bad," Addison called out. "We're here to lay out, not to work out!"

"Overachiever!" Lily accused and I laughed. I smoothed my hair back and went to my chair, ready for the sun to warm me.

"Did we bring snacks? I'm starving," Debra said.

"It's almost lunch time. We could run by my parents' house and see if my mom will feed us," I offered.

"Excellent idea. I'm feeling sufficiently toasted." Debra inspected the tan line on her shoulder. I grabbed my phone and sent my mom a quick text to make sure she was there. Regardless, I had a key and knew stopping by wouldn't be a problem. Without waiting for a reply, the four of us loaded up our towels, magazines, water bottles, and sunscreen, and drove in single file two streets over to my parents' home. The door swung open and my mother beamed.

"Girls! I'm so happy to see you!"

My mother. Always ready.

We followed her into the kitchen where, in the span of ten minutes, she'd set out chips, dip, and a plate filled with ham and cheese sandwiches. A pitcher of iced tea sat on the counter. As I watched my mom flutter about the kitchen, pouring drinks and asking all about Addison's wedding plans, it occurred to me that she really *was* so happy to see us. A pang tweaked my heart at the thought of her being lonely.

Addison asked her a million wedding planning questions, while Lily, Deb, and I helped ourselves to second helpings of chips and sandwiches, tossing in our two cents regarding the wedding as needed. When the bridal talk had finally subsided, Addison grabbed another sandwich.

"Do you guys know that Jason's bringing a date tonight? Someone we've never met!" Addison told us.

This was big news.

"What? Who? Why haven't we heard about her?" Debra exclaimed.

"I think he's hiding her from us until he knows if he really likes her," Addison replied. "You know he hasn't been serious about anyone since..."

"Sara," Lily finished. I glowered at her.

"What? It's true!" she said. Thankfully, my mother was wiping crumbs from the counter and pretended not to hear—though I knew she was listening to every word.

"Is she someone from his cooking school?" I wondered aloud.

"Maybe. I asked him if he was coming to dinner with all of us, and he said yes and that he was bringing a date. And that he expected the four of us to like her and make her feel welcome." Addison raised both eyebrows.

"We're always nice!" Lily huffed.

"Why did he say that about the four of us? He should expect that from Luke and Sam too," Debra said.

"They're guys. They're always nice to new girls. It's us he's worried about." Addison grinned.

"I wonder what she's like," I said.

"We'll know in just a couple of hours." Debra jumped up. "I better get going. I need to shower and run errands before dinner tonight."

Knowing that Jason had a date made me all the more relieved that I would be Everett's date for the evening.

"Is Everett riding with you, Sara?" Addison asked.

"Yes, I told him I'd pick him up. We may go out for coffee afterward."

"Everett?" My eyes popped at my mother's question. I'd forgotten about her.

"You mean you haven't told your mom about your new romance with Everett, Sara?" Debra said with a crafty grin.

"Well, she mentioned him, but I didn't hear about any romance," my mother said.

"Oh yes," Addison joined in with a wicked smile. "Sara's dating my twin brother, Suzanne."

"He's a pilot," Lily added. "And gorgeous. And they've already—"

"Guys!" I said loudly, my face flaming.

"If you're *dating*, Sara," my mother said pointedly, reminding me that we'd pretty much already had this discussion, "why don't you bring him over for dinner tomorrow? Your father and I would love to meet him."

"Um, because we've been dating for ten minutes, and dinner here's not even a remote possibility."

"He's leaving soon!" Addison countered. "You should totally bring him over, Sara. He lives in North Carolina," she explained to my mom. "You'll love him, Suzanne. My brother is a great guy."

This conversation truly needed to end, but somehow—well, by being bullied by my best girlfriends—by the time we all left, I'd agreed to invite Everett for dinner the following night.

Someone should warn him to run in the opposite direction.

I pulled up at Addison's house at six o'clock that evening, and Everett jumped in my car.

"Addison already told me. I'd love to have dinner at your parents' house tomorrow."

"Seriously?" I growled. "This is crazy. You're lucky you live in North Carolina."

He laughed.

"I was just thinking the very opposite. Well … but I'm not sure I could get used to this level of humidity on a regular basis again. It's been a long time since I lived in Texas. To your point though, I can see how Addison, Lily, and Debra could be overwhelming."

"It's just that they're all settled in serious relationships." I felt a tiny urge to defend them. "Jason and I are fair game when it comes to meddling, I guess."

"Well, Debra and Luke aren't even engaged, right?"

"Yeah, but they'll probably end up getting married, eventually." The words sounded hollow, even to my ears.

"Do you really think so?"

"Yes."

Once we'd reached La Velita Blanca and parked, Everett reached for my hand. We walked through the restaurant. Honestly, I melted at the fact that he obviously liked holding hands with me. Jason had been just like that—affectionate and confident and comfortable with anyone and everyone knowing that he liked me. I had missed that sort of demonstrative attention.

I spotted the long table from across the room. Only Addison and Glen hadn't arrived yet. Everyone else smiled and waved when they saw us.

Except Luke.

His eyes stayed on the menu in front of him. As we got closer, it seemed that the corners of his mouth tightened. I wondered if perhaps he and Debra'd had an argument or something. Or maybe it was just my imagination. Everett and I sat down across from Luke and Debra, and right next to Jason and his date.

"Mia, this is Sara and Everett."

I smiled as I sat down next to Mia. I wasn't sure what I'd been expecting—maybe subconsciously I'd expected someone a little like me. But Mia looked more like Lily. Short blond hair, though the tips of Mia's hair *were pink*, unlike Lily's. She grinned at me, and her diamond nose ring glittered. I liked her smile right away.

"Sara, I've heard lots of nice things about you." She sipped a salt-rimmed margarita.

"Well, I'm very happy to meet you," I told her. "Any friend of Jason's is a friend of mine."

"Thanks for that."

Glen and Addison joined us then, so there were more introductions. Halfway through the meal, I was finishing my Tex-Mex cheese enchiladas as the whole table laughed at Mia's hilarious retelling of how she and Jason met at the watermelon stand at the Whole Foods near her house, right as she accidentally knocked a slew of melons to the floor. Next to me, Everett tugged me close to speak into my ear.

"My supervisor is calling me, Sara. I need to take this call. I'll be back, okay?"

I turned to him. Everett was leaning close to me, but he didn't pull away at all. He hadn't shaved the last couple of times I'd seen him, and now he had this ruggedly handsome shadow on his face. His eyes were dark and serious. I nodded.

"Sure, of course." I watched him get up and walk through the restaurant.

"So, he's really cute," Mia commented.

"We're not … I mean, this is only our third date. And he lives in North Carolina. So, we're really just friends at this point, but, yeah, he's great."

Mia winked at me. "North Carolina or not—he seems to really like you."

I looked back over my shoulder, but Everett wasn't in the room. Across the table, Luke was mid-conversation with Glen, but I saw his gaze follow mine.

A few minutes later, Everett slid back into his chair.

"Hey, is everything all right?" He nodded, but I still noticed the tense hold of his shoulders.

"Yes. No. Well, a friend of mine was laid off this week, apparently. I hadn't heard about it. So the airline's a bit shorthanded and calling in more pilots." He glanced at his phone.

"I'm sorry about your friend," I said. "Do you know what happened?" Everett shook his head.

"No. Maybe I'll call him later tonight."

I touched his arm. "They're calling in more pilots? Will you need to go back early?"

He nodded grimly. "Unfortunately, yes. I'd planned to leave later next week, maybe Friday, but I'm going to need to head back Monday or Tuesday."

"Don't even worry about dinner at my parents' house," I was quick to say. "If you're leaving Monday or Tuesday, you need to spend time with Addison."

"No, I really want to, Sara. It's just dinner. I can spend all day Sunday with Addi. And Monday. I'd like to meet your family."

I shook my head; now everything was way too rushed.

"Everett?" Addison's voice popped up. I realized she'd been watching us. "What's up?" she asked him. From where she sat on the other side of Glen, Everett couldn't really talk to her without everyone hearing him. The table quieted.

"Well, something's come up with work, and I may need to go back early," he answered, his voice calm and steady, though regretful. Addison's face fell.

"Oh, that's too bad!" Debra said; she gave me a sort of pitiful look. It registered with me then, he'd be leaving in just a couple of days.

Talk about a fleeting romance. Like an ominous gray storm cloud, a sweeping heaviness hovered over me and wouldn't leave. I had to fight off a crazy urge to cry. Finally, *finally* I meet a guy who I'm interested in and who actually reciprocates my feelings—and he has to take a plane ride to go home.

Disappointment.

Conversations slowly started back up around the table, and Everett nudged my shoulder.

"I'm sorry I have to go, Sara."

I shook my head. "I understand, of course. But I know Addison will be really sad to see you leave. She misses you."

He glanced across the table at Addison. "I miss her too. I never thought we'd live so far apart. I guess life takes us in different directions sometimes."

"You'll be back for the wedding," I reminded him.

"Four months. That reminds me, Sara, I know we're both in the wedding, but I was hoping you'd be my date."

I smiled. "It's a little early, don't you think?"

"I can't chance some other guy asking you while I'm gone," he said, looking up. I watched his gaze shift to Luke for a brief moment.

"That's not likely to happen," I told him. "It doesn't matter anyway. I'm happy to be your date. What will that be? Date number four for us?"

"You're forgetting tomorrow night."

"With my *parents*? That's not a date, Everett."

"Then four, I guess."

"Though you did fall asleep on our second date."

Everett shook his head and covered his face. "That's embarrassing. Really, please forgive me."

I laughed.

"Four months is a long time," Everett mused.

"It is." A sense of desolation swept through me.

"What if I wanted to fly you out to North Carolina? I don't know of any laser light shows … but there's this great Chinese restaurant by my apartment."

Flutters rushed through my stomach. "I love Chinese food."

Everett smiled. "Do you? That will be date number four then."

Chapter Nineteen

"How's Sam's dad?" I asked Lily. The two of us were trying on our bridesmaids' dresses post alterations.

"I think this is still too long!" she whispered to me. "What if I trip or something?"

I looked at her dress. "You'll be fine. Just hold on tight to whosever arm you're holding. Who are you walking down the aisle with?"

She shrugged, turning to the right and then the left in front of the mirror. "Glen's cousin or someone. What about you?"

"Um. Everett." I waited, knowing exactly how Lily would respond to the notion of my walking down the aisle with Everett.

Her eyebrows shot up. "Well, we know *you'll* be holding on tight to his arm."

"Back to my question. How's Sam's dad?"

Lily stepped off the platform. "I guess if my heels are high enough, I'll be okay. Oh, Sam's dad is doing somewhat better. Recovery has been slow—especially when it comes to mobility in the leg that broke—but Macy's been such a trooper. She has a maid service coming in once a week to help with the housework, and Sam's still taking care of the business."

We shuffled back to the dressing rooms to change.

"What's happening with your trip to North Carolina?" Lily asked from the room next door.

I pulled my jeans and shirt back on and then tried to smooth away the static from my hair.

"Everett suggested the second weekend in October." I grabbed my dress and met Lily right outside the door. She held her dress as well.

"In two weeks? How can you just now be telling me? Let's get coffee or smoothies or something," she said. We deposited our dresses in my car, then walked down to the Starbucks on the corner.

"It's been more than a month since he left. Do you still feel fireworks?" she asked before slurping down half her vanilla bean Frappuccino.

I tapped the straw to my caramel Frap. "Well, yes. We talk and text almost every day. We FaceTime. I'd like to see him again in person, though. I *really* like him."

"Enough to go to North Carolina? That sounds serious to me."

To me too, which stirred all sorts of nervous and excited feelings in me. My heart still jumped when I saw Everett's name pop up on my phone, and I enjoyed every text I received from him. Seeing him again stayed in the forefront of my mind, but the thought also sent me into panic mode. The long-distance factor didn't help with feeling sure about anything. Still, panic or not—I wanted to see him.

"He's great, Lily. I know if I go see him, we'll have a lot of fun."

"Your parents liked him too, right?"

"He won my mother over immediately. Both of them really."

"I need to tell you something," Lily said after finishing the rest of her drink.

"You literally drank that whole thing in less than three minutes, Lil."

She shrugged. "I was thirsty. Why can't we ever have a normal fall? I want it to be fall. It's ninety degrees."

"I saw a red leaf on the street."

"You should have pointed it out to me."

I grinned. "So what do you need to tell me?"

She shook her empty cup. "Debra called me last night and told me that she and Luke looked at rings."

"Excuse me?" I said, my voice spiked up a notch. My inner self kicked into gear and sternly told me to calm down.

"Don't worry. Nothing's happening right away. Deb has wanted to do this since their first date."

"They've been dating for six months," I reminded her. "It could be happening."

Lily wiped her hands on a napkin. "It could, I guess," she agreed. "Have you talked to Luke lately?"

I shook my head. She'd tapped on a source of tension that ran deep for me. "We never talk anymore. Other than random texts. Everything's changed. There's nothing between us at all."

"Oh, Sara," Lily said in a tight voice. She reached across the table and grabbed my hand. "Don't say that. There's still friendship. He'll always care about you as a friend. Look at you and Everett… You've moved on too."

But I hadn't. Not to the point where hearing that Luke and Debra were shopping for rings didn't make my hands sweat and my heart pound in my ears.

"He's going to marry her," I said, my teeth clenched. "I have to tell him."

Lily's eyes widened in alarm. "Sara—I think it's too late for that. You don't even know how you feel right now. You just told me how much you like Everett."

I forced my breathing to get back to something resembling normal. "You're right. I don't know why I said that." I looked out the window for a minute, my thoughts on overdrive and my conflicting emotions battling inside me. How had I gotten to this point? "I *do* like Everett. A lot. I guess I just wasn't prepared to hear that they . . . that they're getting closer to marriage. As much as I hope my relationship with Everett keeps evolving—well, I've loved Luke for a long time. I can't just shut that off. But maybe my feelings have changed. I try not to think about his relationship with Debra much. I try not to think about him."

Lily nodded. "I understand. I do, but maybe it's time for some soul-searching. You and Everett—if you're going to give him a real chance, there's no room for leftover feelings about Luke."

"What did Debra say? About shopping for rings, I mean?"

"Sara," Lily began.

"Just tell me."

"Okay, okay. All she said was that they'd been talking about the future lately. Debra said she told Luke straight up that at this point in her life she's looking for a real commitment. He told her that he's obviously taking their relationship very seriously. At that, she said she wanted to look at rings, and he agreed. So they went. But you and I both know she's known what kind of ring she wants for years. So I doubt it will be a difficult search."

My mouth felt like sawdust. "What's wrong with me, Lily?"

Her eyes narrowed. "Don't go there. There's not a thing wrong with you."

"Then why not me? He and I could talk about anything. We did everything together. Maybe it comes down to attraction. He just wasn't attracted to me like that."

Lily squeezed my hand. "Sara, maybe you guys were just better as friends. Think about you and Jason. We all thought you guys were a perfect fit. He was so nuts over you, but you couldn't change your feelings just because it made sense on paper. Maybe Debra's the one for Luke. I don't know. I *do* know you're a beautiful person, inside and out, and if anyone else knows that, Luke does."

Suddenly I didn't want my latte anymore, and I closed my eyes.

Pull yourself together. They're looking at rings. You need to prepare yourself for the real deal. The engagement. The inevitable—

"Oh no. She'll expect me to be a bridesmaid." I groaned, horrified at the thought of standing by Debra, holding a bouquet of flowers while watching her and Luke exchange vows.

"And you'll be strong enough to do that," Lily responded. "Go to North Carolina, Sara," she said gently. "Give Everett that chance."

Everett.

I wished he were here now; his presence would be the distraction I needed from Debra-and-Luke marriage talk.

After dropping off Lily at her house, I drove home slowly, so on edge that I didn't quite trust myself not to do something irrational—like call Luke. I couldn't nail down my feelings. Sad? Maybe. But the sensation felt a whole lot more like anger.

He should have told me. We'd been best friends. Best. Friends. He could have at least talked to me about his feelings for Debra. *He* didn't know that it would have killed me to hear it, and I would have listened and been supportive. Hadn't I already done as much?

After all that time spent as the closest of friends, he'd been able to just let me drift out of his life. I'd been replaced … easily.

Yep.

Anger.

I drove to his apartment.

Lord, help me.

"Sara?" Luke opened the door, green eyes round in surprise.

"We haven't talked in a while. I just thought we should catch up." If my voice hadn't been shaking and communicating vehemence—maybe he would have believed me.

He stepped aside. "Come in. Let's talk," he said quietly. He shut the door behind me. "Can I get you something to drink?"

I thought about saying I'd take a shot of anything he had but decided to try to control myself. Now here, in front of Luke, I had no idea what to say. I just shook my head and gripped my purse like my life depended on it and stood in the doorway, wound up like a stick of dynamite.

"Are you okay?"

"I'm great." My voice squeaked and sounded unnatural. He just nodded, as if that sound was normal.

"Want to sit down?" he asked, one eyebrow raised at me. I hoped it wasn't all that obvious I currently felt like a coil about to spring. I shook my head again.

"We could move out of the hallway if you want," he said, his voice careful. "Let's go into the kitchen." He led the way, then pulled out a barstool at the kitchen island. "Sit down, Sara," he said, apparently moving to commands since suggestions weren't working. I perched on the stool. He stood at the counter across from me.

"I heard you and Deb looked at rings."

He nodded. "Well, it wasn't really a secret, I guess. And news travels fast in our group."

My fingers tapped the granite island. "There was a time when I would have thought *you* would have at least told me. I would have thought close friends shared that sort of thing."

His jaw flexed but he didn't say anything.

"You were my go-to person for everything." I couldn't steady my rising voice. "You were my best friend. I could tell you anything—"

"Anything?" Luke interrupted sharply.

Did he know too? Had he pulled away because he knew my feelings went beyond friendship?

My face burned at the thought. As if I hadn't been humiliated enough already, the feeling began to choke me. My pulse raced and sent my feet to the floor.

"I shouldn't have come here."

"Sara," he said, sounding tense. "I know we were—I wasn't sure how to balance my friendship with you and my relationship with Debra. You knew this would happen before I did. Back at the lake house … you said things would change. They had to. For both of us." He drew in a fast breath. "But I never meant to hurt you. I would never—you must know that, right? I would never want to hurt you."

Prayers started pouring out of me at that point. Begging God to help me not cry. Begging God to hold my heart together, for Him to take away the embarrassment and hurt and loneliness that I shouldn't be feeling. Not with a life full of friends and family and even Everett.

I stepped back from the island. "I have to go."

"Sara, I didn't expect things to change so much."

I had to say something. So much weighed on me that I couldn't leave without letting off some of the pressure. "You stopped talking to me." Hot tears welled in my eyes, and I gulped in a breath. "You changed everything. You just left me behind like I didn't mean anything to you."

His eyes widened.

"No, Sara—I didn't—"

I walked to the door, trembling, wanting desperately for him to follow me.

But he didn't.

I cried all the way home. When I got back to my apartment, I washed my face, then cleaned the kitchen and living room. At dusk, I put on a light hoodie, sat out on the back porch, and watched the sun sink away.

From the rising of the sun until the going down of the same.

It occurred to me God must ache with love for us. Hurting for us. Wanting us. And sometimes we respond to Him in kind. Other times we reject Him.

Love is love, after all. In that moment, I felt God so close to me. Calming me. Reassuring me He loved me and that I wasn't alone. That there would be more for me. If He hadn't shown up, I don't know what I would have done. If He hadn't held me. If He hadn't promised to stay no matter what…

But He did.

Love is the undoing of all of us, my heart whispered. I thought of the painting, that girl staring out at the water, her ribbon falling. I sat outside till the last light of day faded. Before I fell asleep later that night, I made a decision about North Carolina.

I took my phone from the nightstand, shocked to see that I'd missed a text from Luke.

Two words.

I'M SORRY.

My heart ached as I stared at the words. But he'd made his decision, and now I had made one as well. I pulled up the string of texts between me and Everett. The light from the phone illuminated my face as I punched in one word.

YES.

Chapter Twenty

"What do you think?" Everett asked. I looked out the window at the season that never seemed to truly exist in Houston. Bushy, golden trees lined the highway, with auburn leaves drifting all over the road.

"It's gorgeous. It's..."

"Fall. It happens everywhere, you know."

I laughed. "Not like this. It was eighty-four degrees when I left Houston. I actually need to wear a light jacket here. That's something."

"You look great. I don't know if I told you, but you do, and I'm happy to see you." He held out his hand from the driver's side, and I grasped it.

"I'm happy to see you too. So we have two days. What are we doing besides eating Chinese food?"

"Well, we're going to The Old Stone Winery this afternoon, then back to Charlotte for Chinese food tonight. Tomorrow I thought we could go to my church and then out for lunch. I have a surprise for you tomorrow evening before you fly out Monday morning."

"Am I staying with your aunt and uncle?" I asked, knowing he'd mentioned it before. But Everett shook his head.

"No, they live outside of the city. They would absolutely love for you to stay with them, but my neighbor Kayla is great and said you should just stay with her. It's more convenient and more time for us together. Kayla's our age and a lot of fun. I'm good friends with her and her fiancé. You'll be right next door to me."

He squeezed my hand.

I relaxed in the passenger seat. My anxiety level had reached epic proportions that morning as Lily rushed me to the airport. I'd spent the flight worrying about everything from my flat hair to whether this trip was a good idea, but here I was. The moment I'd seen Everett waiting for me at the airport, the crescendo of my nerves had come to a crushing halt, leaving me only breathless and giddy as he'd pulled me into a crushing hug.

The winery was less than an hour outside of Charlotte. I tucked my yellow scarf around my neck and buttoned my light navy jacket as Everett and I walked up the gravel pathway to the building. Taking any opportunity to wear fall-ish fashions, I'd worn my knee-high light-brown leather boots.

We sampled an assortment of wines and cheeses, and toured the showroom and the barrel room. After the tour, we sat outside together at a round black iron table, enjoying two more glasses of a Pinot Noir that Everett and I both fell in love with. I drank in the view of the vineyard. Rows of grapevines covered the rolling-hill landscape for as far as I could see. The Blue Ridge Mountains sat far in the distance. Red- and yellow-leafed trees surrounded the stone buildings, and with every breeze that whipped through the air, leaves danced their way down to the ground. The cool air, the autumn surroundings, the fragrant and delicious wine—I basically had stepped into a romantic movie.

Across the little table, Everett reached for my hand. His hair curled up at his neck. Slim, dark-blue jeans hugged his lean frame, and a gray long-sleeved shirt complemented his brown eyes. The atmosphere of the winery couldn't help but convey romance. But it was the company—Everett's infectious laugh and shining eyes and his warm fingers playing with mine—that sent jitters through me.

After the winery, we drove back into the city, and Everett showed me his studio apartment and all his favorite spots. I could see the appeal. Charlotte was beautiful, and shops, restaurants, and crowds of people surrounded his downtown apartment. The city pulsated with movement and life. Evening seemed to come quickly. We walked to the small Chinese restaurant, amid the people going every which way and the lights bright against the darkness.

At a quiet booth, over fried rice, spring rolls, broccoli and beef, and sweet and sour shrimp, Everett and I talked about work, Addison and Glen's upcoming wedding, our family traditions, our hopes and dreams, everything. An hour passed easily and the dining room filled to capacity, with a line of people gathered at the front door, waiting for tables. The room warmed with the crowd, and mouth-watering smells of Chinese food filled the intimate space. We laughed over fortune cookies—Everett's assured him that he would soon be receiving a large sum of money; mine informed me that money was the root of all evil—and ended the meal by sipping delicious, spicy hot tea.

In fact, every moment Everett and I spent together reminded me of how much I enjoyed being with him. From hanging out at Kayla's apartment till the wee hours of Sunday morning, to Sunday services at the large church Everett attended, to the surprise he'd planned for me late that afternoon. We took a carriage ride through the Fourth Ward, and I oohed and ahhed over the architecture of the buildings and the old Victorian homes. I especially enjoyed seeing The Square, with bronzed sculptures representing commerce, transportation, industry, and the future. The clip-clopping sound of the horses' hooves on pavement, along with the wind and rustle of autumn tree leaves drifting over the city, filled my ears during our adventure.

After the tour, we bought pretzels from a street vendor and walked around uptown. With Everett's arm casually across my shoulders and occasional impromptu kisses we both initiated, over the course of the day I couldn't help thinking the attraction between us had grown even stronger, in spite of the Texas/North Carolina distance … or maybe because of the distance. I wasn't sure.

Things started to go somewhat south later that night. Worn out, I yawned and tucked my feet under me on Everett's sofa. A warm coffee cup filled my hand.

"So, how's your group back home?" he asked me. I told him about Lily and Sam, Sam's father's recovery, what Addison and I needed to finish regarding the wedding details, the fact that as far as I knew Jason was still dating Mia … and I mentioned Debra and Luke shopping for rings.

"Really? Ring shopping, eh? So they *are* getting serious."

"I told you they were. Or are. I told you I thought they'd get married."

"You did," he agreed, his eyes on the coffee mug in his hand.

"Why do you seem surprised?"

He shrugged. "You know them better than I do, Sara."

"I know, but what is it about them? You have an opinion. I can tell."

He sat his mug on the coffee table. "Fine. When I was in Houston, it seemed to me like Luke had feelings for you. It was just a feeling I got, Sara. The way he looked at you. The way he looked at *me* once he knew we were dating."

"He's looking at engagement rings with Deb. He's obviously in love with her." My words came out more defensive than they should have been.

"Fair enough. Though it's not as obvious as you think."

I curled up tighter on the sofa, chilled. "I never would have pictured Luke with Debra," I admitted, knowing Everett deserved my honesty. "But they're together and he loves her. It was a little … shocking to hear that they're shopping for rings. Luke and I used to be so close, it hurt that I didn't hear that from him. Still, I'm okay. I have to trust that God has a different plan for me. Really, at this point, I'm realizing that Luke couldn't have been the one for me."

"Why not?" Everett asked. He stood up and flipped the switch to turn on the gas fireplace in the corner of the room. Blue flames whooshed to life.

The large windows in his small apartment revealed scattered city lights in the night.

"Because I want what every girl wants—the right guy to fall madly in love with her and pursue her until she falls in his arms," I said, unable to keep from sounding exasperated. "I don't want some guy to take years to decide if he likes me or not. I want fireworks and attraction and love and shared values and…" My words trailed off into silence. I had just described this entire weekend spent with him.

Everett gave me a half smile. "So, I'm hoping you feel some of that with me?" He looked a bit shy. I smiled back.

"Absolutely."

We were both quiet for a moment; I could hear the wind blowing outside. Warmth from the fire slowly heated the room and added ambiance.

"You said you couldn't tell Luke how you felt—before. Why?"

"I just couldn't. I knew he was dating Debra. It was pointless to tell him I'd had a crush on him for years when he'd already chosen someone else. That would have been humiliating for me and awkward for him."

"Years?" Everett echoed in surprise. I set aside my coffee mug too.

"It doesn't matter now. I've let that go."

"Have you?"

"You know I have. I'm *here*, Everett."

"You are and I'm glad. But if Luke wasn't with Debra—or if he broke up with her tomorrow and told you he loved you—what would you do?" Everett studied me.

I shifted on the sofa. "That's a crazy question and never going to happen. How could I know what I'd do?" I tried to keep from sounding prickly, but his question annoyed me.

He looked thoughtful—and a little concerned. "I need you to think about it."

"Think about hypothetical situations that will never happen? Everett, what's the point of that?" My voice rose, and I unfurled my feet and stood up, walking to the kitchen to get a glass of water and take a breath, hoping that would calm my jumpy nerves.

"Where is this coming from?" I asked as I walked back to the sofa. "You don't have to be worried about Luke. He's with Debra. You're wrong about him. He doesn't have feelings for me—we used to be friends, now we're barely that." I hoped he didn't notice the wobble in my voice.

"I'm not worried about him. Well, not entirely," Everett said, and my stomach tightened.

"I want to know you *wouldn't* choose him, given the choice. I want to know that what's starting here between us—that *this* is what you want."

"Oh." It was all I could muster.

"I have an idea." Everett moved closer, lightening his tone to, no doubt, lighten the cloud that had come over us. He placed one hand on my knee. "Let's keep talking—doing what we've been doing. And when I come to Houston for the wedding, maybe you can answer me then. You'll have had time to really examine your feelings, and you'll know what you want."

"Okay," I said in a small voice. "And you'll know what you want too."

Everett squeezed my knee and just stared at me. My defensiveness dissipated, leaving me vulnerable from the emotional upheaval. Those brown eyes of Everett's took me to the edge of feeling unhinged.

"I'm pretty sure I already know what I want," he finally said. Then he kissed me. After the initial surprise of his lips on mine again, I returned the kiss with good measure, hoping to disperse any doubts from his mind.

And mine.

Chapter Twenty-One

Jason picked me up from the airport Monday afternoon.

I stood on the curb. "Where's Lily?"

A grin spread on his face. "I volunteered. I get to be the first one to interrogate you. Believe me, the girls were fighting over the honor." Jason tossed my suitcase in the backseat, and I slid into the passenger seat.

"So?" he said as we left the airport.

"So," I answered.

"Are you in love?" I closed my eyes, and my left hand shot out and punched his shoulder.

"Ow!" He laughed.

"What's up with you and Mia?" I opened my eyes again. Jason shrugged.

"You know, we're dating. It's casual right now. She's cool." He switched lanes. "Did you have a good time at least? In North Carolina?"

"Yeah, I did. I had a great time."

"That's good, right?"

"It's good," I confirmed.

"What's your week look like?" Jason asked me, seemingly moving on from the topic of my trip. Lily, Addison, and Debra would never have given up so easily.

"Helping Lily plan Addison's lingerie shower."

He squirmed. "Please don't tell me those things, Sara."

I laughed. "Sorry. Forget I said that."

"I'll try," he said uncomfortably. "How long till the wedding?"

I mentally counted. "Like two months? Gosh! That feels so soon." Anxiety washed over me.

"Two months is a long time."

"Not in the world of weddings. Have you nailed down the menu?"

"Pretty much," he said, unconcerned.

"Are you bringing Mia to the wedding?"

"It's two months away. How can I know yet?"

"Everett asked me."

"Well, you and Everett might be a little more serious than me and Mia. You flew to North Carolina to see him recently, remember? I don't know that I want a date at the wedding. I'll be preoccupied with taking care of the food."

"You have to dance with someone."

"Maybe Everett will share you with me for one dance," he said, and I smiled.

"Dream on."

He laughed loudly. As Jason pulled into my apartment complex parking lot, I examined my nails, not quite ready to be alone.

"Has Luke ... um ... said anything to you? About a conversation I had with him before I left?"

Jason parked the car. "What have you done?"

"Nothing. I heard he and Debra went shopping for rings. I was a little annoyed he didn't tell me."

Jason's forehead wrinkled in confusion. "Why would he?"

"Never mind."

"Sara." Jason leaned back in his seat and squeezed the bridge of his nose. "No, Luke hadn't said anything to me."

"I was just wondering."

"Are you okay? What can I do?"

"I need closure. I don't know how to get it," I said in a small voice.

"Time. Space. Moving on. Dating other people. Prayer."

Markedly absent from his list was anything about having a conversation with Luke.

"What about Everett? Could this be real between you guys? Do you see possibility?"

My heart tugged with affection and attraction at the thought of Everett. "Yes," I said honestly. "I didn't see it coming, though."

Jason smiled at me. "That's the best way sometimes."

Once in my apartment, I put on a load of laundry and made a cup of hot tea. Lily called on cue, and I gave her a much more thorough rundown of my trip. Finally, the conversation meandered to Addison's lingerie shower at Lily's house that Friday night.

"I'll need you here early. You should take off work by four o'clock," she told me.

"I'll be there as soon as I can," I promised. "We've planned out the menu. It will be fun and low-key. Don't worry, Lily."

"I'm not. But there are lots of other girls coming from our church, Addison's new church, and her school! I'm not great at hosting things."

"I'll be co-hosting with you. Deb's helping too."

"You should come Thursday night, and we'll decorate ahead of time."

"Okay," I agreed. "But then you need to cook dinner for us."

"Done. I'll order pizza or something."

After a second, Lily took a breath. "Luke talked to Sam."

I bit the inside of my mouth and winced. "Really? What did he say?"

"I don't know. Sam wouldn't tell me. He only said that Luke was upset."

I groaned. "What should I do?"

"Nothing. Just pray."

"You sound like Jason," I mumbled. She chuckled softly.

"I'll pray too. It will be okay. Let's get through Addi's wedding, honey. Then we'll deal with Debra's—if there is one."

"All right," I agreed, thankful for Lily's calm voice in the face of impending doom.

It rained Tuesday off and on, from the moment I walked through the museum doors until I left. My mother texted me at ten that morning, telling me she wanted me to come for dinner. Another Everett interrogation, I assumed. But since I felt lonely, I was happy to go home and let her feed me.

I smelled beef stew the minute I walked through the door. My mother is a firm believer that some meals are meant only for certain seasons. She'd only serve chili and beef stew from late September to February. My father and I, both fans of her stew, would beg for it other times of the year, but she didn't like to give in. I stood in the foyer and breathed in the scent deeply.

"Sara?"

"I'm here." I walked into the kitchen and dropped my purse on the island.

"Is it still raining?"

"Drizzling. Did you make cornbread?" (Texas, y'all.)

"Of course," she answered, as though there couldn't be a different answer.

"The stew needs fifteen more minutes. Tell me about your trip," she insisted. So, I told her all about my trip to Charlotte (minus any kissing parts). My mom's eyes brightened as I described the highlights of wine tasting at the gorgeous vineyard, dinner in the city, and the romantic carriage ride through uptown Charlotte. The eagerness in her voice as she asked questions clearly indicated my mother's excitement for any romance for her unmarried daughter. She and I both howled with laughter when I told her about the fortune cookies.

We paused for a moment at the sound of a thunderclap overhead.

"Where's Dad?"

"On the phone upstairs. A colleague called him for a consult. He'll be down in a second. Let's set the table and I'll dish out bowls."

Five minutes later my father came downstairs, and the three of us sat down to dinner together. I had to rehash most of what I'd already told my mom regarding my trip to my dad (though this version was even less romantic than the one I gave my mother). By the time we finished eating, the drizzle outside had turned into a full-on thunderstorm.

"Just stay the night," my mom insisted. "You have extra clothes here. I don't want you driving in this rain."

I was inclined to agree. While she finished cleaning the kitchen, I wandered back into my parents' study and found that album again—the one filled with pictures from the year I was born. I studied my parents' faces, again looking for signs of marital strain. But they seemed happy. Faces beaming. Granted, the infant version of myself was between them or in someone's arms in nearly every photo. And I assumed parents of newborns were usually beaming and happy, though sleep-deprived.

My mom walked into the room, stood next to me, looking over my shoulder at the album with a smile.

"Oh, I like that one." She pointed to the photo below of my dad holding me in their old living room.

"Mom, how did you trust him again?" I asked, my voice quiet. She reached down and turned the page.

"It took time," she finally answered. "But I believed the effort was worth more than the alternative. He worked hard to earn my trust again. That helped. Marriage can be difficult, Sara. But that doesn't mean you have to let go."

"I thought I would be married by now." The statement popped out of my mouth unexpectedly. My mother just nodded.

"That's all right. Life rarely goes according to our plans. It will happen for you. This is a waiting season in your life. It's not easy to choose contentment when we want things to be different from what they are. Believe me, I've been there."

I kept my eyes on the album. Why in the world did my mother have to know me so well? I wanted to protest that I was plenty content, but it would have been pointless. I also held back from telling her that Luke and Debra were now looking at engagement rings. I knew she'd be disappointed, just as I had been. No reason for both of us to be sad. I ran my hand over the plastic page of pictures of my parents and me. An intact family, forged through the fire.

"Sara," my mother said, her voice soft but firm. "Concentrate on what God wants you to learn through it." She left me alone in the study.

I closed the album.

All right then. God, what do you want me to learn right now?

No answers came down with the thunder, but I had a feeling I was at least asking the right question.

Friday morning I swung by Starbucks to grab a latte and, standing in line to order, I got a text from Luke.

> Still sorry about our last conversation. Can we talk sometime?

I just stared at the message, trying to decide how to answer and how I felt … relieved, in a way. I'd worried I might never hear from him again after our argument at his apartment, and that could get awkward since we'd inevitably be around each other for Addi's wedding festivities.

I stepped up to the counter and ordered a chai latte, then moved to the corner to wait.

> Sure. Maybe after the holidays.

Wickedly, I smiled at the text. Knowing Luke's propensity, like mine, to avoid unresolved issues like a swarm of mosquitoes, I had a feeling he wouldn't like my response.

> Where are you now?

An unbidden smile crossed my face at his response. I pictured him, forehead wrinkled and eyes narrowed at his phone.

> Picking up a latte, about to go to work.

The barista called my name, and I grabbed my drink before heading out the door. My phone rang as I stepped onto the sidewalk.

Luke.

The humor I'd felt a moment ago disappeared, replaced by anxiety. Banter through text was one thing, but verbal confrontation was another. I licked my lips as I raised the phone to my ear.

"Luke?"

"Sara, I can't wait until after the holidays."

I closed my eyes at the sound of his voice pleading with me. After a moment, I sank down on a bench a few paces away from Starbucks.

"Everything you said keeps going through my mind. I didn't mean—I never meant for you to feel like I just left you behind."

"I have to be at work in a few minutes, Luke. I don't think I can talk about this." The stupid impulse to cry rose in me.

"Sara, my relationship with Debra—it happened so fast. But I haven't stopped caring about you. You—we—our friendship—" His words broke off.

"Just say what you need to, Luke." The bitterness in my tone eased a little. "You could always talk to me about anything before."

"That's what I mean. You know how close we've been. It did feel … like staying that way would be a betrayal to Deb once we were in a relationship."

I sucked in a shaky breath, willing my emotions not to get the better of me, wanting to be able to accept his honesty even if it hurt. And hadn't I thought the same thing?

Thick silence lasted for a moment.

"I heard you went to see Everett," Luke said, his tone apprehensive.

My fingers hurt from the tight grip on my phone. "Yes." I waited, practically daring him to ask about my relationship when he'd never offered anything about his.

"Did you have a good time?"

"Yes." The latte cup now felt lukewarm in my free hand.

"I'm glad for you. I want you to be happy, Sara."

Not crying just got a lot harder.

My shoulders slumped as I breathed out. "I want you—and Debra—to be happy too." Because no matter what, the friendship among all of us ran through the deepest parts of me, and I loved them both. I couldn't stop.

"I know you do," he said, his voice gentle. "And I'm still here, Sara. If you need me for any reason, you can call me and I'll come. Wherever you are, I would come to you. We may not talk as much as we used to—or hang out together—but that doesn't mean I wouldn't drop everything if you needed me."

Oh, Lord. I wiped away a runaway tear. That was the Luke I loved.

"I'd do the same for you."

I needed to get to work and so did he, so we said goodbye, at least leaving a slight sense of peace between us. But his words dominated my thoughts all day, even as I drove to Lily's house that night for Addison's shower. However, as I walked up the driveway, thoughts of Luke had to be set aside. One of my best girlfriends was about to get all kinds of sexy lingerie, and it was absolutely time to party.

Debra threw open the door for me and squealed. "This is so exciting!"

I smiled back. She grabbed my arm and pulled me in. Lily came around the corner, wiping sweat from her forehead and tying her hair in a ponytail while asking me why I couldn't get there earlier. The three of us set out platters of appetizers and desserts. Pink and black streamers and balloons filled the living room and dining area. A huge cake sat in the center of the dining table, flanked by bottles of champagne and a huge bowl of pink punch. The house filled up fast with Addison's many friends from church and work.

Low-key never seems to really be a good way to describe parties. I hadn't been able to sit down once since arriving at Lily's around 4:30. Laughter and conversation reached every corner of the house. I organized the gift table, kept the food platters filled, and started making coffee and slicing cake once everyone finally settled into the living room in order to watch Addison open gifts.

Parties also always seem to last much longer than the "end time" written on the invitation. At 9:45, I collapsed on Lily's couch as Addison said goodbye to the last guest. The four of us girls were alone. Debra stretched out on the floor.

"Is there cake left?" Addison asked from her spot on Sam's easy chair. I opened one eye.

"Yes."

With a groan, Addison pulled herself to her feet and made her way to the dining room table, which housed the leftovers for the moment. Apparently, cake was more important than rest.

"I think that was a great success," Lily said, already tidying up. "Everyone seemed to have a fabulous time."

"And you got so many beautiful things!" Debra said, propping herself up on one elbow. "You must be so excited to get married, Addison."

Addison emerged with a piece of chocolate cake and sat cross-legged on the floor, leaning against the sofa.

"I can't wait. Six weeks! That's all. Six weeks and I'll be a married woman."

"Those six weeks will fly by," Lily told her. "I remember when Sam and I got married. I kept thinking the day would never come. Then I blinked and it was there in front of me. Think of it, Addi, this Christmas will be the first one you and Glen spend as a married couple!"

"How romantic!" Debra sighed. "I wish it were me. Maybe I'll at least be engaged by Christmas."

My spine straightened. *By Christmas?* All three of us girls looked at Debra, our eyes bulging. Without warning, Luke's voice replayed in my head. *I would still drop everything if you needed me.* I reached for my champagne glass on the coffee table.

"You think so?" Addison said.

"I *hope*," Debra clarified. "I've found the ring I want. Why shouldn't we go ahead and get engaged? I already know I want to marry Luke. He's the one always taking everything so slowly."

"What do you mean?" Lily asked in a light tone.

"Well, I think he's ready, but he's so hard to read. You know me—I put everything out there. I tell him how I'm feeling five times a day. Luke's so quiet and circumspect."

"Do you like that about him?" I asked cautiously.

She just shrugged. "It's part of who he is. I hope he'll open up more the longer we're together, but I know better than to try to change him."

"What *do* you love so much about Luke, Deb?" Addison asked with interest.

Debra's eyes took on a dreamy look. "I like the way he makes me feel. He's strong and safe and smart. Obviously, I'm attracted to him. I've always thought he was handsome. I like his blond hair and green eyes. I can always count on him. If I need him, he's there. He's dependable, you know? He's…"

"Steady," I finished for her. Debra nodded.

"Yes. He's steady. And I like that about him. I don't mean to say he's perfect, of course. I mean, I wish he'd be more open and transparent. And I'm spontaneous, but he's not really. I think he tries to be sometimes. He's everything I need."

I blinked my suddenly dry eyes several times.

She sees the real Luke and she loves him. She doesn't want to change him. Not really.

"Do you think he'll propose by Christmas?" Lily asked.

Debra laid her head back on the floor. "Maybe. But Luke is sort of unpredictable when it comes to that. He could decide tomorrow and ask me. Once he's sure of his decision, I don't think he'll take long to ask. He knows without a doubt I'll say yes. But he's also romantic when he wants to be, and Christmas is a very romantic time, so he may do it then. Oh, I hope!"

Something clicked inside me at that moment. It felt like a door closing. It felt like letting go.

And it hurt.

Chapter Twenty-Two

"All right then, team. I know we've just barely hit November, but we need to nail down our plans for the holiday season. As you know, we'll be setting up a slew of Christmas trees, and different corporations will sponsor and decorate each one. Also, we're having a special Holiday-Around-the-World exhibit!" Jeanie told the team leaders as we met for a staff meeting. She tucked her dark-blond bobbed hair behind her ears.

"I think it will be great," she continued. "We've got some incredible paintings coming in on loan. Most are coming from a private collector—one, specifically, of the Nativity, is supposed to be strikingly beautiful—as well as some historical artifacts and pieces that originated in Germany." Jeanie tapped her finger on her iPad. "The holidays are busy for us. People come in while the kids are on winter break, so be prepared for big crowds.

"We need to know right away if you're going to need time off, so make sure you turn in your requests early. I'm looking forward to a fun holiday season here at the museum. All right, people, let's get to work."

Jeanie dismissed the staff from our monthly meeting, and I headed straight for my cubicle. I pulled up my calendar on my phone once I reached my desk. November first. Five weeks until Addison's wedding. My bridesmaid's dress was ready. Nearly all the wedding details had been sorted out. Other than a wedding shower to be held at Addison's new church in two weeks and a small, intimate bridal tea that Addison's mother was hosting the week before the wedding, everything seemed to be in place for Addison and Glen's big day.

Everett would arrive the week before to be part of the last-minute wedding frenzy, which relieved me. Since I'd taken on the role of pseudo-wedding-planner, I'd probably have to spend every spare minute with Addison's family that week. Everett would be a welcome source of support.

Everett.

A twinge of worry struck me. His schedule had been busy since my trip, and we'd talked less frequently. With both of us preoccupied with work, communication had to be pushed to the backburner, so to speak.

And I missed him.

After Addison's lingerie shower, I'd waited daily to hear news of Luke and Debra's engagement, but so far, nothing. Now a week later, the thought wasn't in the forefront of my mind.

With November came the busyness of family gatherings and such, and I doubted I'd be in touch with our group too much. We all tended to go our separate ways for holidays. But this being the craziest season of Addison's life, she seemed to need us around her more than ever. So the Saturday before Thanksgiving, I found myself at Shipley's Donuts at ten in the morning, having coffee with Addison and the girls.

I devoured a sausage-and-cheese kolache while Addison had a slight meltdown. (Texas, y'all.) The spicy sausage wrapped in a melt-in-my-mouth roll was so delicious that I ordered another one, along with a dozen glazed donut holes that the girls and I shared.

"So it's beginning!" Addison said with panic in her voice. "I told my parents I was spending Thanksgiving Day with Glen, and they freaked out. My mother said that it's my last Thanksgiving as their unmarried daughter, and they absolutely expect me to honor them by spending the whole day with them. What do I do?"

"Well, you could always spend half the day with Glen's family and half with your parents. That seems fair," Lily proposed.

"But both families have a big Thanksgiving dinner on Thanksgiving Day. Not lunch. Not the night before. Dinner on Thursday. So I have to miss one or the other. But I don't want to spend it away from Glen. That's unthinkable!"

"Would he spend it with your family?"

"His mother would be heartbroken. Like mine. How do we please everyone?"

"You can't." Lily's voice stayed calm but filled with empathy. "It comes with every marriage, Addison. What do *you* want to do?"

"I want to be with Glen and my parents, of course. My mom is right—though she's not being very fair—that it's my last Thanksgiving as their unmarried daughter. And as thrilled as I am to be marrying Glen, I understand how my parents feel. I feel all kinds of mixed emotions too. Even though I've been on my own for a long time, it feels as though I'm severing this final tie. My last name is changing. My loyalties are to Glen now. We'll be starting our own traditions, eventually. My parents are my parents, and I love them so much, but things are changing."

We were all quiet for a moment, munching on kolaches and donuts and sipping our lattes, contemplating the issues that come with girls growing up and getting married.

"I know it's not ideal, but do you think your mom would change the time? Or Glen's mom? While family together is a must, it doesn't seem that dinner should have to be set in stone at six. You could do an early dinner, like at four thirty, with your parents—Glen too—and then go to Glen's later in the evening. If not for the full meal, at least to join in on dessert," Debra suggested.

"You could even stay the night before at your parents' house so you could spend most of the day with them." I tacked on my two cents. "Then it's only reasonable that you should spend some time with Glen's family in the evening."

"That may work," Addison mused. "My mom used to love for us to watch the parade on TV together in the morning. We haven't done that in a few years, and it would be special to do it for this year's holiday. Since Everett's not coming home for Thanksgiving—he's flying that day—it'll be me and my mom doing most of the cooking. My grandparents are coming over later, along with my aunt and uncle and two cousins. I don't see why we couldn't have an early dinner."

"At least ask and make the case for it, Addison," Lily told her. "And it may be a good time for discussion with your mom about expectations and the changes that will come with your marriage."

"Those are not topics she likes to think about," Addison said with a shudder. "But I'll try."

"Well, Luke's going to Colorado for Thanksgiving," Debra said with obvious disappointment.

"Are you going with him?" I asked.

"He didn't invite me! Can you believe that?" Debra's tone rose in frustration. "He said his mom needs him right now—you know, first major holiday since her divorce and all that, and his sister and her husband will be there, so he told me it's a family thing. His mom likes me. I know she wouldn't mind if I came! I'm so frustrated by the whole ordeal. We've looked at rings, we've talked about getting married, we love each other… At this point in our relationship we should be spending holidays together. Why doesn't he understand that? I want to be with him and his family." She pushed her curly hair out of her face with a huff.

I gritted my teeth and determined to stay out of the discussion. Lily and Addison jumped in to calm Debra, carefully defend Luke (without seeming to take sides), and assure her that every family is different and having just been through a divorce, Luke's family's needs had to be respected.

For my own family, the Thanksgiving agenda hadn't changed since I was five, so I doubted that it would this year. My mother and I would do all the cooking and decorating, followed by dinner at my parents' house with my grandparents and at least part of our extended family. Thanksgiving being one of my very favorite holidays, I looked forward to all the cooking and family time.

By the time the four of us left Shipley's, Debra seemed slightly less offended by Luke's choice not to invite her to spend Thanksgiving with his family, though still not happy. Addison sounded determined to find a compromise for the Thanksgiving dilemma, and Lily had to leave to pick up lunch for Sam and his crew on a job.

I had the whole day free and really did not know quite what to do with myself. Seeing as how Everett would be flying into town in a week, I decided to go shopping. A new outfit for the rehearsal dinner sounded like a good idea, especially since I knew I would be attending with a very attractive date.

I spent the afternoon walking through Market Street near the Woodlands Mall. Despite the still rather warm temperatures, fall was in full effect in Texas. Autumn décor filled the window displays; some were already decked out for the Christmas season. I walked slowly, enjoying the (very) slight breeze and the festive decorations.

"Sara Witherspoon?"

I turned around. "Miss Alana!" I was face-to-face with one of my mother's best friends. The tall, thin African American woman with poise that matched my mother's smiled warmly at me.

"Doing a little shopping, are we?" she asked. I shrugged.

"My friend's getting married. I thought I may find something new for the wedding."

"That's right. Suzanne mentioned that one of your friends was getting married. How exciting!"

"Yes, I'm so happy for her." I smiled wistfully. "I sort of wish it were me."

I froze.

Where did that come from?

I wanted to suck the words back in. Alana nodded, studying me.

"I haven't had any lunch. Let's you and me stop at Portobello's and have some sandwiches. My treat."

Oh dear. Pep talk ahead. Still, I didn't feel I could say no at that point. Alana had been my mother's best friend for several years, and I'd just made myself sound like the lonely, unmarried, twenty-seven-year-old that I happened to be. As much as I liked Everett, I wanted us to be part of each other's daily lives, to be there for each other in tangible ways.

Fifteen minutes later I was sitting at an outdoor café, taking a big bite out of a club sandwich.

"So your mother tells me you're dating someone. A pilot?" Alana said. I wanted to roll my eyes. *Thank you, Mother.*

"Yes. He's actually the twin brother of my friend who's getting married. We've only been dating a few months. He lives out of state, so I'm using the word 'dating' pretty loosely. Mostly that means talking on the phone."

"Are you serious about him?"

"Yes. I mean, I really like him. I wish we lived closer." I popped open a bag of baked chips.

"What are you looking for in a husband, Sara?"

I blinked. Well, let's get straight to it then.

"The usual," I said lightly, and Alana laughed. I smiled too.

"I guess I'm looking for what most women are looking for—that guy who's my match. Someone who knows me better than anyone else. Someone who sees my flaws and still thinks I'm worth it. Someone who will love me faithfully for as long as I live."

Alana nodded. "You're right. That's what most women are looking for. What about personality? Character? What are you drawn to?"

I sipped my Diet Dr Pepper and thought about the question. "I need someone strong."

Alana folded her hands on the table. "Go on," she said.

"I need someone who knows when I just need to be quiet. But I want someone who pushes me to talk when I really need to. I want to be with someone who shares my values and beliefs. A man who will tell me he's praying for me, and I can trust he means it. I want a guy who would rather spend time with me than do anything else. I want someone who thinks about me at random times all throughout the day. Someone who wants to have children with me. Someone who sees me as beautiful even when I'm not. I want my heart to pound when he touches me. I want someone with integrity. I need a man who's dependable, who takes me seriously, who will love me in a way that makes me completely fulfilled."

Alana put her hand over my wrist and squeezed gently. I stopped talking and realized my eyes were wet.

"I'm glad you know," Alana said.

"What kind of husband I want?"

She smiled. "No. What kind of woman you are. A woman who knows what she needs, knows who she is."

Words escaped me.

"Sara, I'm sure your mother never told you this, but the truth is that I was married once before. Paul is my second husband. Everything that could go wrong in a marriage did go wrong that first time. I didn't know myself back then. There was a messy divorce, a season of mourning what was lost. A time of picking up the pieces and finding out what I was made of. By the time God brought Paul into my life, I knew myself in a different way."

My eyes stayed on her, intent on giving Alana my undivided attention. I felt honored she would share such personal information with me.

"The end of my marriage devastated me—I couldn't believe that God would let that happen to me. Looking back now, though, I can see how God carried me through. How he used all of it to turn me into the woman I was meant to be. He'll use whatever you give him, Sara. Your fears. Your weaknesses. Your hopes. Your dreams. Your disappointments."

I thought of my mother.

"Some days I feel that at this point in my life, I know myself; I know what I want. Then other times, I'm completely unsure," I told Alana. She just smiled.

"That's true for all of us, Sara."

I looked out at the people walking down the sidewalk. "I *do* know that I want to be in love. I want to be married. I want that in my future."

"It will be," Alana assured me. "Be patient. There are a lot of good men out there—horrible ones too, by the way. You need the *right* one. You'll know, sweet girl, and you'll be ready when the time comes. I can see that clear as day."

We chatted for a few more minutes and finished our lunch, then Alana brushed my cheek with a kiss and told me she was off to buy a birthday gift for her niece. I stopped at a few more stores and ended up finding a cute, simple, black dress to wear to the rehearsal dinner. The wedding felt just moments away, and for some reason, the thought of it made my stomach clench.

More change.

The wedding was yet another reminder our group would never be quite the same again.

Chapter Twenty-Three

Two weeks before Addison and Glen's big day, I was running on fumes. As much as I adored Addison, if I never helped plan another wedding, that would be fine with me. We even recruited my mother to help with arranging the bridal tea and finding a new deejay when the one Addi had booked for the reception canceled. December seemed too jam-packed to squeeze in even one more activity, but when Lily and Sam asked us all to have lunch together after church, I knew they'd been just as stressed out as the rest of us, if not more, and needed to connect with the group. So, exhaustion notwithstanding, I drove to the gas station where Sam asked us all to meet. Luke stood on the sidewalk in front of the glass doors.

I stared for a moment at the sight of him standing there. Dark-blue jeans and a white collared shirt, aviator sunglasses hiding his eyes. I supposed he couldn't help being gorgeous. He smiled when he saw me, and I took that as a good sign, considering our last two conversations. I got out and joined him.

"Sam and Lily aren't here yet? Where's the restaurant? Nearby, I hope. I'm starved."

Luke bit back a grin. "We're already here."

I shaded my eyes and looked at the adjoining sign to the gas station. "The Rusty Armadillo?"

"Yeah. Jason, Sam, and I had lunch here the other day. The barbecue is amazing."

I looked at the busy gas pumps. "Um. We're eating at a gas station? You're saying that the three of you, on purpose, meet at gas stations for lunch?" Jason's truck pulled up at that moment and he hopped out.

"Dude, Sam's not here yet? Why the heck are you two standing outside?"

"I'm still confused by the fact that the plan is to *eat at a gas station?*" I looked from one guy to the other and rolled my eyes at their wide grins.

Jason led the way toward the door. "Texas, baby. We know how to do barbecue. I swear, it's the best chopped beef you've ever tasted. And the house barbecue sauce—"

"Trust us. It's good," Luke piped up.

We walked inside and pushed *all three* tables together. Sam and Lily walked in, Lily wearing a perplexed look on her face and groaning out loud that, "This is ridiculous and it *better* be good, y'all." She then proceeded to tell me that there was a faculty luncheon at Glen's church, so he and Addison weren't going to make it for lunch. For a split second, I worried again that Debra would arrive and it would be a triple date, with me and Jason inevitably paired off, but to my surprise, Debra had to cover someone's shift at work.

So the five of us sat down to eat together in a gas station (Texas, y'all.), and yes, it was the best chopped beef I'd ever tasted. I begrudgingly told Jason that he had been right. Luke sat next to me and for just a little while, over potato salad and chopped beef sandwiches drenched in barbecue sauce, things seemed normal again. Jason and Luke and Sam joking and teasing with each other, Lily and I chatting, a table and good food between us.

Luke was eating his second sandwich when I nudged his shoulder. "How's your mom doing?"

He wiped his mouth. "Better. I hope to see her sometime during the holiday season. It's taking time, but I think she's finding herself."

I grabbed my Styrofoam cup and his, then went to the counter for refills of sweet tea. When I came back, Lily, Sam, and Jason were arguing about whether or not we should all risk hypothermia and go tubing in the spring. I took my seat next to Luke, and he accepted the drink.

"Thanks, Sara."

"Do you miss Colorado?" He gave me a side glance.

"Sure. Sometimes."

"Would you ever want to move back?"

"Trying to get rid of me?" he teased, and I poked him.

"For real. Tell me. Do you want to stay here?"

"Yeah, I think so. I mean, it's hard to get used to the mosquitoes, but what can you do? And the humidity is killer. Still, there's a lot to love, as I'm sure you know. I've never met a Texan who wasn't fiercely loyal to their state."

"What do you love about Texas?" I chewed on the end of my straw and waited for his answer.

His eyes met mine. "You."

I blinked in surprise at his answer, and my heart nearly stopped. He coughed. "And Deb and Sam and our group. I like the friends I have here. I like my job. The fact you can find stellar barbecue in a gas station is pretty cool too."

He smiled that smile of his, and I sighed a happy sigh. I grinned back at him. "Yeah, just a hop, skip, and a jump away from scratch cards, Cheetos, and Skoal."

"See? Only in Texas can you find a girl who says 'a hop, skip, and a jump.'" He winked at me and I laughed. And it felt so good. So normal.

"Hey." Debra stood at the end of the table, her narrowed gaze zeroed in on me and Luke.

"Deb! Hi!" I jumped up and moved to the empty seat next to Jason.

"We thought you had to work!" Lily said as Deb slid into the chair by Luke.

"No," she replied slowly. "Someone else had already agreed to cover the open shift, so they let me go."

"Are you hungry? Despite our unfortunate surroundings, the food is delicious," Lily assured her. Debra looked at Luke.

"I texted you."

He pulled out his phone and scrolled downward. "I'm sorry. I didn't hear it. Do you want anything to eat? I'll get it for you."

"I'm not hungry," she answered, glancing at me. The table quieted. She didn't say anything else after that curt, short answer, and Luke quickly finished his sandwich. Debra's usual bubbliness seemed to have been replaced by moody annoyance. The silence alone on her part told me something was off. And where a few moments before Luke had been laughing and talking, now he didn't take his eyes off the sandwich in his hands. Jason and Lily and Sam picked back up their conversation like nothing was wrong. That left me awkwardly silent with Luke and Deb for a few minutes. I pulled out my phone and checked Facebook.

"How's Everett doing, Sara?" Debra finally said. I dropped my phone back in my purse.

"He's really looking forward to the wedding. I think he flies in the middle of next week."

"You must be excited to see him."

My head bobbed up and down. "Definitely."

She turned her gaze back to Luke, but he stood up to throw away his empty cup and plate. I leaned in toward Jason.

"I've got to get going," I said in his ear. He nodded.

"Yeah, me too." We both stood up and that started the round of goodbyes. Luke asked Debra a question in a low voice, and she answered in a hurried whisper. The rest of us discreetly left them behind for some privacy. Luke barely looked my way when I said goodbye to him. My last glance before getting in my car was of the two of them, still sitting at the table inside. Who knew what they were talking about … but I had a feeling there was trouble between our lovebirds.

"All right then, Sara and Everett, the two of you are next," the church coordinator for the wedding ceremony instructed. This would be our third walk down the aisle together. The rehearsal seemed to never end.

I held tightly to Everett's arm as we walked down the long aisle. If we had to keep walking together, at least I was going to enjoy being so close to him.

"Third time's the charm, right?" he said through clenched teeth. I smiled pleasantly.

"We can only hope," I whispered back. We slowed our step as we reached the altar and went our separate ways, with Everett giving me a quick wink. Addison and Glen went through the ceremony, and then again we all filed out to the sound of the wedding recession music. Standing side-by-side in the lobby, Everett and I waited to hear the verdict.

"Okay, guys, let's head to the restaurant for dinner," Addison announced after talking with the coordinator.

Everett threw his arm around my shoulders as we walked through the church's dark parking lot. I unlocked my car and drove us to the nearby steakhouse where the rehearsal dinner was being served.

"You've got to be exhausted, Sara," Everett said, massaging his neck once we were in the car. "This wedding stuff is completely draining, and you've been holding Addi's hand through every step! The two of you have *breathed* wedding plans for days."

I chuckled. "It's not so bad, and it will all be over in a matter of hours! I can't believe it. It feels like yesterday that Addison told us she was engaged." I paused for a moment, thinking of the other announcements that had been made that night. "How do you feel, knowing your sister will be married tomorrow?"

He shrugged. "I'm a guy, Sara. My sister's getting married to someone I really like. I feel fine. I'm happy for her. She and Glen are a good team."

"She's crazy in love with him," I said, and Everett nodded.

"That's obvious." He reached over and played with the ends of my hair. "Is it obvious I'm crazy about you?"

I giggled. Again with this guy making me giggle! Good grief, he was cute.

"No," I answered. He leaned back and smiled.

"Well, maybe I'm being too mysterious then. I'll have to work on that."

We parked at the restaurant and made our way to the reserved banquet room where Addison and Glen's families and most of the bridal party were already mingling. We ended up sitting next to Addison and Glen and across from Luke and Debra. Lily and Sam sat at the opposite end of the table. My nerves heightened as I glanced at Debra, who looked uncharacteristically tense, then shot a look down at Lily. She shrugged as though she couldn't help where they were seated.

The room buzzed with multiple conversations. Oblivious to Debra's slight change in temperament, Everett seemed to still be feeling flirty and in great spirits.

"Luke and Debra," he said after our meals were served, "Sara says it's not at all obvious that I'm crazy about her. What do you think?"

I blushed and poked his shoulder. "They wouldn't know!"

"Sure we would," Debra answered, her voice wavering. "I think it's obvious. Don't you, Luke? Isn't it obvious that Everett is crazy about Sara?"

Luke slowly cut the steak on his plate.

"It *should* be obvious when someone's crazy about you," Debra continued, the waver in her voice noticeable enough now that I was sure Everett sensed the tension as well. Under the table, my hand found Everett's.

"I think I need more salad dressing," I stated. Everett and I both looked around for a waiter, our heads turning back and forth like standing, rotating fans. Everett flagged a waiter down. Across from us, Debra and Luke didn't say a word. The four of us ate in silence while we waited for the waiter to deliver an extra side of ranch. I had about three pieces of lettuce left, but I doused them in the dressing once it came.

"How long have you two been dating?" Debra asked, her words sharp.

"Not as long as you guys," Everett answered in a smooth voice. I nudged him, trying to telepathically communicate to him to change the subject.

"Well, that's true," Debra said. "Luke and I have been dating for about eight months. Which is a very long time—to me, at least. And we've known each other for years. Of course, we've all known each other for years, right, Sara?"

Why did this feel like a strange question leading me down a dark path at night? The inclination to run in the opposite direction hit me full force.

"Um, you mean our group? Yes, we've all known each other for several years," I agreed. "Will they be serving dessert soon, do you think?"

"We may need to ask someone. I'd like some coffee as well," Everett said. There was another moment with our heads rotating in search of a waiter. In search of any distraction, really.

"So Sara," Debra said, her voice again taking me to that dark path. "Are you just as crazy about Everett as he is about you?"

I felt my cheeks flame.

"Deb," Luke said softly, "I think you and I should step outside for a minute."

Her eyes watered. "Why? Here's what I want to know. Is it obvious that you're crazy about me, Luke? Is it? What do you two think?" She looked at Everett and me frantically, but I didn't think she really saw us. She kept blinking and breathing hard. Everett and I just gripped hands and didn't speak.

Luke stood up and held out his hand to Debra. "Come with me, please," he said in a quiet, calm voice. "We're okay, Deb. Just come with me."

She looked at his hand. I could almost see the invisible pull and the inner fight happening right in front of me. Her desire to be angry versus the longing to be reassured. She couldn't fight it, and even I felt relief when she placed her hand in his. Luke's hand closed over hers, and he pulled Debra to her feet and led her out of the room.

Everett and I both exhaled.

"That was…" He couldn't seem to find the right word. I nodded my understanding.

"They probably just had a little argument before the dinner. It's always worse when you're trying to act normal in front of a crowd of people," I said.

"That's true." The waiter finally came and offered us coffee and dessert. "I hope she's okay." Everett and I sat side by side. I scooted as close as I could to him, needing the support of feeling our shoulders pressed against each other.

"Should I go check?"

Everett looked at me and shook his head. "No, Sara. Definitely not."

Luke and Debra didn't return to the table, and my worry over them continued to escalate. During dessert, people started getting up and making speeches and offering their best wishes to Addison and Glen. It was a special time of reflection and laughter. Addison wept during every speech. During a small break, I found myself dragging Lily to the restroom with me, where I gave her an overview of what had happened. Lily's brow creased with concern.

"Oh no. That doesn't sound good at all. What can we do? Where are they? Have they left?" I shrugged helplessly at Lily's questions.

"No idea. Should I text either of them?"

Lily shook her head. "No, I think you should just go back and enjoy your time with Everett. Let me text Debra."

I went back to my seat after our conversation.

"Any sign of Luke and Debra?" I asked Everett.

"No. They probably just needed some time alone to talk, Sara. I'm sure they're fine," he said, his voice soft.

Part of me agreed with him. Another part of me kept seeing the frantic look in Debra's eyes and the unsteadiness in her voice. It wasn't my business, of course, but I couldn't help wondering what was going on between them. They'd just been looking at rings, for goodness' sake. What could be wrong? I supposed they could have had a disagreement about something, though I wondered what could cause so much tension. I thought back to the day when we'd had barbecue—there had definitely been tension that day as well. The look on Debra's face a few moments ago kept flashing in my mind, and the tightness in Luke's tone—I hoped Lily managed to get ahold of one of them at least and help somehow.

The rehearsal dinner went well into the night, and Luke and Debra never reappeared. A quick whisper from Lily told me she'd text me later if she heard anything. Everett and I walked back to my car and drove to Addison's townhouse.

"You're worried about them, aren't you?" he asked during the drive.

I nodded. "Debra seemed so upset."

"She did," he agreed.

I realized in that moment that I was obsessing over Luke and Debra rather than being present with Everett. I tried to shake off the worry.

"I'm sorry, Everett. I'm sure you're right. They'll be fine." Everett raised my hand to his lips and kissed my fingers.

"They're your friends, Sara. I know you can't help being concerned." He looked up at Addison's townhouse, its porch light softly glowing in the darkness. "Addison's home. I better go in. I need to make sure she gets some rest before tomorrow. Big day, you know." He smiled at me. Impulsively,

I cupped his face in my hands and kissed him. When I pulled back away, Everett's lashes fluttered with pleasant surprise.

"What was that for?"

I laughed. "I couldn't seem to help myself. You must be irresistible." I touched his face. "Thank you for being so understanding," I added.

Everett ran his thumb across my lips. It seemed like there was more he wanted to say, but he didn't.

"I'll see you tomorrow, Sara. Save a dance for me."

I kissed him once more. "You're my date, Everett. They're all for you."

The morning of the wedding dawned bright and beautiful. A clear Texas December sky and just enough of a cold front to make things feel festive for all of us. I threw on a sweater over my jeans and blouse and left early for a hair appointment. I was having my hair done at my mother's favorite salon before heading over to Addison's house. The bridesmaids and a few of Addison's female relatives were all grouping together at her house for brunch, then we girls would get ready together.

By 10:30 a.m. the hair stylist twirled the salon chair around for me to see the final results of my hairdo.

"Kelly," I said, lightly touching the braid, "it's so gorgeous."

"Well, it's a good thing you came in so early. Your highlights really needed help."

I laughed. "True enough." I looked at the blend of blonde and light-brown chunks of hair, woven together in a loose but classically elegant braid that swept over my shoulder. I grabbed my purse, paid the bill, and rushed to Addison's house, which was already bustling with activity. I picked up a breakfast sandwich and took the stairs two at a time.

"I'm here!" I announced as I walked into the bedroom.

Addison sat on the bed, crying. Lily and Debra stood on either side of her, both looking pale and nervous.

"Um, what's going on?" I asked, setting aside my sandwich.

"I don't know why I'm crying." Addison hiccupped. "I'm really happy. I promise!"

"We believe you, sweetheart," Debra said in a comforting tone, placing a hand on Addison's shoulder.

There was a tap on the door and then Everett pushed in; he fit the theme of pale and nervous too.

"Here's your tea, Addi," he said gently, crossing the room and handing her a mug. When she didn't move to take it, I reached for it and set it on the nightstand. "Everything's going to be okay, sis. Do you not want to go through with it? You don't have to," Everett said.

"I do! I want to!" Addison cried out. All of us stepped back.

"Thanks for the tea, Everett." Lily dismissed him. "We've got this. Just keep everyone downstairs for a few minutes, all right?"

He nodded his immediate agreement and disappeared downstairs.

Lily sat down next to Addison. "It's just nerves, honey." She spoke in that calm way of hers. "And that's okay. We've got hours before the ceremony. I promise you'll be ready by then. Glen is God's sweet, precious gift of a husband to you, Addison. He's yours and you're his. That man loves you with all of his heart, and men like Glen don't come around very often. Weddings are stressful, love, but tonight, after all the fun of the ceremony and reception, you'll lay down next to Glen and nothing will be more wonderful than that. You'll wake up next to him tomorrow, and you'll smile—you may even cry because you're just so darn happy. And it's all God's blessing on your life."

Lily's words mesmerized all of us.

"Oh, Lily," Addison whispered. She laid her head on Lily's shoulder. Debra sat down on the other side of Addison and held her hand. I knelt down right in front of Addison and placed my hands on her knees.

"You can do this, Addison," Debra said, holding her hand tight.

"We're here, Addi." I looked up at my sweet, beautiful friend. After a few moments, her breathing steadied.

"I know you don't feel like it, but you need to eat a little something. That will help. Carol from church will be here soon to do your hair and makeup. We need a fresh cup of tea, Sara," Lily ordered. I nodded obediently, but before I could stand, Addison covered my hand with hers.

"I love all three of you so much. You know that, right?"

I smiled at Addison, emotion rushing to my face. "We love you too." I stood up and leaned over, kissing the top of Addison's head, then ran downstairs for food and more tea. Everett, his mother, his aunt, and another woman I vaguely recognized as a relative of Addison's stood around the breakfast table, looking terrified.

"It's okay," I assured them. "She's doing better. I'm under strict orders to bring up some food and tea for her."

The doorbell rang at that moment. "That must be Carol," Addison's mother said. "I'll let her in. Thank you, Sara. Thanks to all of you girls. Addison surely has some special friends," she said to me with a slightly less worried look on her face. I heard her open the front door and then greet both Carol and Addison's cousin.

By four o'clock, all of us bridesmaids and Kinley, Addison's cousin and maid of honor, were ready. We fluttered around in our cranberry-colored dresses, enjoying the excitement as the ceremony drew near. Addison turned from side to side in the full-length mirror in her parents' bedroom.

Her auburn hair was swept into an elegant bun, with beaded bobby-pins tucked in the elaborate twist. Flawless makeup smoothed her cheeks and emphasized her eyes. The white, lace-covered bodice complemented Addison's curves, and the wide skirt flowed easily as she moved, swishing back and forth with every step. She looked gorgeous down to her silver stiletto sandals and white toenail polish. The dress helped with the nerves. The minute she put it on, a fixed smile filled Addison's face, and relief settled in the house.

I left her parents' bedroom right as Everett walked out of the guestroom. We stopped, just looking at each other. *Wow.* The man should consider a new career as a tuxedo model. He raised his eyebrows at me.

"Well? What do you think?" he asked, tugging at the tie.

"Don't pull at that," I scolded lightly, walking up to him. "I think … well, you look great."

He looked back down at the tie, then he looked at me. His eyes started at my hair and made their way all the way down to my shoes. I blushed.

"You look beautiful, Sara." He kissed my cheek. "My dad's here now. We're all heading to the church."

"Right," I said, stepping back. "I'll meet you at those double doors in the back of the sanctuary. Don't walk down the aisle without me," I teased.

He smiled. "Don't worry."

The previous night's situation with Debra and Luke hadn't completely slipped my mind, but she seemed calm and collected, so I figured the fight must have blown over. Regardless, I barely had time to think with all the wedding hoopla going on. A long black limo pulled up in front of the house—a surprise for Addison from Everett. She squealed and all of us piled in for the ride to the church. Once we arrived, there were last-minute issues to take care of and pictures with the bridesmaids.

I decided that a December wedding had been a fantastic idea. The church was already beautifully decorated for Christmas with wreaths hanging and poinsettias everywhere. I had worked with the church staff to arrange minimal added decorations for the wedding, but the sanctuary had been festive and striking to start with.

The wedding began at five thirty. I could hear the music from where I stood in the lobby, and I knew guests packed the sanctuary.

"Are you nervous?" I asked Everett.

"A bit, yeah," he answered. "Wait here." He went back to where Addison was standing at the back of the procession line with their father. I watched as Addison threw her arms around Everett, and he whispered into her ear. The scene stirred emotion in me. I saw the photographer trying to inconspicuously snap a few photos of the sentimental moment. The double doors opened just as Everett took his place back by me. I slid my hand through his arm and squeezed. He looked at me with a sad sort of smile. Whatever he'd said before, I could clearly see the emotional weight of the moment all over his face now.

The church coordinator stepped up. "It's time!" Everett squared his shoulders, then led me down the aisle.

Chapter Twenty-Four

I sidestepped the dancing flower girl to get back to my seat, two pieces of lemon cake in my hands. I set one plate in front of Everett and sat down next to him.

"Oh! Thanks, Sara."

I twisted in my seat to watch Addison dance with Glen. The Vineyard reception hall was even more beautiful than I remembered, and I gasped in delight at the sight of the dimly lit ballroom. The crystal chandelier, the polished floors, the crown molding—I felt like I was suddenly in a Jane Austen novel, at *the* ball of the season.

"Let's dance." Everett wiped his mouth and dropped the napkin on his chair as he stood.

"What?"

I looked back at his plate, which held only crumbs. "You devoured that cake," I told him.

He shrugged. "It was good. Come on."

I took a quick bite of my own piece of cake and then obligingly placed my hand in his and let him take me to the dance floor.

"Look," he whispered. "To the left."

I glanced to the side and saw Debra and Luke on the dance floor. While I wouldn't say Debra radiated happiness, things looked less tense than they had the night before.

"Everything must have gotten resolved," he surmised. I wondered about Everett's words. Lily hadn't said anything to me about our friends' argument. I scrutinized Luke and Debra for a moment—the tautness of his neck, the way he kept looking at Debra. Her gaze darted around the room, seeming to settle anywhere but on him.

"I hope so. They look a little more at ease." My gaze lingered on them.

"And how are we, Sara?"

I looked at Everett, surprised by the curious tone of his voice.

"What do you mean?"

We moved slowly around the dance floor. "Well, I told you back in North Carolina that I needed to know where we stand."

"Oh. Right." Conversation paused as Everett twirled me, then pulled me back to himself. "How do *you* think we are?"

I felt his arm around me tighten. "I think we—"

At that moment, the deejay came over the microphone as the music changed to a country line dance song. The floor filled up with people. Addison came up to us, breathless and grinning. She pulled Everett away to dance with her, and I gladly watched the two of them together. I made my way back to the table and sipped champagne.

"Hey!" I said as Debra sat down next to me. "I thought you loved line dancing!" I scanned the room for Luke. She shrugged.

"I don't feel like it right now."

"Where's Luke?"

Her face hardened. "He's talking to Jason at the moment."

"Deb, is everything all right?" I asked gently. She shook back her curly hair.

"We're okay," she answered, her tone unconvincing. I offered her my glass of champagne, and she took a long sip.

"You look beautiful," I told her. Her dark curly hair, held back by a gorgeous black-sequined headband, looked stunning against the cranberry dress and spilled over her shoulders. Smoky eye makeup highlighted her eyes and long lashes. Pink blush gave her rosy cheeks, and every time she turned her head, her long, dangly earrings shimmered. She didn't respond. I wasn't even sure she'd heard me.

"I don't know." She squinted as she looked across the ballroom. "Here we are in this romantic setting—everything should be perfect. I finally found the love of my life. Why does he hold back, Sara?" Her voice quivered.

I couldn't find any words.

"Maybe he's not holding back," I finally said. "You know Luke. He's reserved. He's cautious."

"I thought I did," she answered. "Reserved, cautious—that's all well and good. But when you love someone, you have to dive in eventually. Throw caution to the wind. Buy the ring."

Her voice jumped erratically, and my unease grew at her obvious anguish. "Maybe he has. Bought the ring, I mean. He can be hard to read sometimes; that doesn't mean he's not ready. He could just be waiting for the right time to propose. He loves you, Deb." She tipped her head back and finished off my glass of champagne.

"That's true," Debra said, her eyes on the dance floor. "And I love him with all my heart. The problem is that by this point, I should be able to read him. I shouldn't have to guess. I shouldn't have to ask."

"What if he proposed tonight? Or on Christmas, like you were thinking? What would you say?" At that, she looked at me, her eyes red.

"I'd say yes, of course! I'm in love with him. He's in love with me. I want to marry him more than anything. I'm tired of the waiting."

"It will work out, Debra." I touched her arm.

"What if it doesn't?" she whispered hoarsely.

Oh Lord. What if it doesn't? I jerked as though a cold blast of air hit me. *I know he loves her. We all know it. What's wrong?*

"There's something keeping him from making a commitment to me."

"He's committed to you, Debra," I assured her.

"Not like I need him to be."

Out of the corner of my eye, I saw Luke coming our way.

"Maybe we were never right for each other," Debra said, that same frantic tone coming back from the night before.

"You don't believe that." All my worries from the other night flooded back as she stood up.

"You do, though." Her clipped tone held a hint of bitterness, but she never looked my way, obviously distracted. I couldn't move; my heart had just been sucker-punched. Debra moved toward Luke. They met halfway, near the window. Luke's head bowed to hers as he listened to her. I wondered desperately what she was saying. Then Luke straightened. She walked past him and he followed her.

Everett sat down next to me, his chest heaving. "I haven't line danced in forever. Thankfully. Addison's always loved it for some reason. I definitely feel like I'm back in Texas."

He gulped down half a glass of water, and I reached over and smoothed back his tousled hair.

"You looked like you were having fun out there."

He nodded and drained the glass of water.

"Hey, what's wrong?" He touched me. I didn't answer for a moment.

"Sara." Gentle pressure on my arm. I sighed and relayed everything that had happened. He got quieter and quieter as I told him everything.

"Maybe you need to talk to Luke," Everett said after a few moments. I looked at him.

"Luke? Why? Talking with Debra didn't help at all. I need to stay out of it."

He placed both hands on his knees and didn't say anything for a moment. Another upbeat song came on and the crowd cheered.

"Let's worry about it tomorrow. It's my sister's wedding, and I want to dance with you."

The abrupt shift in his tone surprised me, but I nodded. "You're right. It's between Luke and Deb. Let's dance."

He stood up and reached for my hand. "Come with me, Cinderella. I'll be your prince. At least for tonight."

I slept late Sunday morning, aching with exhaustion. I finally made my way to the kitchen at eleven, only because of my intense need for coffee. In my robe and slippers, I glanced at the clock. Addison and Glen had a plane to catch at one o'clock to the Virgin Islands. I smiled at the thought of Addison's beautiful wedding. Despite her nervous tears the morning before, she and Glen had danced the night away at the Vineyard, and I had never seen her so happy.

My smile vanished as I thought about Debra's final comment to me.

Father, what do I do?

I sat down on the sofa and drew my knees up, holding my warm cup of coffee and thinking about Luke and Debra. Luke and I hadn't really talked since the day he'd called me. Now Debra seemed on the verge of her own not-so-mini meltdown.

What's he waiting for?

I knew Luke well enough to know that if he'd dated Debra for eight months, he had long-term intentions. He would never be able to just date casually. I had no doubt he planned to marry her, but knowing him as I did, I knew he wouldn't ask until he was ready to. Debra had a lot of pull with him, but he'd propose when he felt it was right.

My thoughts moved to Everett. The night had ended well between us—both of us exhausted and exhilarated from the wedding. A light kiss and he'd sent me on my way home, promising to see me sometime today before his flight home tomorrow. Still, there'd been something in his eyes that worried me a little.

I finished my coffee and headed for a hot shower, hoping the steaming water would help rinse away my anxiety.

When Everett showed up at my apartment that night, I knew immediately from the look in his eyes that something was indeed wrong.

"Do you want to go out for drinks or anything?" I asked him, pushing open the door. He walked in, wearing a wrinkled T-shirt and shorts and running his fingers through his messy hair.

"No, I just want to talk."

"Okay." I closed the door and followed him to the sofa. My shoulders tensed slightly at his serious tone. "Did Addi and Glen make their flight okay?"

He nodded. "She texted me once they were on the plane."

"Good." I sat cross-legged on the couch. "Tell me what's wrong, Everett."

He blew out a breath and leaned back. "I think we need to hold off on us for a while."

My stomach sank like a stone in water. Panic and disappointment coursed through my veins at breakneck speed. Everett placed a hand on my knee, and I instantly uncrossed my legs and stood up.

"Sara—"

"But—we just—last night—I don't understand," I argued, trying to keep the desperation out of my voice.

He looked at me. "I'm crazy about you. Seriously. I am. But you're not ready, and seeing Debra and Luke—seeing how much pain she was in—I can't do that."

"What?"

"He's pulling away from her. I'm afraid you would do that with me eventually, Sara."

"I wouldn't." I crossed my arms and sat back down, this time on the chair, leaving plenty of room between us. He leaned over, his elbows propped on his knees, his hands folded. Concern shadowed his face and seriousness replaced all the playful exchanges I'd enjoyed from him during the past few days.

"You may," he said, a tiny, sad sympathetic smile on his face.

"I thought … I'm just surprised. I thought you were into this." My anger was seeping through at this point—we had such a good thing going. Why did he all of a sudden want to break up?

He sat up straight. "You're not hearing me! I'm *so* into this. Into you, Sara. I need you to be sure. And I'm not convinced that you are. So let's take some time."

I released a pent-up breath. "You think I should talk to Luke."

"I think you should have talked to him years ago! I think he picked the wrong person, and he's realizing it, and he's in a really bad situation. I don't envy him that. But don't think for one minute that I want you to end up with him. I want us to take some time and for you to come to the conclusion that *you're* into this."

"Okay," I said, my racing pulse slowing at the assurance that he wasn't saying goodbye forever to me. "I've been consumed with wedding stuff and work obligations for weeks. Maybe a little time will be good for us." I didn't see how, but I wasn't going to beg. If he wanted time, I'd give him that, and I'd find a way to reassure him that my heart was ready for more. I couldn't, wouldn't, lose him over Luke.

Everett stood up and walked over to where I sat. He took my hand and pulled me up next to him, then placed one hand behind my neck and brought me close, kissing me gently.

"You looked so beautiful at the wedding, Sara," he told me, his voice tender. "I think you're an amazing woman."

His words warmed me and lent me some hope, but I couldn't manage to smile. Fear and frustration surged through me—and worry that the adorable pilot in front of me was about to slip through my fingers. I hugged him tight. "How about if I call you sometime after the holidays?"

"You do that." But his voice and embrace left me knowing he wasn't entirely convinced. I hated to let him go.

Chapter Twenty-Five

That's not really breaking up," Lily said after a moment. I'd gone straight to her house Monday after work and told her Everett's break-up speech to me.

"Really? What would you call it?" I asked, sitting at the kitchen island in Lily and Sam's house.

"He wants you to be sure."

"Breaking up with me is a strange way to find that out."

"Maybe. Maybe not."

"Have you talked to Debra?" I asked. Lily's face scrunched and she pushed her hair out of her face.

"Yes."

"And?"

"I don't know. Couples fight. Maybe they'll be fine, but he needs to make a move if he's going to. The waiting is killing her."

"What is he waiting for?" I rested my chin on the palm of my hand.

"I wish I knew."

The front door opened, and Sam and Luke walked in. Lily and I looked at each other, our eyes like saucers.

"Sara!" Sam exclaimed, obviously shocked to see me.

"Luke, hi." Lily shifted into hostess mode right in front of me. "I didn't know you were coming over. Can I get you something to drink? I just made a pitcher of sweet tea, and I've got a homemade pizza in the oven. You and Sara should stay for dinner."

"Oh, um. Well—" Luke looked at me for a minute.

I stood up. "Thanks, but I can't stay, Lil. I need to get home."

She glowered at me, but I wasn't staying to hear her argument. I grabbed my purse.

"I'll walk you out," Luke said suddenly. Goose bumps prickled my arms as he walked me outside. At forty-five degrees, it was for sure the coldest day we'd had in December. (Texas, y'all.) That, along with my shaking anxiety, had me freezing and trembling all over. Not the perfect time to have a conversation. I tightened my coat as we stopped at my car.

"First," he began, his eyes locked on me. "Are you and Everett in a serious relationship?"

I blinked. "Really? No, that can't be 'first.' Surely you have something else to say to me, besides asking about my boyfriend." My words came out heavy with sarcasm.

"Is he your boyfriend then?"

Oh right. Except he broke up with me last night.

This is awkward.

I breathed in through my nose. "No, he's not. We're dating. Sort of. We're kind of taking a break over the holidays, but we're dating."

Yes. I know. It didn't come out as a very good description of a normal relationship. Luke frowned.

"What's happened with you and Deb? Why are you fighting?" I asked point-blank. He'd set the precedent for awkward questions.

"She wants us to get married."

"Of course she does!" I threw my hands up with exasperation.

He crossed his arms, forearms flexing, his face white from the cold. His jaw clenched and unclenched, and the corners of his eyes tightened, almost as though he were preparing for impact. "Tell me the truth, Sara. Did you ever want us to be more than friends?"

I was shaking like a twig in a rainstorm. Hurt and rage and every emotion I'd withheld came pouring out of me. He would ask this of me now?

After all this time, I needed to tell the truth. He'd asked me, and I had to tell him.

"Yes!" I nearly spat out the word.

He winced and sank backward against the car. "For how long?"

"Since the day we met." I bit my lip, wishing I didn't feel so cold and my entire body would stop quaking.

"Then why did you date Jason?" He unfolded his arms, pushed off from against the car, and shouted the question. I stepped back, shocked. Then I balled my fists, ready to fight.

"Because he asked me!" I yelled back. "You didn't seem interested. So I set aside my feelings and tried to stay open. I dated Jason because I liked him. He's fantastic. But in the end, I couldn't force something that wasn't there. So we broke up." I struggled to control my voice.

Luke ran his fingers through his hair violently as I talked.

"Have you ever wanted us to be more than friends?" I asked, bracing myself for the answer but needing to know.

He closed his eyes. "Since the first day I met you."

My mouth fell open. For so long, I'd assumed I'd be overcome with joy at the sound of those words coming out of Luke's mouth. But I was wrong. My stomach turned and I felt sick.

Sick.

"Why … why didn't you say anything?" My hollow voice sounded like a distant echo in my ears. Nothing behind it, just emptiness.

"Because Jason is like my brother. Because he staked his claim the minute you walked through the door." Luke fell back against the car.

"That doesn't—"

He held up his hand to silence me. "You don't get it. He's one of my best friends. I couldn't do anything. And once you guys finally broke up—well, we all knew he was still crazy about you. Knowing and respecting Jason as much as I do … I wasn't sure how I could ever ask you out at that point. It would have changed things forever between me and Jase. Then you and I became best friends, and I didn't want to chance ruining that. And you seemed happy just being friends, so I didn't think you wanted more!"

"If *you* wanted more, you should have said something," I said, ice in my words. How could he tell me this now?

"Why didn't *you* say something? At the lake house, I told you to tell me the truth!" he said, his voice shaking with anger.

"I couldn't." I nearly choked on the words. "You'd chosen her! You had never shown the slightest romantic interest in me." The truth in those words physically pained me, and I clutched my stomach. "Do you know how much that hurt?" My voice rose and cracked.

He held his head in his hands.

"You've been dating her for months. You've taken her to look at rings. She's—"

"I can't marry her." He said the words, and I tried to speak. I opened and closed my mouth twice before words actually came out.

"How can you say that? It's been months. She's expecting—"

"I know!" He turned away from me for a moment and placed both hands on the car. "But I can't! I thought I could … but I just can't."

My teeth chattered so hard that my whole head seemed to rattle. I rubbed my hands up and down my arms.

"How can you even think of hurting her that way?"

He turned back to face me, pain searing his eyes, his mouth grimacing. As furious as I felt, still, the clear torture on his face wrecked my heart. "Because

I know what it looks like when someone marries the wrong person. I can't do that. I've lived it already."

"You're just *now* realizing that? After eight months? After looking at rings together and talking of marriage?" My eyes rounded in disbelief.

"I know! I'm ashamed, and I'm sorry, and I've made mistakes. I let it go further than I should have. I kept going when I should have stopped. But I can't marry her, Sara." The tone in his voice shifted there at the end. I could hear it. He was begging me to understand. But I didn't. This wasn't Luke. To take it this far, to hurt Debra, to hurt me … it seemed so unlike him.

"Are you in love with Everett?"

"Maybe," I answered. He flinched.

Let him hurt, I thought. Lord knows I've hurt enough over him.

"At least he liked me enough to pursue me," I said, unable to hold the words back. Luke stepped close to me, and I couldn't breathe.

"And I didn't?"

"No! You didn't!" I shouted, pushing him back. "And how do you think it's been for me? Watching you date Debra for months and months? Listening to her tell all of us about her love for you? Having a front-row seat to every moment of your romance with her?" My frustration spewed out like venom, but Luke just glared at me.

"I had to watch you with Jason—and hear all about it from him nearly every day for a year. How do you think that was for me?"

"Obviously I wouldn't know, since you never told me. Anyway, that was forever ago. And if it bothered you, you should have done something about it. Jason and I broke up. You had every opportunity to tell me how you felt."

"I know," Luke said again, his arms dropping to his side helplessly. We were both quiet for a moment, still breathing hard.

"I should have but I didn't," Luke said. Now I see you with Everett—and I feel it all over again."

"Feel what?" I shoved my hands in my coat pockets.

"It doesn't matter." He tentatively stepped closer to me again; this time I didn't push him, and I didn't move. I couldn't meet his eyes. The desires to both hit him and throw myself in his arms simmered right below the surface.

Unspoken words lingered between us. Thoughts of Everett and Debra hovered in the back of my mind. Still, even now, it seemed we couldn't say everything. I finally glanced up at Luke's face, white with cold but cheeks flushed red, his deep-green eyes holding mine.

"Sara." His low, desperate tone reverberated all through me.

"How can you do this to me?" I cried. "Say all this now—wait until the worst possible time."

He didn't respond.

"What will you do?" I asked, frightened at the thought of Debra's disappointment.

Luke folded his arms again. "What I have to, Sara."

"Will you break up with her?" I whispered in horror. "You can't! And what do you expect to happen after? Don't do this for me. It's too late for that."

What little color was left in his face drained away. "Whatever I do at this point, it will be for myself. As for what happens after—God knows, but I sure don't."

"You could have told me how you felt," I insisted. "Before. And everything would be different now. I waited and hoped and you never said anything."

My disappointment registered with him, and I could see the helplessness in his eyes. "You could have said something too," he pointed out. I looked away.

"I needed it to come from you."

He sighed.

"Now what, Luke? Where does all of this leave us? We can't even be friends anymore. I was your best friend, and you were mine, then suddenly I was nothing to you."

The despondent look on his face reached me at my core.

"I know you felt that way—but it wasn't … I still … I couldn't…" Luke looked at the ground, his shoulders slumped forward.

God, how can this be happening? Finally. Finally, he tells me this. When nothing can come from it.

Tears cascaded down my cheeks.

"I better go. This all feels wrong." I rubbed the back of my hand under my eyes and across my cheeks. The movement blocked my view of Luke, but that was okay. I couldn't look at him any longer.

"I'll go." He stepped toward his car, then turned and looked at me, his dejected green eyes piercing my heart. "It hurts, Sara. But it's honest and real, and that finally feels right to me."

He drove away, and I went back and pounded on Lily's door. Sam opened it, his eyes darting behind me.

"He left," I said simply. "I need Lily."

Lily came around the corner.

"Did you know?" I demanded of her, walking inside. She exhaled and exchanged a look with Sam. "Did you both know?" My voice grew shrill.

"Back at the beginning, Sara," Sam said after he closed the front door. "I knew Luke felt frustrated that Jason had asked you out so quickly. Jason told Luke and me that first day that he was interested in you. After that—I thought Luke had just moved on. Every now and then, I thought … maybe he hadn't. But you guys were so close, I figured if it was meant to happen, it would."

Lily nodded her agreement of his assessment.

"Then he started dating Debra, and we both thought he must have really moved on. You never actually told any of us how you felt about Luke, Sara," Lily reminded me, and I scowled at her. "You kept it a secret. But I could see it after a while. So could Jason."

"How could he not tell me? Now he says something, after all this time, when Debra's waiting for a proposal!" I shuddered and sank down on the sofa. Lily sat by me. "Debra. Oh, Lily, this is terrible." I closed my eyes. "What can I do?"

Lily shook her head. "Wait. Trust. Pray. Things are about to get messy."

Chapter Twenty-Six

A week went by and I didn't hear anything. I texted Lily daily, but she hadn't heard anything either. I couldn't eat. The thought of Luke breaking up with Debra when she was anticipating a proposal made me queasy.

Addison and Glen returned from their honeymoon a week and a half before Christmas. She invited all of us girls over for coffee to tell us about the trip. Having no idea whether Luke and Debra were still even a couple, and knowing that Everett had probably told Addison that he had broken up with me—I felt as though going to Addison's house was like walking into a room full of explosives.

But Lily made me go.

She picked me up, and we rode over to Glen's house. I suppose I should say Glen and Addison's house, though that still felt weird to me. Addison's parents had hired movers to move all of her things over to Glen's house while they were away, and a For Sale sign now sat in the yard at Addison's old townhouse. Lily's car came to a stop in front of their house.

"I can't do this. I feel nauseous," I told Lily.

"You can and you have to. We're going in. We would have heard by now if Luke and Debra had broken up. That would be like World War Three, honey. Not a quiet situation. So they're still together, and maybe they'll work things out. Who knows? Luke is really unpredictable at the moment." Lily said that last line with marked disapproval. I couldn't blame her. "And Addison can't be mad at you about Everett. He's the one who decided you guys needed a break."

Having finished her speech, Lily got out of the car and waited for me at the base of the driveway. I groaned and got out, and we walked up together. Addison and Debra were sitting on the sofa, scrolling through honeymoon pictures. Addison jumped up and hugged both of us. A smile crept up on my face at the sight of her beaming in all her newlywed bliss.

"The honeymoon was *perfect*! Come look at pictures!" she squealed. I glanced over at Debra, trying to maintain control of my nerves. She seemed quiet, but not on the verge of crazy. That was positive.

For the next hour, Addison gave us the complete overview of her honeymoon, and we all gushed over the pictures. Glen came home, and Lily and Deb and I offered up more congratulations and such. It felt new and strange to see Addison at home and already so settled with Glen.

I knew I'd miss our girls' nights around the table at Addison's old house. The barbecues out on the back deck … movie nights and Bible studies in her living room … but seeing her here with Glen, I felt happy for her.

Happy for her, and lonely, and a little sad.

The conversation around me shifted, and my ears perked up as I heard Addison ask Debra how Luke was doing and what their plans for Christmas were. Having been preoccupied during the wedding festivities, I realized that Addison had no idea of the current strain that surrounded Debra and Luke's relationship. For that matter, she might not know that Everett and I were cooling things.

Oh dear.

"Luke is … Luke. We're okay, I guess."

The room went silent. I knew Addison would pick up on the tension immediately, and it wouldn't matter to her one bit that she'd just returned from an idyllic honeymoon. If someone in our group was hurting, that would take precedence.

"What's going on?" Addison set aside the ongoing slideshow of pictures. She turned toward Debra and touched her hand. Debra shook her head, eyes welling up.

"I don't know. He's really distant and says we need to slow down. Slow down?" she repeated, her voice shaking. "We looked at rings a few weeks ago, and now he wants to slow down?" She was losing it, her tone spiking. "He won't tell me what's wrong! Slow down after eight months? Now he's not sure—after all this time?!"

No one moved.

"Has he talked to you, Sara? Has he told you what he's thinking?" Debra asked suddenly, eyes on me.

Oh, Lord. Help.

"Really, Debra. He's hardly talked to me at all for months." That was the most truth I could muster.

"But has he talked to you recently? Do you have any idea of what's going on with him?"

Mercy. Mercy. Mercy.

"I talked to him the other day, and I agree that something seems really wrong. But I—" My words stopped, and I looked at Lily desperately.

"I know he's talked to Sam," Lily broke in, and Deb leaned forward urgently. "Sam thinks Luke is just doing a lot of soul searching right now."

Debra leaned back with a huff. "What does that *mean*? I thought we'd be engaged by Christmas! He's scaring me with this talk of slowing down!"

My heart hurt.

"Did Everett talk to you, Addison?" I asked, distressed enough to use my own situation to change the subject. She nodded.

"He called me last night to hear about the trip. And he mentioned that you guys were going to be cooling things for a while. Are you okay?" she asked with concern. Debra's eyes rounded in surprise.

"But … why? He's crazy about you, Sara. What happened?"

"It was Everett's decision, really," I said, "for us to slow things down, and he was right. For one thing, the distance factor is a problem. We hardly ever see each other, and I think because of that, it's hard to feel sure." I felt a twinge of guilt. "It's hard for *me* to feel sure," I corrected. "We both love our jobs, we're rooted in our communities and everything—" I realized in that moment that I *was* unsure. Not surprising that my best friends would bring this out of me.

I didn't want to move to North Carolina. Everett loved his job and his church and his friends out there. He didn't really want to move back to Texas. The geography issue was a big one for both of us.

The perfect guy who just happened to live more than a thousand miles away.

"So we're slowing things down, and maybe we'll talk in the new year."

"But you're okay?" Addison pressed, worried. I nodded.

"I'm okay, Addi. Everett is truly a wonderful guy, and I like him. He's also observant and perceptive, and I trust his judgment. So slowing things down is the right thing." I said the words and knew them to be true.

"Not for me and Luke," Debra said after a moment. "We should be moving forward. It's time, and if he's not ready … then I need to know why."

"Is he going to Colorado for Christmas?" Debra's face fell at Lily's question.

"I don't know. He said he's not buying a flight, so he'll just decide last-minute if he wants to drive up to the mountains. I wanted us to spend the holiday together, of course. He suggested I go to Minnesota. I asked him to come with me, and he said he can't make it this year. Unbelievable! And just why can't he? The only ticket I could find that wasn't already outrageously priced was for Christmas morning. I'm leaving at 5:00 a.m., and I'll be out there till after New Year's. This is not what I envisioned for my holiday."

My neck and shoulders ached from the tension. "Do you have coffee, Addison?" I asked. She nodded and jumped up.

"Coffee's a good idea. Let me make some."

"I'll help," I insisted, following Addison into the kitchen and leaving Debra and Lily in the living room.

"I was so hopeful you and Everett would work out." Disappointment tinged her words. I rolled my neck and wished I had some Tylenol.

"It could still happen. We're just going to take a little time. Meanwhile, you seem to have a newlywed glow about you."

Addison blushed. "Well, I suppose love does that to you."

"Where are the spoons, Addi?" At her townhouse, I'd known the kitchen like it was my own. This felt different—sending a wave of sadness to hit me again. Things had already changed so much. And now with Luke and Debra's fragile relationship on the brink of disaster—I had a feeling things would never even be close to the same again.

Addison turned from the coffeemaker to look at me. I was reminded that, just like Everett, Addison had a keen sense of perception.

"Second drawer on the left." She placed a hand on my shoulder. "And you'll soon know this kitchen like you did my last one. Because we're family, Sara. Now and always."

I put my arms around her.

"Now and always."

I hoped.

Lily and I didn't say much on the way to my apartment. A sense of heaviness over what was happening with Luke and Debra hung around us. She dropped me off, and I walked through my apartment. I wanted to call Everett. Like Luke had been once upon a time, Everett had been my go-to person to talk to for weeks now. Phone calls after work, e-mails and text messages daily. But since calling was not really an option, I just turned on HGTV and went to the pantry in search of Nutella.

Luckily, I didn't have all that much time to dwell on worrisome thoughts. The week before Christmas ended up being a busy one at the museum. People flocked to the see the Holiday-Around-the-World exhibit. Families, probably entertaining out-of-town guests, kept coming in to see the gorgeous oil paintings as well as photos and descriptions of Christmas celebrated in different countries. The Germany display drew me back again and again with its enchanting and colorful depictions of Christmas street markets, Advent wreaths, and polished boots awaiting treats from Santa.

Four days before Christmas, I checked my watch as I walked down the corridor of the Christmas exhibit. Twenty minutes till closing. Just one or two stragglers were still milling about in the museum. I walked to the Nativity painting and stopped, as I had done every day since it had arrived. I stepped close to the painting and studied every detail.

I think it was the use of light that drew me in. The soft yellow hues of the stars, along with the yellow glow from a lantern hanging in the stable. Something about the warm, radiant light pulled me into the scene. The artist had captured the simplistic setting of stable, animals, and straw in rustic realism. I could almost feel the animals' warm breath, the cold chill of the air, the confusion and interest of the shepherds, the quiet stillness that comes after the chaos of birth.

I kept going back to Joseph's face. Mary and the Christ-child looked serene, though I'd argue Mary looked exhausted, understandably. But the look on Joseph's face captivated me. Was it awe and wonder? Or did the artist mean to capture a sense of trepidation and fear? Or all of the above?

His tender gaze was directed on the baby. Joseph held a staff in his hand, and the faint whiteness of his knuckles, the taut rigidness of his enclosed fingers, showed his tight grip.

He looked to be a man of nervous apprehension and enormous responsibility.

There was something else I couldn't quite place just yet. As often as I'd looked at the gorgeous painting, I'd contemplated the look in Joseph's eyes.

I took one last look at the title of the painting on the gold-plated label below.

Immanuel: God with us.

"There you are, Sara." I turned to see Jeanie walking toward me.

"Jeanie!" I exclaimed, shocked at the sight of her meandering the hallways so late and so close to Christmas. During all of December, she'd taken to leaving the museum by three thirty and had been using much of her vacation time. "I thought you were off today."

She shrugged. "My sister and her husband are in town. They wanted to see the holiday exhibit so we came in a little while ago. My nephew is enthralled by the fossils."

I smiled. "What did they think of our Christmas artwork?"

"Oh, charming. My sister loved it. She's a believer—like you," Jeanie said, a little awkwardly. I just smiled and nodded.

"Were you looking for me?" I asked. She nodded as though she'd forgotten.

"Oh, right! Yes. I wanted to tell you that I'll be out tomorrow. My mother, sister, and I decided at the last minute to drive up to Galveston to see Dickens on the Strand."

"That sounds fun!" I'd been to the same holiday street festival in the coastal city of Galveston several times with my own mother. The Charles-Dickens'-inspired parade, based on nineteenth century Victorian England, was a hotspot for holiday entertainment.

"You'll help handle things here then?" Jeanie's eyes darted to the few guests walking past us. "We're closed Christmas Eve and Christmas Day, but tomorrow—"

"We can handle it, Jeanie," I assured her. "Don't worry about a thing."

She nodded, still not looking convinced. "All right then. Have a good holiday."

"Jeanie, we pulled Danny away from the dinosaurs." A weary-looking couple with a toddler in tow came headed in our direction. Jeanie's obviously very pregnant sister paused for a moment, her husband and son stopping with her, then continued walking.

"Heather, this is one of our team leaders, Sara Witherspoon. Sara, my sister, Heather, my brother-in-law, Joel, and my nephew, Danny."

We all said our hellos. "Jeanie told me you like the holiday paintings," I mentioned to Heather. Her eyes lit up.

"They are breathtaking! I'm so glad I got a chance to see everything. Especially the Nativity painting. It's … something special."

Heather let go of Danny's hand and stepped closer to me in order to take one more look at the painting. I turned with her, both absorbing the beauty and message of the art.

"There's something in Joseph's eyes," I said, scrutinizing his facial expression again. "Don't you think? He looks kind of nervous, a bit overwhelmed—even frightened. And something else…"

Heather looked at me. "Oh, yes. Can't you see what it is? Acceptance, of course."

Then I *did* see it. Amid the fear and worry—complete and utter acceptance.

"Acceptance," I repeated, barely above a whisper.

Heather touched my arm as she moved to return to her family.

"We all get there, eventually."

Chapter Twenty-Seven

I left work late on December 23 and drove to my parents' house. As per our family custom, I'd spend December 24 with my parents, cooking and preparing for a Christmas Eve dinner with our extended family and usually a friend or two. My mother and I woke up early. The house had been decked out with Christmas décor for weeks, of course, but it never failed that my mother found more things to set out, ornaments to move around, and other such things to do before our guests arrived.

I was tasked with baking Christmas cookies for our neighbors while my mother began the arduous job of cooking the turkey, along with our family's special stuffing recipe. My grandparents arrived by midafternoon, along with my aunt and uncle and two of my cousins. I was surprised but pleased to see Ms. Alana and Paul show up for dinner. Apparently, their family celebrations were held on Christmas Day, so they'd decided to spend the evening with us.

After feasting on turkey and stuffing and all the trimmings, we sat in the living room. Paul had a beautiful baritone voice, and when he began to sing "Away in a Manger," the moment segued into all of us singing Christmas carols as we admired the tree. Since it was fifty-seven degrees outside, my mother had decided to take the opportunity to have a roaring fire in the fireplace. (Texas, y'all.)

Sitting next to my grandmother, Mimi, I looked at my mother's lovely Christmas tree and joined in singing "White Christmas," relishing the comfortable feeling of family and tradition.

I knew my mother was in her element as she set out a large tray with hot cocoa and then served homemade pumpkin pie to all of her guests. She motioned for me to stay with Mimi when I moved to get up to help. So I snuggled back next to my grandmother, holding on to the moment that embodied so much of what I loved about Christmas.

Our guests stayed late. Sometime after ten o'clock, once my grandparents were settled in one of the guestrooms and my aunt and uncle and cousins had left for home, I helped my mother finish cleaning up. Once the dishwasher was whirring and the food was stored in the refrigerator, my mom disappeared upstairs. I sat on the sofa to enjoy the last few minutes of the fire as the embers burned low.

The glow from the Christmas tree filled me with wonder, as it had every year since childhood. My mother loved themed trees, and she'd gone with an all-gold theme this year. Her nine-foot, snow-flecked artificial tree dominated the corner of the living room. Gold ornaments of every shape and size covered the tree and glittered among the white lights and gold mesh garland. A gold peacock sat regally at the top, its long, beaded, sequined, intricate tail curving down around the tree. Beneath the tree, gifts wrapped in sparkly gold paper, some with large bows and ribbons, beckoned to be opened.

My mother. Even her tree was a work of art.

I glanced at the clock over the mantel when I heard my phone beep from where it sat on the end table. 11:45 p.m. *Fifteen minutes until Christmas.* I reached for the phone and read the text I'd just received from Lily.

IT'S OVER.

PRAY FOR DEBRA.

I didn't breathe for several seconds; my eyes started to burn as I stared at the text.

Debra.

Alone on the couch, firelight barely flickering into the room, I tried to sort out my feelings. But I couldn't.

I could only cry for my friend—the one whose hopes for an engagement were now as unlikely as snow falling in Houston.

I woke up to the smell of ham frying and the sound of my parents and grandparents downstairs. The covers were wrapped around me as tight as a swaddled baby. I had to kick to get them off. Then I sat up and it hit me again that Luke and Debra had broken up on Christmas Eve, that Debra was on a flight to Minnesota, and that she was, no doubt, devastated and having the worst holiday of her life.

I wished I could talk to Lily about everything, but it was Christmas morning and I just couldn't bother her. My phone beeped again from somewhere in the tussled blankets. I frantically searched for it.

Everett.

WISHING YOU A MERRY CHRISTMAS, SARA.

I typed back something similar quickly and scrolled down to see if I'd received any other texts during the night. Nothing.

What had happened? How was Luke? Was he driving to Colorado? Was he home alone in his apartment? Was Debra crying on the flight? Was she furious? Was it really over? I groaned as I swung my legs over the edge of the bed and stood up. I smoothed back my hair, grabbed my robe, and padded downstairs. My father made me a plate of scrambled eggs and ham and biscuits, and I ate quietly, tuning out the conversation all around me.

My mother came up behind me and touched my hair. "Everything all right, dear?"

Might as well tell her.

"Luke and Debra broke up last night," I whispered. Her eyes widened in alarm.

"Oh no. She must be heartbroken."

I nodded glumly. "I'm sure. I doubt it's an easy day for Luke either."

"Where is he?" she asked. I shrugged.

"No idea. If he didn't drive to Colorado, he's either home alone or he's gone over to Sam and Lily's."

"Should you—" my mother began, but I shook my head firmly.

"No. I shouldn't do anything." She nodded.

"Well," she said and smoothed my hair again, "I know your heart is heavy for your friends. You should go take a hot shower. That may make you feel a bit better."

I finished my breakfast and did just that. Afterward, I suppose I did feel a bit better. Ready to join my family in celebrating the birth of Christ, at least. My grandpa read the Christmas story, and we opened a few gifts. My aunt and uncle and cousins returned as we pulled out all the leftovers for a Christmas lunch.

Lily called me around two o'clock. I stepped out on the back deck as I took the call.

"What happened?"

"Debra called me at ten last night, crying. I think she would have called Addison, but, you know, her being newly married and her first Christmas Eve alone with Glen—well, Debra didn't want to drag Addison into it. She said that Luke had been at her apartment; she was packing for her trip to

Minnesota. She just started letting him have it—saying that they should be together for Christmas. That he needed to make a decision about their relationship. And then, apparently, Luke said that he *had* made a decision and that they needed to break up."

I winced.

"I would imagine there was a bit more to it than that, and knowing Luke as well as we do," Lily continued, "I'm sure he was apologizing and trying to explain, but she didn't tell me any of that. Just that he said he didn't think they were right for each other and that it wasn't going to work. Jason may know more at this point; he drove Deb to the airport at four this morning."

"She was crying?"

"She was sobbing, Sara. And angry. Very angry. I think it's good that she was going home, actually. It may help, her being surrounded by her family, I mean. It gives her a little time away from here, which I'm sure she needs."

"Where's Luke?"

"He's here," Lily said. "He's downstairs with Sam and our families."

"How is he?"

"He told me he doesn't want to talk about it."

"Oh."

"I better go. I hear someone calling for me. Sara—" I could almost see Lily struggling with what to say. "Give this to God, okay? Don't fret. Don't obsess. All we can do is pray for our friends and be there when they need us. Worrying won't help, honey. I know it's impossible not to worry somewhat, but I want you to try to focus on being with your family. None of this will be resolved quickly. It's going to take time."

I breathed heavily. "You're right. I'll try, Lil. You go have Christmas with your family. I'm glad Luke's with you guys."

"All right. Love you."

"Love you too."

I tucked my cell phone back into my pocket and sat down on the swing, gliding back and forth.

What happens now? The question rolled over and over in my mind. So many emotions kept colliding through me. Lily had said that Debra was angry. I was somewhat surprised to find that anger was the main emotion I felt toward Luke as well.

I finally let myself absorb the fact that Luke had liked me—as I'd liked him—since that first day in the Sunday school classroom. The thought was a painful one.

So much wasted time. All those days and minutes and hours, he'd wanted from me the same thing I'd wanted from him.

Anger flashed again. Why hadn't he *said* something?

Then I cringed.

Why hadn't I? Fear of rejection, most certainly. Like him, I'd worried that he didn't feel the same and that I would ruin our friendship in the process. Hope, as well, I thought. Hope that Luke would pursue me and make me feel loved on his own. The dream of being swept off my feet by the man I desired. To me, Luke was such a great leader. I wanted to see that strength while being romanced by him. I'd wanted what he'd given Debra—cards and flowers. Date nights and kisses. I *didn't* want to have to declare my feelings for someone who hadn't yet pursued me.

Even now, I had no idea what he intended. Surely he felt Debra's wrath and devastation, and he knew he was the source. I didn't think he'd come to me—not now, if ever. Even if he did, would I accept him? How could I? Debra would never forgive me. What about Everett? Yes, we were sort of on a break, but I hadn't thought that was the end of the two of us. I just thought we needed a little direction on how to make our relationship work.

But Luke…

God, what are you trying to teach me right now? What am I supposed to learn from all this? Everything feels wrecked right now. It's Christmas—but I don't feel peace.

A cool wind rustled my hair and brushed past my face. I pushed myself up off the swing and went back inside.

Sunday I went to church, my eyes scanning the sanctuary for Luke, I'll admit. I didn't see him, but I did see Jason, Sam, and Lily. The four of us sat together. Afterward, we talked quietly while people filed out.

"Is there anything we can do?" I asked. "Maybe they'll get back together. Couples break up and get back together all the time."

"That's not going to happen, Sara." Jason stood up and pulled on his jacket, tugging on the sleeves as though the coat brought discomfort.

"They both need some time. We need to give them space." Sam rested his arm across the back of the empty row of chairs. "Who's picking up Debra from the airport after New Year's?"

"Addison," Lily answered, shuffling through her purse and pulling out a tube of Chap Stick. "I think we just have to wait and see what happens. Luke will resurface when he's ready."

I agreed with that, but I wished I knew how he was doing. I had no doubt he was dealing with some strong feelings of guilt.

So was I.

He'd said any decision he made was for himself, and I believed him. Whether or not he and I might ever find a way to starting over, I knew he would have broken up with Debra regardless. Once Luke believed in his heart that they weren't right for each other, he'd never willingly enter into a marriage with her. His words to me about living through that once—I knew that stemmed from a life with volatile, unhappy parents. Luke wouldn't marry unless he felt 100 percent sure about the relationship.

Could he be 100 percent sure about a relationship with me? And if he could be, would Debra ever forgive us for taking away the happy marriage she thought she was going to have with him?

I wasn't sure if my guilt was rational or not, but I couldn't shake it. I'd hoped, at times, that he and Debra wouldn't work out. I'd been jealous of Debra, and now she was heartbroken. The crushing weight of blame blocked out any glimpse of hope I had for my own reconciliation with Luke.

Jason and Sam headed out of the sanctuary, and Lily and I trailed after them slowly.

"I feel like it's my fault somehow," I confessed.

Lily shook her head. "Well, it's not."

"Do you think … I mean, the last time I talked to Luke, we shouted at each other. We left things so damaged between us. I hate that."

"What do you think you should do? Do you feel like you need to talk to him?"

I stopped walking. "I feel like there's a lot that needs to be said between us, but just like before, I feel like I need to wait."

"To wait on him? I'm not sure that helped very much last time." A shadow of doubt crossed Lily's face. I pursed my lips for a moment.

"I know. Maybe I should have told him how I felt before. I couldn't seem to do it. And now, eventually, we'll have to talk. If he doesn't initiate that, I'll have to, I guess. He's got to be reeling from the breakup. But right now … this is about him and Debra. I can wait on our conversation, at least, for a little while longer."

I went home and took down my Christmas decorations, stored everything away, then whipped up an easy stir-fry for dinner that night. Every time my thoughts started to meander in the direction of replaying my argument with Luke—hearing him again say that he'd wanted to be more than friends since the beginning—I quickly redirected my thinking. And I started making plans to redecorate my apartment.

Chapter Twenty-Eight

Two days after New Year's, I called Jason and asked him to come over. He knocked on the door that night after work and walked in, his eyes rounding at the sight of my apartment. Most of the furniture was covered by plastic slipcovers. I waved off his astonishment.

"I told you I needed help."

"Doing what exactly, Sara?"

"Moving furniture. I've just repainted the living room and kitchen. Now I need to move the sofas around, and the last time I did that on my own, I hurt my back. So just lend me your muscles for a few minutes and you can be on your way."

He raised his eyebrows. "Use me for my muscles and send me off, huh?"

"Basically. I can also give you a zucchini muffin as payment."

He pushed up his sleeves. "The things I'll do for a zucchini muffin. Fine. Let's move your furniture. You know I think you're crazy, right? When we were dating, I moved all of your furniture around at least three times. There are only so many places to put these sofas, Sara. What's the point?"

"I need a new vibe in this room. I know what I'm doing. We should get started."

Thirty minutes later, Jason was exaggerating about his sore shoulders while he sipped a bottle of water. I walked around the living room.

"This really does look so much better," I murmured. He ignored me. We both jumped at the sound of a loud knock at the door.

"Are you expecting company?" he asked, standing up. I shook my head and went to the door. Since Jason was there, I didn't bother looking through the peephole. I just opened the door.

"Debra!" I exclaimed, shock running through me. She barely glanced in my direction.

"Can I come in?" She walked in and paused mid-step at the sight of Jason. "Jason? What are you doing here?"

He looked just as stunned as I felt. "Sara needed me to move some furniture around for her."

"And you came right over. How sweet." Sarcasm dripped from her tone and I flinched.

"Deb, can I get you something to drink? How was your time with your family?" I asked cautiously. She dropped her purse on the plastic-covered couch.

"No, I don't want anything to drink. And my vacation was about as you'd imagine it, having just been dumped by my boyfriend."

Right. My heart was starting to pound in my ears. Jason pulled the plastic from the sofa, loveseat, and chair so we could all sit down. The overwhelming tension in the room left me wishing I could open a window for some air. The smell of fresh paint hadn't bothered me earlier, but my senses must have been heightened because it was overpowering at the moment.

"I'm so sorry about the breakup, Deb." It seemed ridiculous to ignore that topic since I felt certain it was why she was in my living room. "How are you?" Sympathy rose in me at the sight of her disheveled curly hair and the gaunt look on her face. Debra liked to wear bright, bold colors. She liked jewelry and even at her most casual, she would wear pink lipstick. The girl before me now had on a long, plain gray sweatshirt over black leggings and not a drop of makeup. I sat down next to Jason on the sofa, and Debra sat on the edge of the loveseat.

"I'm shattered, Sara. That's how I am. What has Luke said to you?"

It was disconcerting to meet her cool gaze, so I kept looking at her and then at Yoda on the floor in the corner of the room. "He hasn't said anything. I haven't seen him or talked to him since before Christmas."

A wave of nausea hit my stomach. Had Luke brought my name up during the breakup conversation with her? I couldn't imagine him doing that.

Guilt gnawed at me again.

"Deb, what's this about?" Jason broke in, his voice composed and curious. She flicked a glance at him, seemingly annoyed by his presence.

"This is about Luke, of course. And Sara stealing him from me."

My breath stopped short.

"I haven't—Debra, this has nothing to do with me." My protest came out in high-pitched squeaks.

"Really? Are you going to tell me you haven't been jealous of my relationship with Luke? That you haven't wanted him for yourself?"

The hairs on the back of my neck stood straight. Next to me, I felt Jason lean forward, his eyes directly on Debra.

"Debra," he began, but she held up her hand.

"Let her answer, Jason."

"Debra," I began, trying to find my words. At that point, I could do nothing but tell the truth. "You're right. I was jealous. Just like you, I did like

Luke as more than a friend, but then he chose you. So I backed off. I did! He and I used to do everything together. Once you two started dating, my communication with him became almost nonexistent. So this is between you and him. It's not about me." That last sentence came out like a plea.

"It is about you! You've done this somehow. You turned him against me." Debra visibly trembled and tears clouded her eyes.

I shook my head and cried, "No, I wouldn't do that!"

Jason frowned. "Where is this coming from, Deb? Did Luke blame Sara when he ended things with you?"

I was so glad he asked. She took an unsteady breath.

"No, he just said a lot of nonsense about how he'd realized that this wasn't going to work out. He didn't feel that our relationship should go any further. He kept saying he was sorry and that it was all his fault, but I know the truth." She looked at me with blazing fire in her eyes and rose to her feet.

"You wanted us to break up!" she yelled. I shrank further in the couch cushions, both horrified and heartbroken at Debra's overflowing anger.

"I—tried to be supportive," I argued weakly. "Yes, I cared about Luke, but you're my friend too. I never wanted you to be hurt. And he hasn't contacted me at all since you guys broke up, Debra. I promise."

"He will," she said. "Don't pretend you care about me. Everett wasn't enough. You still wanted Luke. And even before that, you hurt Jason!" She pointed to Jason next to me. "You know she hurt you, Jason! She's hurt everyone in her pursuit of Luke!"

I covered my face with my hands.

"Debra," I heard Jason's calm voice. "Sara and I broke up years ago. That's between her and me. This is about you and Luke." His words were gentle but non-negotiable.

"He loved me! I know he did. What happened?" she cried out and collapsed back on the loveseat. I felt Jason stand up, and I peeked out from my covered face. He moved to sit next to Debra.

"That's something for you to discuss with Luke. I care about you, Deb. Sara cares about you. We all do. I know you're hurting." Unflustered—and by that I mean he was the only person in my apartment not crying or yelling at that moment—Jason put his arm around Debra.

I saw her resist Jason for a moment, then bury her head in his chest and weep. Silent tears continued to roll down my cheeks as Debra kept murmuring that Luke loved her and she loved him. Jason just held her tightly, saying quiet, soothing words. After several minutes of this, Jason stood up and pulled Debra to her feet. "Give me your keys, Deb," he told her. "I'm driving you home."

She fumbled through her purse and handed him her keys, gulping for breath. I wondered how Jason would get back to his car, but I didn't say anything, knowing he'd figure something out or call me if he needed a ride. Instead, I just watched as they walked together out my front door, Debra clinging to Jason like a woman drowning. I could hardly bear to watch.

I closed the door and stood there, unable to move. I didn't think I could pray, but then suddenly I was sitting on the floor, crying out for God to help, completely undone by Debra's anguish and by my own guilt for all the times I'd wished Luke had chosen me.

The next day at work, I rushed to look at the *Immanuel* painting once more, knowing it would be packaged up and returned that night. I stared at Joseph's face.

Heather had been right. I could see behind the heaviness in Joseph's eyes, all the way to the point of acceptance. This was no small feat, and I felt nothing but admiration for the talented artist who had captured so many levels of emotion in one face.

We all get there, eventually, Heather had said to me. The words kept crossing my mind like a blinking marquee. It occurred to me as I looked at Joseph—his clenched grip on the staff, the unseen weight on his shoulders—that the acceptance in his eyes revealed his inner strength or maybe his strength came at the point of surrender. Acceptance of his situation, of the truth before him, and then surrender of his original plans to God's will for his life.

And then peace.

The startling thought came from somewhere inside me, like a whisper to my heart.

My soul thirsted for peace at that moment. With my circle of friends cracked beyond repair, peace felt out of reach. My shoulders fell at the fresh reminder of Debra's words to me. She blamed me for the breakup. All those months of biting my tongue and trying to appear nonchalant about Luke and Deb's romance—apparently it hadn't worked. She still held me responsible in the end.

Lily called me around eight o'clock that night.

"How are you, Sara?"

"Not good. I feel like everything is ruined."

"Well, things are less than peachy, that's for sure. I heard about the drama at your apartment last night."

"From Debra or Jason?"

"Sam had to pick up Jason at Deb's apartment late last night. Sounds like it was a rough time," she said, her tone as soft as a blanket.

"She said I was jealous, and she was right. I was."

"So was she," Lily said. "Debra's angry because she was jealous of you, just like you were jealous of her. That's why as soon as Luke broke up with her, she jumped to the conclusion that it was your fault. She's obviously always been a little worried he would choose you after all."

"He hasn't. Chosen me, I mean. He would have broken up with her regardless."

"You're right, I think. I'm not sure what he's going to do now, Sara." I understood Lily's hesitance.

"Don't worry. I'm not expecting him to come fall on his knees and declare his love for me."

"What would you do if he did? Would you choose him at this point?"

I was quiet for a long moment. Lily didn't push.

"I don't know," I said, my words barely audible.

A week passed and I didn't hear from Luke. A second week passed and still nothing. Lily and Addison texted me regularly, but we all seemed to stay busy with our work schedules. I finally sent Everett a long e-mail, telling him that he had been right—I wasn't ready. I told him everything—all about Luke and Debra and how our circle of friends felt shattered, about my conversation/fight with Luke and that while I wasn't sure where that left Luke and myself, I knew I couldn't be in a relationship at the moment.

Everett's response only reminded me of the fact that he was an amazing man. His understanding and tenderness and friendship eased what could have been yet another source of guilt and remorse for me. He reminded me of Jason, accepting my decision and still offering what he could: his friendship.

I felt crazy all over again, as though I'd let another phenomenal man slip through my fingers. How many did I think would just happen to come into my life?

A full three weeks passed before I saw Luke.

Chapter Twenty-Nine

It was Friday and I'd promised my mother I'd come over for dinner. I walked through the parking lot and stopped in my tracks at the sight of Luke standing next to my car. Once I recovered from the shock of seeing him, I walked closer. With about six feet between us, I stopped and looked at him.

"What are you doing here?"

"I wanted to see how you are. I know … well, I know this has been difficult for everyone. And the last time we talked, it didn't go so well." At the sound of his voice, I bit my lip.

"How is Debra? Have you seen her?" I watched as he folded his arms and leaned back against his car, parked in front of mine.

"I'm not sure how she is," he said. "I did see her—once—after she came back from Minnesota. We talked. It wasn't a very helpful conversation, I'm sorry to say. I haven't heard from her since then, but she's spent time with Addison lately, which I think has probably helped. I've met and talked with Glen a couple of times—he's really good at putting things in the right perspective. Talking with him has been positive for me."

Neither of us said anything for a moment.

"I'm sorry about—well, the last time we talked—" he began.

"You mean, when we were screaming at each other," I said, with barely a hint of a smile.

The corners of Luke's mouth twitched, and I thought he was holding back a smile as well.

"There was some yelling, I remember."

"It's okay. I'm okay," I told him. "How are you?"

He sighed. "I'm here. I just feel like I've destroyed Debra's life. And I've ruined all the friendships that mattered the most to me."

My heart tugged.

"She blames me," I said. His eyes darted up to my face.

"I know she says that, Sara. But it's really me she blames, as she should. It's not your fault."

"You haven't ruined all your friendships, Luke," I said after a moment, softening toward him. "I've been angry with you, but I'm still your friend. I couldn't stop if I wanted to."

His lips pressed together, and I saw him take several deep breaths.

"Are you still angry?" he asked.

"Sometimes. Yes, I am." I jingled the keys in my hand. "I have to go. My parents are expecting me for dinner."

"Okay." He stood up straight. "Can we talk again sometime, Sara?"

The half-hopeful, half-nervous tone in Luke's voice was new to me. He seemed shy. There was a time we'd been so comfortable together—shy felt strange.

"Yes," I answered, knowing there was more to be said but that I wasn't up for it yet.

The delightful smell of fried chicken greeted me as I walked through the front door of my parents' house. (Texas, y'all.) I dropped my jacket on the sofa and washed my hands at the sink while my mother stirred a big pot of baked beans.

"Where's Dad? That smells delicious."

"He'll be down in a second. Set that bowl of macaroni salad on the table, will you? And pour three glasses of tea."

I did as she told me, my mouth watering at the smells wafting around the kitchen.

"So, what held you up?" I rolled my eyes at her not-so-subtle question.

"Mother, I'm ten minutes later than I told you I'd be."

"I know," she answered, all innocence. "So, what held you up?"

I stuck a serving spoon into the macaroni salad and sat down at my place at the table. "Luke was waiting for me in the parking lot at work."

That stunned her. I almost laughed at the way her mouth opened into a large O.

"What did he say?"

"What did who say?"

I turned my head in the direction of my dad's voice. He grinned as he joined me at the table.

"Luke was waiting for her in the museum parking lot after work," my mother said, her voice hushed as if she were sharing a great secret.

"Was he now?" my dad said, winking at me as he plopped a rounded spoonful of macaroni on his plate.

"Yep," I answered curtly, taking my turn at the macaroni bowl, then reaching for a chicken leg. My mother sat down, her eyes like huge question marks.

"What did he say?" she repeated.

"Let's pray over the food, Suzanne. Then you can pester Sara." My dad reached for my and my mother's hands and closed his eyes to pray. Once the prayer ended, he squeezed my hand before letting go.

"Well?"

"It was not a big deal, Mom. We talked for maybe ten minutes, hence why I was ten minutes late. We're not dating. He's not in love with me. He just wanted to apologize for—well, for the way things went down the last time we talked. We had an argument before Christmas."

"About what?"

I gave my dad a pointed look. "Stuff."

"Oh, good to know." He chuckled.

"Anyway, we just said that we're still friends and we'll talk again soon."

My mother let out the breath she'd been holding and allowed herself to sit back and fill her fork with macaroni salad. "What about Debra? How is she?"

I looked down at the baked beans on my plate. "I don't know. Probably still heartbroken." My mother nodded solemnly.

"How did Luke seem?" I could tell my mother had kept my dad well informed of the Luke-and-Debra situation. One of the joys of being an only child: your parents follow your life and the lives of your friends as though they were characters on soap opera episodes.

"He seemed … okay, I guess. A little sad."

My dad studied me. "How are *you*, Sara?"

I managed a smile under my dad's scrutiny. "I'm okay too. A little sad, as well."

After dinner, my mother and I sat on the sofa to watch a period-piece movie that she'd rented. My father couldn't escape fast enough to his study. Halfway through the movie, my mother paused the screen to make popcorn. I followed her into the kitchen and poured a glass of water.

"Do you think… I just wondered…" My mother struggled to ask the question I could read all over her face.

"Mom, I have no idea what's going to happen at this point."

"Do you still have feelings for him?" I sipped my water.

"Yes. I do," I answered at last. "But I'm frustrated with him!" I continued, surprising myself. I guess I needed to talk about it because I kept going. "He told me before Christmas that he was interested in me since the very first day that we met. That was years ago! If he'd only said something to me before—we wouldn't be in this situation. I'm almost terrified of him actually asking me out at this point. Debra would hate me forever if I said yes."

My mom leaned against the counter, listening.

"How could I say yes? But if he never asks … well, I don't know what I'll do. Wait around for another perfect guy like Jason or Everett, I guess."

She repressed a smile. "Well, that's an option."

"I'm mad at Luke. I'm disappointed in him." My voice started to climb. "I hate feeling that way, but it's the truth. I've loved him and admired him—and now, I don't know. He let me down. I'm upset that he hurt Debra, even though I wouldn't have wanted him to marry her just to avoid a bad breakup. I feel"—I paused, struggling not to cry or shout or hit something—"devastated that what used to be a seamless circle of friendship is now fragmented and will never ever be the same! I know I've lost Debra as my friend. I had no idea that this was the last summer we'd all be together at the lake house. Everything has changed forever." My throat thickened, and I busied myself with finding a bowl for the popcorn.

"Things change, Sara." She took the bowl from my hands and looked straight at me. "People end up going in different directions. Friendships change as we get older. Our lives change. It's hard, I know."

I sniffed.

"You're angry and disappointed with Luke right now…" My mom seemed to be thinking through what she wanted to say. I interjected.

"Yes! I am. This can't be my love story, Mom!"

She blinked but didn't say anything. I turned away from her.

"I can't have a relationship that comes from other people being hurt. I doubt Luke could do that either. Where does that leave us? I'll tell you—nowhere! Why couldn't he have pursued me from the beginning? We might even be married by now if he had!" I choked on my emotion and had to take a few breaths to calm down. "I needed him to be strong and brave for both of us, but he wasn't. He wasn't!"

My mom reached out and stroked my arm. "I guess he's only human, Sara."

Only human.

My rapid breathing stopped for a moment.

I had placed him on a pedestal and hadn't left room for mistakes. I opened my mouth, then closed it again. The pain in my heart hit me so strong.

But I wanted a perfect love story.

"I know you feel like Luke failed you," my mother said. "The truth is that there will be moments when he fails you and moments when you feel like you've failed him too. There will be times when he disappoints you and times when you frustrate him. It's human nature."

I rubbed my eyes, weariness coming over me. "We're a tragic, broken mess. This isn't what I hoped for."

"Oh, honey. Haven't you learned by now? I told you, we're a broken people, Sara. All of our love stories have imperfect chapters. But sweetheart," she said and tipped my chin up for me to look at her. "God can fix broken things. He uses broken people for His glory. You'll see." I could see moisture glisten in her eyes. "When you do, Sara, remember to praise Him."

Chapter Thirty

I rolled out the print I'd ordered online from its scrolled package, pressed it into the frame I'd bought, and hung the framed print across from my bed, where I could see it clearly every day. I used my level to ensure the picture was straight then sat back and admired the end result.

The Undoing.

My phone buzzed, snapping me out of my moment of reverie. I looked at the text from Lily.

> BIRTHDAY DINNER FOR ADDISON AT HER HOUSE FRIDAY NIGHT. THE GUYS WILL BE THERE TOO.

I set the phone aside and sat on the edge of the bed. We hadn't gathered together as a group since the wedding eight weeks before. And while I knew Debra had stayed in close contact with Addison since the breakup, she had distanced herself from the rest of us. Would she be there? Would Luke?

I hadn't seen Luke since that day in the parking lot, nearly three weeks earlier. He'd texted me twice, just polite *How are you?* messages. Nothing more.

After the conversation with my mother the other night, I'd made a decision, however. I would wait—not necessarily on Luke—but on God. And like Joseph in the painting, I'd struggled with acceptance of my situation, surrender of my broken expectations to God, and finally found a kind of peace that came from letting go.

The thought of Addison's birthday dinner *did* stir anxiety in me, but I refused to let it consume me. Friday night, after swinging by my apartment to change clothes and grab the birthday gift, I drove over to Addi and Glen's. Luke's car was parked on the street in front of their house. I took ten calming breaths before walking up the driveway.

Addison flung open the front door and grinned at me. "Sara!" She pulled me into a warm hug, and I hugged her back. For a long moment we stood there, holding each other without speaking. It was the silence of a friendship that ran deep.

"Come in," she said at last with a smile. We joined Lily in the kitchen. She was inspecting the food. I could hear Glen, Jason, Sam, and Luke talking in the dining room.

"Addison, are those jalapeno peppers in that casserole?" Lily asked with doubt.

"Just a few," Addison said reassuringly. "It's not too spicy, Lily, I promise. Glen loves spicy food, but I don't want you crying and guzzling water all through dinner."

"Hmm," Lily replied, unconvinced.

"Debra?" I finally just went ahead and asked. Lily and Addison exchanged a look.

"No, she couldn't make it," Addison said, her voice sad. I nodded with understanding.

"How is she?" I asked Addison.

"She's … well … she's unhappy right now. It won't be like this forever. I know God has a plan for Deb's life, and I believe things will get better for her. But right now, she's unsure of a lot of things. Pray for her every day, okay?" Addison looked from me to Lily, and we both nodded our acquiescence.

The seven of us sat down to dinner. I noticed that Lily only took a small portion of the casserole and had a full glass of water by her plate. Luke sat at the opposite end of the table from me, and I made a point of not looking at him, instead focusing on chatting with Lily and Addison.

"So we're celebrating more than just my birthday tonight," Addison said after a while, loud enough to draw the attention of the guys.

"What else are we celebrating?" Jason asked.

"My townhouse finally sold!" Addison exclaimed. "The buyers close in three weeks. I'm so relieved to have that behind me. We were thinking we'd need to start renting it out if it didn't sell soon. It's the best birthday present I could have received."

There were rounds of congratulations from all of us.

"Well, while we're adding to the celebration list," Lily began slowly, looking at Sam. He nodded.

"Sam and I are expecting." Lily smiled as jaws dropped around the table.

"We're having a baby!" Addison shouted, and Lily burst out laughing.

"Yes, I suppose we are. The first baby born into this group."

I clapped my hands with delight. Addison and I inundated Lily with questions: How far along was she? (Eight weeks.) How long had she known? (One week.) Had she been to the doctor yet? (Her first appointment was to be on Monday.) The three of us couldn't stop smiling.

A baby. I felt the cloud that had been discreetly hanging over all of us lift somewhat. Maybe everything wasn't quite so ruined. While a baby would undoubtedly bring more change, there was nothing but joy in my heart at the thought of it.

We had birthday cake and coffee and sang to Addison. Somehow I'd managed to say no more than four words to Luke by the end of the night, but still, things hadn't felt too strained. He'd mostly engaged in conversation with the guys, and the baby news dominated my conversation with Addison and Lily.

Any contact with him made me feel as though I were betraying Debra. I wasn't sure how we could even go back to something resembling our former friendship. Every scenario that ran through my mind had Debra hating me forever, leaving me stuck in limbo. It was bad enough Luke had broken up with Debra... If he and I were to start dating ... I shuddered at the thought of Debra's despair.

The moment Sam and Lily packed up to leave, I jumped up to do the same, hoping to avoid any opportunities to speak alone with Luke. But just as Sam and Lily walked out the door, Addison held me back for a moment, wanting to be sure we collaborated when the time came for a baby shower for Lily. Then she wanted to show me the wedding pictures that had come in. Jason, Glen, and Luke were deep in some theological discussion in the living room, so I didn't see the harm in scrolling through pictures on her computer in the kitchen.

The wedding pictures were lovely, but my heart hurt at the sight of some of them—Luke and Debra together, me and Everett, one special photo of our entire group, laughing and looking every which way and looking so ... together. I was crying before I knew it. I laughed at myself with embarrassment, wiping tears away until I realized that Addison was crying too.

"I know you put some of the blame on yourself," Addison said, once we both had our emotions a bit more under control. She took my hand in hers. "But that won't help. Just like you and Jason—sometimes relationships don't work out."

I nodded. "I don't think they're going to be friends afterward the way Jason and I are."

She sniffled. "No, I don't think so. Maybe one day. I know better than to put limits on what God can do. Still, for now, Debra can't be around Luke. It hurts too much. And I think something in her knows that you and Luke—well, that you two may come together eventually. That will be a lot for her to take."

"We may not. He still doesn't talk to me," I said, my voice just above a whisper.

"He can't yet, Sara. You have to understand," she said, her own voice low as well to keep from anyone hearing us.

"It doesn't matter. I don't know what I would even say. How could I hurt Debra even more?"

"I watched you all these months, Sara. I know you pushed down your own feelings to support Deb and Luke as best you could. I *know* it. Don't think I didn't know."

Apparently, everyone in the world knew. Except Luke.

"You were hurting and disappointed for months. So *you* know, on some level, how she's hurting right now. You survived it. She will too."

I felt overcome by emotion.

"Luke and I together—I used to dream of such a thing. Now, how can that work when everyone else's life is ruined?" I propped my elbows on the table and lowered my head in my hands.

Addison tugged on my arm. "Not everyone, Sara. Are you still—do you love him?"

I straightened my head and ran my hand across the surface of the table. Did I love him?

Does he love me?

"I don't know. Maybe. I'm not sure we could get past all of this, though. And even if I do love him, is love enough?" My voice strained. "Is it? Is love enough to cover all the hurt and pain? Because I think maybe it's not."

Addison looked quiet and thoughtful for a moment.

"If it's not," she said, "grace is."

My lips sealed shut.

"When the time comes, and it will, Sara, hear me on this—there's nothing grace can't cover."

I bowed my head, knowing she spoke truth to me.

"How long do I wait?"

"For true love? For the person you were meant to be with?" Addison smiled. "You wait as long as it takes. He's worth it. So are you."

Addison's words sparked a glimmer of hope in me, hope that true love was still within reach. By the time I left, Luke and Jason were already gone. The memory of the wedding photo of our group stuck in my mind as well—a bittersweet reminder of what may never be again.

I laid in the dark, prayers swirling out of me.

God, can I love him even now? Can I offer him grace—will Debra ever offer me the same? How could she?

Deep inside my heart, these words welled up like a spring, reassuring me, holding me:

I can offer you Mine, daughter. It will be enough.

My mother was right. We are a broken people.

Will You heal my heart? Will You heal hers?

For some reason, I kept thinking of my parents … and my mother's words to me. I had a feeling I knew what it was I needed to learn.

God fixes broken things.

Chapter Thirty-One

Two weeks later I received this text from Luke late Friday night:

CAN WE MEET FOR COFFEE TOMORROW?

I needed to see him.

During the time since Addison's birthday party, my thoughts and emotions had run the gamut, from appreciating the space and time to think, to worrying when, if ever, I would hear from Luke, to desperation for some sort of resolution.

I arrived early at Starbucks the next morning. Standing in line, I thought about ordering him a coffee, then wondered if his tastes had changed. We used to go out for coffee often, and he always ordered his black. Such a small decision made me nervous now.

I ended up buying a mocha latte for myself and a black coffee for Luke.

We'll see, I guess.

In the back corner, there sat a small table for two where I waited. When he walked in, wearing light jeans and a V-necked baby blue T-shirt, my stomach flip-flopped. I was that girl all over again, sitting in a Sunday school classroom, her heart stopping when this blond-haired, green-eyed guy walked through the door. He sat down across from me, and I pushed the coffee cup toward him.

"Thanks," he murmured.

I sipped my latte. He drank about half his coffee in two gulps. Then we looked at each other.

"I've missed you," he said, and, have mercy, it was enough to make me cold all over.

"I've missed you too," I responded, trying to keep my voice from wobbling. I clasped my hands together underneath the table.

"I know this may be awkward for you." His brow furrowed, and he pushed his cup around the table, as if he didn't know what to do with his hands.

I shrugged, but I'm pretty sure it looked like a weird, violent jerk. I took another sip of my steaming latte, trying to feel less tense and more at ease. It didn't work. "For you too, I guess."

"Maybe a little."

"It's been a while."

"It has." He looked at the long line at the counter for a moment. "I've missed talking to you, Sara," he said.

"I've missed talking to you too."

"I've even missed grocery shopping with you," he said, and I laughed out loud at that unexpected comment. The corners of his mouth finally lifted and the tension cracked just a bit. My eyes locked on to that hint of his beautiful smile.

"How have you been?" I asked.

"All right. How have you been?" He fiddled with the watch on his wrist.

"Fine," I answered. "Things have been steady at the museum."

"Oh. Good." I could see him swallow twice.

"What's up, Luke?" I pushed gently. He let out a wheezing sort of laugh and looked at the table for a moment, shaking his head. The golden hair on his forearms caught my eye as he moved. I watched his hands clench, then release.

"I've thought about this for so long that I didn't think I'd be nervous. I guess I was wrong."

Well, I was a bundle of nerves myself and had been all morning. It had taken forever for me to choose what to wear—in the end, I opted for comfort with my favorite stretchy skinny jeans and a long, loose white top. Rushing, I didn't have time for breakfast. The surge of caffeine on my empty stomach had now taken my nerves to the next level.

"Just tell me," I said.

He nodded and steadied his gaze on me. "Sara, I remember exactly what you were wearing the day that we met. Your hair was just a little shorter then. I remember how anxious you seemed. Being the new person was hard for you. I remember thinking that you were so beautiful. I looked at you, once, across from where we were sitting, and you were watching me."

My breath stopped.

"You only caught me once, huh?" I said, biting back a smile. Luke smiled back at me—this time it was the smile I knew so well. The one that reached his eyes and warmed me.

"I wanted to ask you something that day, but I never got a chance."

"What did you want to ask me?" I asked, curious. He leaned over the table and looked right at me.

"Would you like to have dinner with me, Sara?"

I tried to swallow but couldn't seem to manage.

"Are you asking me on a date?" Butterflies swirled through my stomach.

"I am."

I felt completely ridiculous, but my eyes wouldn't stop watering. Luke kept staring at me; my restrained tears didn't seem to faze him. All the waiting faded into this one moment where we could be ourselves.

"Do you think—I mean, is that a good idea? Is it too soon?"

"I've waited for more than four years. I'm not waiting anymore. Unless you want to," Luke said, after a moment. "I'm asking you now, Sara." There was a crack in his voice that pulled at my heart.

In all truthfulness, I had no idea if it was too soon. I only knew right then that my chance was sitting across from me, and I couldn't say no, not even if I tried. Despite everything, despite the heartbreaking, winding road that had led to this place, Luke sat across from me. And the way I felt when he said my name told me that I hadn't stopped loving him. Not for one moment.

He was my match.

"Why wait for dinner? Let's go find some breakfast," I answered.

He exhaled, his nostrils flaring for a moment, emotion filling his face. Then he stood up next to me and held out his hand. My trembling fingers slid across his palm, and that simple touch was enough to make me dissolve right there where I sat. He pulled me up. By this time, the small Starbucks had filled nearly to capacity, but I didn't hear anything. We might as well have been alone.

Suddenly, Luke put his hands at the base of my neck, his fingers tangled in my hair, and he lifted my face to his. He leaned down fast, pressing his lips hard and rough against mine. I could feel the tension in his body; I could feel him holding back what he could. The waiting, the jealousy, the hurt, the anger—it came through in that forceful kiss.

I wrapped my arms around his neck and held him tight. My eyes were closed, but one tear trickled down my face. When he finally released me, I gasped for breath. He leaned down, his forehead against mine.

Well. I'll never be the same after that.

"Forgive me, please, Sara," he whispered.

I could feel his chest rise and fall.

"Oh, Luke." I opened my eyes and pulled away just enough to look at him. "Forgiven."

Then he kissed me again. This time just a little more gently, and I melted into his kiss, wanting more.

And we were, both, covered in grace.

Luke stepped back after a moment, holding my hand. "So, breakfast, right?" he said with a small smile, his eyes glassy.

I tightened my grip on his hand, never wanting to let go. "Right. I'm starving."

"Breakfast, then lunch sometime after, then dinner tonight. I have a lot to say to you, Sara."

I laughed. "Let's start with pancakes."

Chapter Thirty-Two

She should be out of her appointment by now!" I glanced at the clock on my phone.

Luke chuckled. "Be patient, Sara. Lily will call you soon."

"They better not try to be one of those couples who keep it a secret," I said with worry. He smiled.

"As if Lily could keep a secret like that."

"Hmm." He was right. I glanced at the phone again.

"Did Addison tell you about Debra's new job?" Luke asked from where he sat next to me on the loveseat in my apartment. I nibbled on my fingernail nervously.

"No. What job?"

"She applied at a radio station in Denver. She told Addison she hopes to move soon."

I couldn't quite read Luke's body language and expression. Remorse? Pain? I reached over and squeezed his arm. "I'm sorry," I said quietly.

"Me too."

We were both silent for several minutes.

My phone buzzed, and I scrambled to answer it.

"Well?" I demanded. Lily laughed.

"I'm doomed to a lifetime of football games, I think. It's a boy!"

I squealed. "It's a boy! Hooray!"

Luke's phone rang and he answered it. I could tell it was Sam, telling him the same thing. After both of our conversations ended, I curled up next to Luke, tucking my feet underneath me.

"So, I have to plan a blue baby shower now. Maybe I'll go with a jungle theme. That would be cute. Or something like trains. What do you think?"

"If you're planning it, Sara, I'm sure it will be beautiful and fun no matter what." Luke lifted my hand to his lips and kissed it. He glanced over at me. "How long have we been dating?" I tried to think.

"Maybe two-and-a-half months? Is that all? It feels like longer," I said, leaning back against the cushion.

"It does," he agreed, then he stood up. "I have errands to run before tonight. What time should I pick you up? We're doing dinner and a movie, right?"

"Right. Let's leave for dinner around six."

He nodded. "Okay."

He didn't move. He just kept looking down at me.

Not for the first time, I wished I could tell what he was thinking.

"Luke, whatever it is, just say it," I said with a teeny smile.

"I'll pick you up tonight."

I nodded and pressed my lips together. "Sounds good."

"Okay then."

"Okay."

"I love you," he said. I just looked up at him. Then I stood up.

"Do you?" I asked. He smiled.

"I wouldn't have said it otherwise."

I touched his face. "Say it again."

"Sara, I love you." He placed his hands on my waist and squeezed, and I yelped. He grinned. "Is there anything you might like to say at this point?"

I pretended to think about it. That got me another good squeeze.

"I love you," I said, and he sealed the moment with a kiss that I didn't want to end. When he started to pull away, I went up on my tiptoes, tightened my grip around him and wouldn't let go. He chuckled, even with his lips against mine, and relented, deepening the kiss until he left me sated.

"It feels a little strange to finally say it out loud," I said after a moment. He cocked his head to the side.

"Really? Why?"

"I've felt it for such a long time. Now I can say it to you."

He pulled me closer. "As often as you want. I'll never get tired of hearing it."

"Me either," I assured him. I rested my head against his chest. "I love you."

June 1st Addison sent out an e-mail to me and Lily, wondering if we'd be up for a girls' weekend at the lake house the following weekend. Lily's immediate response was that she had no intention of anyone seeing her in a swimsuit in her current state, to which Addison replied that Lily would not be required to strip down to a swimsuit, and really, the belly was cute anyway. To which Lily replied that she'd remind Addison of that when Addison happened to be twenty-five weeks pregnant.

The three of us rode together to Lake Shore Woods that next Saturday morning. I sat in the backseat and listened to Addison and Lily chitchat back and forth. I couldn't help thinking of Debra. She'd accepted the job offer from Denver and had moved just four weeks before. Addison, Glen, Jason, Sam, and Lily had helped load the U-Haul with her things. (Well, Lily had brought donuts and helped supervise.) Luke and I obviously had not been invited to the goodbye party.

I missed her. Luke still struggled with guilt. I rested my head on the back of the seat and looked out the window. Now past the city limits, the traffic waned. Under a cloudless sky, pine trees flanked the interstate, interrupted by an occasional gas station or rest stop. Country music played softly in the car. I tuned out Lily and Addison for a moment, my thoughts turning to prayer, asking God to bless Debra, asking Him to go with her.

I closed my eyes.

She's Mine. As are you.

The reminder comforted me.

Once we reached the lake house, I settled my things in the blue room. Lily said she needed the master suite since it had the largest bed, and she could only sleep if cushioned by no less than four pillows. Addison opened windows and started cooking a big batch of Fettuccine Alfredo while I chopped lettuce and tomatoes for a simple salad. The three of us sat outside and ate dinner together. I relaxed and enjoyed the cool breeze, the view, laughter, and conversation.

"How are you and Luke?" Addison asked me. Lily rested her chin on her folded hands and waited for my answer.

"We're..." I couldn't help my smile as I thought on how I could possibly describe my relationship with Luke.

"Good," Lily answered with a wink. "I'm glad to hear it, Sara."

I looked from Lily to Addison in confusion. "I didn't say anything."

Addison grinned. "Oh, your face said it all for us. Love looks good on you, Sara."

My cheeks flushed. "I do love him."

"And he loves you," Lily said.

"The journey to this point wasn't what I expected, but we made it here somehow, I guess."

"You want to marry him, of course?" Addison's sentence ended sounding like a question.

"Oh, every day," I assured them.

Both girls laughed. I poured myself another glass of lemonade.

"Well, Luke knows what he wants. I don't think he'll wait too long to ask you," Addison said.

"I can wait. Just knowing he's mine is enough for now. But I will say that every time he kisses me, I just—"

Addison and Lily both leaned closer. "Yes?" they said in tandem, and I chuckled.

"Where there was friendship before, there's fire now. He lights me up."

Addison and Lily exchanged a glance. "Yeah, I don't think he'll wait too much longer to ask you." Addison's smile was suspiciously knowing, but I let it go. We cleared the table, and Lily promptly sat down in the living room with her feet up while Addison and I cleaned the kitchen. Then we sat together in the living room, drinking coffee and talking about work, about faith, Lily's pregnancy and Addison's love of married life. Through the window, the pink sky over the water caught my eye and I stood.

"I'm going to walk down and watch the sunset," I told the girls. Lily waved me on. I slipped into my sandals and made my way to the edge of the pier, looking out at the rippled water. Dark, tall trees rustled around the lake. Birds flew overhead, calling out in the distance. A breeze blew my hair over my shoulder.

"From the rising of the sun."

I jerked around at the sound of Luke's voice. He stood at the other end of the pier, the setting sun shadowing him in a soft silhouette.

"Until the going down of the same," he continued. "The name of the Lord is to be praised."

My mouth rounded in an O, and I lifted both hands in surprise. "What on earth are you doing here?"

He smiled. "I guess I missed you."

I smiled my response. He walked down the pier to where I stood waiting.

"Well, you missed dinner. There are leftovers in the refrigerator, though."

He shrugged. I reached out, and he grasped my hand. We were quiet for a minute, listening to the water. My shock at seeing him subsided, but it seemed odd to me that he'd shown up at our girls' night away. Still, my heart skipped at the sight of him just as it always did. The sun dipped lower, and the pink sky radiated over the lake. Beneath the wooden pier, the water swished back and forth. Luke's presence intensified the romance of the sunset. I ran my thumb over the top of his hand and breathed in the scent of his cologne.

"Sara." I turned to face him.

"The last time we were here—I think I may have broken your heart," Luke said, his eyes serious. I traced his jawline with my finger.

"I survived." Not only that, I could accept him, flawed, real, imperfect—and yet, strong, passionate, and steady. Everything that I wanted and needed. We could have each other. Our love story might not be perfect, but I would fight for it. And looking into those intense, beautiful green eyes staring at me, I knew he would fight for it too.

"Has it healed then?" he asked me, tucking my hair behind my ears. I ran my fingers across his collarbone.

"Every time you kiss me."

He leaned down, put his lips on mine, and kissed me slowly, his hands cradling my face ... and my heart—all at once. "That's better," I whispered.

"I love you so much, Sara." Luke's eyes took on a look of regret. "I wish I could go back to the beginning and speak up before Jason did. Or arm-wrestle him for you or something."

I chuckled. "It's okay. Looking back won't change anything. We got here eventually, and we spent a lot of time building a strong friendship. I'm thankful for that."

He held both my hands to his chest. "I'm thankful for that too. You're my best friend."

"And you're mine." His hands tightened their hold. My eyes closed.

"I didn't know it would be like this for us," he said in a husky whisper. I sighed.

"I did."

His laughter floated gently along the breeze. He kissed my knuckles and then stepped back, kneeling down. I gasped out loud and covered my open mouth. My heart began to pound like a drum. Luke took hold of my left hand.

"Marry me, Sara. Please. As soon as possible."

Wind whipped through my hair and my eyes burned. "Are you—are you sure?"

He nodded. "I wouldn't have asked otherwise." He tucked one hand in his pocket and pulled out a small velvet box. Cushioned in white satin sat the most gorgeous, sparkly ring I'd ever seen. The large round diamond front and center was mounted in a halo of small ones, flanked by a two-row design of tiny twinkling diamonds set in a platinum band.

"It's so perfect. How did you know which one I'd want?" I brushed away tears even as I couldn't stop smiling.

He took out the ring, and I held out a trembling hand.

"Well, I had a little help from your mom. And Lily. And Addison. Between the four of us, I had a feeling we'd find something that would work." He slid the ring on my finger. "Will you, Sara? Will you marry me?"

"As soon as possible." My eyes were glued to my glimmering ring. The fading light of day cast over us and the diamonds shone. Luke stood up and kissed my hand.

"I'd marry you tonight if I could find a preacher and you would agree to it," Luke said—and I believed him.

"How romantic of you, but I want a big church wedding."

"I know."

"Which will probably be in something like six months." I realized then that his eyes were wet too, and I reached out to touch his face.

"Whatever you say."

"You'll be the undoing of me, Luke Anderson," I said softly, my eyes sneaking another look at my ring.

"I look forward to it." He kissed me until my legs weakened and I faltered in his arms. Then he lifted me up and spun me around. "I'll love you for the rest of your life and mine, Sara."

"I'll love you forever," I promised.

Cheers erupted and we turned to see Lily and Sam and Addison and Jason on the house deck, clapping and yelling and jumping up and down. More tears flowed from my eyes.

"The guys came too?"

Luke grinned. "I tried to talk them out of it, but it was hopeless."

Family.

Grace.

Addison held up a bottle of champagne, and I laughed as Luke and I made our way back to the house, back to our people, his arm snug around me. We'd walked here before, broken and apart. With Luke next to me now, his ring on my finger, his heart tied to mine, we walked together. And he was worth it all to me.

My heart ached with happiness.

Praise the Lord, as my mother would say.

Acknowledgments

Once upon a time, a story showed up in my heart. A story about seven friends who moved in and out of each other's lives, and who loved one another like family. A perfect circle of friendship that ends up being splintered. Anyone who's ever had a close friend knows that this can happen. Love and pain are very real parts of life.

Over the years, these seven characters stayed with me. Until I wrote and rewrote and *rewrote* their story. And finally, *The Last Summer* was finished. I'm so thankful for Lighthouse Publishing of the Carolinas for taking a chance on this book and for Marisa and Meghan, who helped make the story all it was supposed to be. I'm so thankful to Jeff for that night he took me to the Spaghetti Warehouse and the Pink Floyd laser light show in Houston. Best. Date. Ever.

I'm thankful for Texas and tamales and Shipley's and Diet Dr Pepper and people who say *y'all*. I'm thankful for my absolutely wonderful family, from Texas and Louisiana to Colorado and Virginia.

I'm thankful for Jesus.

And I'm thankful for every person who reads this story. Please know that it's so close to my heart, and these characters are practically family *to me* at this point. The fruition of this book is, in a very real way, a reminder to me that God fixes broken things. He uses all the moments and experiences of our lives, if we'll let Him … even the broken ones, especially the broken ones.

And with all my heart, I'm thankful for my children, Ashtyn and Lincoln and Lillian. Because they are all my dreams come true. I breathe them in and breathe them out and love them so much it hurts, and all I can do is praise the Lord.

Made in the USA
San Bernardino, CA
21 August 2017